Flipping
the Script

Also by Paula Chase

SO NOT THE DRAMA

DON'T GET IT TWISTED

THAT'S WHAT'S UP!

WHO YOU WIT'?

Flipping the Script

A Del Rio Bay Novel

Paula Chase

Dafina Books

KENSINGTON PUBLISHING CORP.

www.kensingtonbooks.com

DAFINA BOOKS are published by

Kensington Publishing Corp.
850 Third Avenue
New York, NY 10022

All Kensington titles, imprints, and distributed lines are available at special quantity discounts for bulk purchases for sales promotion, premiums, fund-raising, educational, or institutional use.

Special book excerpts or customized printings can also be created to fit specific needs. For details, write or phone the office of the Kensington Special Sales Manager: Kensington Publishing Corp., 850 Third Avenue, New York, NY 10022. Attn. Special Sales Department. Phone: 1-800-221-2647.

Dafina and the Dafina logo Reg. U.S. Pat. & TM Off.

ISBN-13: 978-0-7582-2586-3
ISBN-10: 0-7582-2586-5

First Kensington Trade Paperback Printing: April 2009
10 9 8 7 6 5 4 3 2

Printed in the United States of America

To my clique: Nick, Mandy, Dirt, Wink, and Big Ed
Two Plus Too till we die

"I drop it all for y'all, if my homies call."
—Tupac, "If My Homies Call"

All I Want for Xmas Is You

"Santa hooked me up this year."
—B2K, "Santa Hooked Me Up"

Closing time!

Well, almost.

Mina eyed the clock on the register, willing it to move from ten-thirty to eleven. She stared at it for a full thirty seconds and the time remained one zero, three zero. She hip-bumped the vacuum cleaner she'd stowed away under the register—totally against the rules—and gave the register's clock one more pleading look before giving up.

Eleven P.M. was taking forever.

It was official, she hated working the holidays with a passion. The extra hour the mall was open was killing her.

At ten-thirty on the last shopping Friday before Christmas, the teen girls who would normally storm Seventh Heaven's were at other stores shopping for their boyfriends or parents, not themselves. It would be another story the day after Christmas. But Mina didn't want to think about that. She was still praying she wouldn't have to work that day, even though Jess said everyone was usually scheduled to handle the onslaught of returns.

I could use an onslaught now, she thought, taking the store's emptiness personally.

Unable to endure the idleness another second, Mina waved at Vic, Seventh Heaven's cutie-pie DJ. She signaled that she was about to turn on the vacuum and he should pump up the music a notch. She ran the dust sucker over the already immaculate floors. Not once had Mina ever felt vacuuming accomplished anything except some inane need of the store's supervisors to check it off a closing procedure to-do list. The floors were clean enough to eat off. She took her time rolling the vacuum down the center aisle past the perfectly folded tees and racks of miniskirts. She smiled over at the brown cord mini. Next pay day that baby would join the rest of her growing Seventh Heaven wardrobe.

The vroom of the vacuum sucked to a dead stop.

Mina frowned down at it, bent to check the problem—probably sucked up one of the price tags—then heard Vic's laughing. She looked up to ask him what he'd done, figuring he was messing around with her, and ran smack into Jessica.

"Mina, I told you to stop vacuuming so early," Jessica said, the vacuum plug dangling from her folded arms, legs in a wide model stance. Her hazel eyes were an eerie contrast to her coffee bean skin.

Vic imitated Jess behind her back and Mina bit back a smile. Seeing the glint in her eye, Jess whipped her head Vic's way, but only caught him bopping his head, ear to the headphone.

"I'm just going to make you vac again at eleven–oh-five," Jessica said, facing Mina once more. She sounded like an exasperated parent chastising a child.

"The store's empty," Mina reasoned. She reluctantly wound the plug around the vacuum, snaking it out of Jess's grip.

"So? We're not supposed to vacuum until we're closed."

"That's seriously the dumbest rule ever," Mina said, more pouty than rebellious. She eased by Jessica, rolling the vacuum with her toward the front of the store. "Friday nights blow."

Jessica's shoulders hitched as she folded an already well-folded shirt. She flicked her long, curly weave over her shoulder, then tucked a piece of hair behind her ear, nearly singing, "If *I've* gotta be here, *you've* gotta be here."

Mina looked over at Vic and rolled her eyes. He winked at her as he spun her favorite song. Singing under her breath, Mina swayed her hips to the beat and dance-walked the vacuum back to the spot where she'd started, on the ready for eleven P.M. A sudden grin exploded across her face. Even over the music, she heard the clique's banter, recognizing the familiar cadence, before they appeared around the corner. She drank in the sight of her friends like a thirsty person sizing up a glass of cold water.

JZ stopped and stooped low enough for Jacinta to climb onto his back. He stood up, popped Jacinta in the spot he wanted her, and caught up with the rest of the clique in two long-legged strides. His biceps bulged when he locked his hands under her jeans-clad thighs. Both he and Cinny were looking fit thanks to a summer of conditioning. He'd taught her how to swim and for reasons only known to JZ, he'd made early morning runs, sit-ups and push-ups part of his lessons. Jacinta, who had already been curvy to a point of distracting guys, now had a tighter waist, toned arms, and a rock-solid butt. Mina noticed that whether he was dunking Cinny in the pool, lifting her over his shoulder for a playful spin, or giving her a ride on his back, JZ couldn't keep his hands off the new firm figure he'd help sculpt.

And Jacinta was the happiest Mina had seen her in a long time. Raheem, her boyfriend of five years, was at Georgetown University—out of sight and out of mind. No sooner had Jacinta said bye than she and JZ began a more open flirtation fest, and it hadn't been that sly to begin with.

Mina couldn't relate to Cinny's giddiness. She fought depression anytime the realization hit that Brian was in Durham, a starting freshman on Duke University's basketball team. Some days Mina spent hours imagining what life would be like if Brian were a regular student instead of a student athlete.

He'd be able to road-trip home now and then and be home for regular holidays instead of on lockdown until Christmas. He hadn't even come home for Thanksgiving because the team played in a tournament in Hawaii. Forget being mad jealous that he was in one of the most beautiful places on earth; Mina only knew he should have been home with her. Instead, she'd watched the television wide-eyed, giddy, yelling "That's my boo" anytime the camera caught him.

Mina wondered how Cinny was going to handle Raheem being home for the holidays, something she'd confided only to Mina that she dreaded.

Mina's eyes scanned the clique quickly, as if needing visual reassurance that Brian wasn't bringing up the rear. He'd bulked up over the summer preparing to go toe-to-toe with some of the country's best college ballers, and Mina couldn't help but stare at his new girth anytime he was near.

She wanted to see him so bad she could taste it. Instead, she focused on Michael, apparently the only one immune to the buffness running rampant among the guys, looking oddly patriotic in a pair of jeans, a red polo, and a pair of crisp, white Air Forces. His kicks sparkled as if he'd just popped them out of the Nike box. Just about five foot ten, he was five inches shorter than JZ and more male-model clean than athletic chic.

Bringing up the rear were the couples—Kelly and Greg, Lizzie and Todd. The girls were petite next to the guys—Lizzie in a frayed denim mini, boots, and a tee, Kelly in a blousey baby-doll top and skinny jeans. Todd, once skinny even with muscles, was now the same size as JZ. He was still the same goofy basketball geek but one who had finally filled out his promising frame. Lizzie was one lucky girl, in Mina's opinion, and she reminded her best friend of that now and then. When she cheered for Varsity basketball games, Mina couldn't take her eyes off Todd. Not in a sleazy kind of way, but in amazement. Over the summer, he'd left Del Rio Bay toned and come back ripped with a surfer's body, complete with a six-pack. On top of that, the Cali sun had bleached his walnut brown hair blond, again. Even with their summer tans fading, he and Lizzie were a cute, sun-kissed, matching pair.

Kelly and Greg were their brown doppelgangers, the preps to Liz and Todd's beach-bum casual. The four of them conversed among themselves between exchanges of conversation with JZ, Jacinta, and Michael, in and out like couples do, making Mina's heart ache.

She missed being part of a couple.

The seven of them were creating the most activity Mina had seen in the unusually subdued corridor all night.

Drawn to their noise, Jessica stationed herself beside Mina. "I figured that was your posse. Could they be any louder?"

Mina knew Jess's annoyance was only for show. Jess was as happy as she was to have a distraction for the last few minutes of their shift.

"Hey, Deev," Michael said, as the clique entered the store. He gave Mina an affectionate shoulder squeeze.

"What's up, girl?" JZ said, in his usual loud voice. He squatted a few inches so Jacinta could slide off his back and threw a "what's up?" fist Vic's way. Vic returned the salute.

"Hey, girl," Jacinta said before heading to the clearance rack.

As their boyfriends stopped to chat up Vic, Lizzie and Kelly joined JZ and Michael in a semicircle in front of Mina and her vacuum.

"Any minute now, your guy will be home. Excited?" Lizzie's green eyes twinkled.

"Please, she practically has a clock over her head counting down," Kelly said, bumping Mina's shoulder.

Jess snorted. "As long as that clock knows it's not going off until eleven-thirty, she'll be fine."

Satisfied she'd gotten in the proper snip for the night, Jess runway-modeled to the cash register. Mina, Kelly, and Lizzie rolled their eyes.

"Wasn't Brian coming with you guys?" Mina asked, unable to resist peeking around JZ but only getting a glimpse of Greg and Todd high-fiving Vic at something they found hilarious.

"He was supposed to." JZ leaned against a rack of holiday dresses, blocking Mina's view of the entrance. "Didn't he text you?"

Mina instinctively pulled her cell out of the pocket of her jeans. There was no message. She shook her head.

"His flight was delayed or something. He won't be here till tomorrow," JZ said. He put his arm around Mina's neck in a light hold. "You're stuck with me."

Mina wriggled out of the hold and shoved him. "Please, don't remind me."

"Now, see, how does that sound?" JZ faked a pout. "We go back to kindergarten, girl."

"But we've only been friends since second grade," Mina said, hands on her hips.

"Oh, that's wrong. You didn't like me until second grade?"

Lizzie stepped between the mock fight. "And I've been refereeing since fourth grade," she said. "Break it up, you two, before I call Cinny on you."

"I am not in this," Jacinta said, peeking her head over a rack of pajama bottoms. "Mi, this is cute. Hook me up with your discount."

"No she's not either," Jess said, from the register. Her eyebrows arched to her forehead in what Mina called her supervisor's stare.

"Like I said," Jacinta continued, raising her voice and purposely not looking Jess's way, "*Mina*, hook ya' girl up."

Mina gave Jacinta a little head shake and smiled when she saw the evil grin on her friend's face. Jacinta always knew how to get to Jessica. She was clearly baiting her. She'd never seriously ask for a discount out loud. She didn't have to. Mina would happily hook any of her friends up. All they had to do was tell her what they wanted, she bought it, and they paid her back. Cinny, obviously in a good mood, was successfully getting under Jess's skin. Any other time she acted as if Jessica didn't exist, and Jess did the same right back.

"Mina, I'll report you. The employee discount is not transferable," Jess said. She walked over, joining the tight circle, hands folded against her chest, and glared across the store at Jacinta, who'd already lost interest in the game and was eyeing Seventh's tiny inventory of shoes.

"Oh my God, Jess, chillax," Mina said. Her eyebrows furrowed as she came as close as she dared to dueling with her frenemy/boss. "Cinny was only joking."

"She'd better be. I'm watching the things she picks out and if you buy any of it, I'll know it was for her," Jess said, narrowing her eyes Jacinta's way.

Mina didn't bother to respond. Jacinta knew how to play the game better than that. Anytime she was in Seventh's she picked up things she didn't like, because she knew Jess was evil enough to spy her selections. Then later she'd tell Mina the stuff she really wanted. If Jess put half as much time into being human as she did being bitchy . . . well, she'd still be a major bitch. Mina hadn't known her any other way. They got along fine at work, but Jess could turn on her bitchiness with the quickness. Mina had learned, long ago, to ride with the flow and hold on quietly during the rough patches.

Her breath hitched as an arm went around her waist. Brian's voice, smooth and deep, was in her ear, "You trying dip early or what?"

Mina screamed loud enough to penetrate the music's booming bass. "Oh my God!" Whipping around, she jumped into Brian's open arms, for once not caring about the mushy PDA. He scooped her up and she wrapped her arms around his neck. They kissed and the tight circle, which had gotten progressively tighter to cloak Brian's entrance, immediately dispersed.

"Awww, ain't they cute?" JZ said with mock adoration. But in four long strides he was at Vic's DJ station, already over the happy reunion. "Vic, I hope you got some fresh mixes for my New Year's Eve joint, son."

In answer, Vic nodded in time to the booming beat.

Lizzie and Kelly joined Jacinta in window shopping. Only

Michael and Jessica remained off to the side, Michael browsing the CDs in the impulse-buying section near the register and Jessica pretending to neaten a stack of tee shirts.

Brian set Mina down. "For real, though. You ready to blow?"

Mina nodded her head Jess's way. "Gotta ask my boss."

"No," Jess said before Brian could ask. She looked at her watch. "She still has ten minutes before closing and another thirty of cleaning."

Brian laid one of his prettiest smiles on Jessica, his brown eyes teasing. "Come on, Jess. You know I'm only home a few days."

"Uh-huh. And?" Jess's hands flew to her hips. Mina saw in her face that Jess was working to keep her gaze steely. Like most girls, she was openly tickled that Brian James's light shone on her. Mina saw it in the hopeful twinkle in Jess's catlike hazel contacts. They brightened more when Brian put his arm around Jess's shoulder.

"You know Mina has curfew. Help a dude out," he said, making Jess his co-conspirator.

"That's what you get for dating a young 'un," Jess said. Her eyes rolled but without the usual annoyance.

"What can I say? I like 'em young." Brian laughed when Mina smacked his arm.

"Come on, Jess. Let her go early," JZ hollered from the front, Vic's earphone up to his ear.

"No," Jess said his way. Her eyebrow rose toward Brian. "Uh-uh."

"Don't be like that, Supe," Brian said.

Mina nearly giggled. Only Brian and JZ could get away with calling Jess "Supe"—short for supervisor. Jessica actually grinned. Everyone loved getting a Brian James nickname.

"She can't leave before eleven-thirty. That's her shift," Jess said, working to sound authoritative. Her lips pursed. "But she already vacuumed too early. So as soon as we close she can roll." She swished her hair and smirked. "But you owe me, Mina."

Mina groaned. "I'd rather stay till eleven-thirty."

"Don't say that," Brian said. His fingers tap-danced down Mina's back, leaving goose bumps along the way. "Supe might change her mind."

"She still has ten minutes," Jess reminded him, as Brian tugged on Mina's arm.

Brian picked up a pink tee and held it up to his chest. "Is this my color?"

"You're only making more work for your girlfriend," Jessica said. She pulled it from his hand and tossed it at Mina, who caught it clumsily.

Mina obediently refolded the shirt, careful to follow the Seventh Heaven formula—right sleeve, left sleeve, left side, right side, two body folds up, neckline last. She did it without thinking; six-hour shifts, four days a week for eight months did that to a person. She shook her head in a firm no when Brian went to grab another tee. He came up behind her, pretending to help her fold.

"Hurry up and clock out," he whispered. His mouth lingered on her ear and nibbled, making Mina grin and her legs rubbery.

"Get a room," Jacinta yelled from across the empty store.

Brian stepped back, threw his hands up in a hands-off gesture, then leaned against a shelf of jeans.

Michael came over, taking his place beside Mina. He draped his arm over her shoulder. "I saw those baby doll flats you were talking about. They're cute."

Jess's eyebrow arched. "What are you? The token queer eye for the straight guy?"

Mina's jaw dropped, but before she could defend Michael, he easily traded barbs back.

"Only if you'll officially join us as the token bitchy, pretending-to-be-rich girl."

The diss escaped his mouth smooth as butter, so casual a passerby would have missed the nasty undertone.

Had Michael backed down it would have been an invitation for

Jess to dig deeper for another venomous diss. It was her way. But game respected game. Jess flipped her weave, her expression cool, and busied herself brushing lint off the folded jeans.

Brian tweaked Mina's side as he said, so only she could hear, "She gon' let you go now. Watch."

Mina pressed invisible wrinkles out of the shirt she'd refolded and pretended to check the other shirts, to make sure no tags were sticking out or sizes out of place. She bit back a grin when Jess, with an exaggerated sigh and eye roll, said, "Just clock out, Mina. Your *clique* is only making more work." Her lip went up in a partial scowl.

Mina's legs worked triple time, just short of a run, as she walked to the store's back room. She grabbed her purse and jacket and was clocked out in three minutes. She breezed by Jess and bid her a hasty, "Thanks, Jess."

Jess's eye roll was halfhearted. She and Mina's bond was a shaky one, based more on their mutual love for Sara, Jessica's twin, than anything else, but that was enough.

Jess followed the louder than ever clique to the entrance, eager to put down the store's glass closure and lock up. When everyone was out, she shouted after Mina, "You still owe me," then let the glass come down on Mina's response.

Brian slid his arm around Mina's waist. They walked in sync, lagging behind the others.

"I got you off work early. So you owe me too," he said, a devilish grin on his toffee-complexioned face.

Mina smiled up at him. Even in his Duke hoodie, she could see he was more muscular than when he left, broader too. Remembering how good it felt to lie her head on his firm chest made her tingly.

Owing Brian, she didn't mind.

The Gang's All Here

*"You gon' make us both get into some things
that'll scare grown folks."*
—David Banner ft. Chris Brown, "Stuntin is a Habit"

It's just like old times, Mina felt like shouting as the clique chilled in JZ's family room. Sitting at the juice bar with Brian, she surveyed the usual chaos, soaking in every ounce of the energy emanating from her friends. Her heart fed off it.

It was like being in a time warp bubble from the summer. Todd, Michael, and JZ on the sectional sofa playing Madden, smack-talking insults and obscenities; Jacinta flitting between plucking with JZ—a happy intrusion to his game that he would have never allowed a year ago—and conversing with Lizzie and Kelly at the arcade-sized Pac-Man game. Greg standing with them, guiding the girls through each level's danger spots, as he waited his turn at the "real" gaming on the sofa.

Greg went with the flow like he'd been friends with all of them forever, fitting in easily since he and Kelly became an official couple over the summer.

Mina knew if JZ or Michael brought a girl around, it would hardly be as nice a match. And they must have known it too because neither of them ever had.

Not that me and the girls wouldn't accept her, Mina thought, checking herself. The fact was, guys seemed to find things to bond over, while girls seemed to focus on the differences.

And then there was the whole competition thing.

She'd run up against her fair share of girls JZ was dating who always seemed to get her and Jay's sibling-rivalry friendship twisted. If she had to explain to one more chicken head that she and JZ were only friends, a choke hold was going to go along with the explanation.

She giggled at the thought. More than likely she'd get Jacinta, the brawn among the girls, to do the choke-holding.

Brian pulled her stool flush against his, forcing Mina's attention back to him. She draped her legs over his to prevent them from being crushed by the bar stools. His hands cuffed her sides as he leaned in, closing off their part of the room with his intimate stare and seductive grin.

"You miss me, Toughie?"

"Nah," Mina said, unable to keep a straight face. An explosion of "aw man," went off from the couch, but Mina barely heard. Brian kissed her gently, pulled back, and in a voice that melted her heart, said, "I missed you."

Her heart trotted as Brian kissed her again, this time longer, his hands pressing against her hips as he leaned in closer. Mina's head swam. She and Brian hadn't been this close since August. If you didn't count the many times she'd watched him play on television, it had been four months since they'd seen each other. The time apart had been all text messaging and phone calls. She kept her phone on so much she'd worn out two batteries already.

Oh my God, I'm swooning, she thought, giddy, and to prove it, lost her balance when Brian eased his hold on her hips.

"Mmm, good hands," she murmured when he rested his hand on the small of her back to steady her.

"Uh-huh." A playful smile lit up his face. "What you know about how good my hands are?"

"A little sumpun, sumpun," she said shyly, suddenly dumbstruck by his presence.

He was really here, home with her again. She quickly zapped the bothersome side note that he was only home for a week before heading back to school. Instead, she stared into his face, taking in the way his long eyelashes framed his friendly brown eyes, wanting to make sure the moment was real. Being up close, very close to her delight, she saw he looked different, somehow older and more mature. A clean thin line of facial hair framed a more square jaw, and his eyes seemed wiser, like he knew things.

How can that happen in four months? she wondered, content to sit there inches from his face, his hands lightly stroking her backside.

His left hand kept up the gentle stroke as the right hand lifted Mina's left hand. His thumb rubbed the silver heart-shaped ring on her finger. He grinned. "Just checking."

Mina squinted. "You thought I was going to stop wearing it?"

"You know how y'all chicks do." Brian's thumb played with the promise ring he'd given her, twisting it around her finger slowly. He gazed at her, his eyes narrowing as if probing into Mina's mind. "You probably just put it on 'cause you knew I was coming home. I need to do one of those spot inspections on you one day . . . catch you off-guard."

"And if you do, you're gonna be all burnt 'cause I'll have it on," she said. Her heart did a small happy dance when Brian squeezed her hand lightly and winked. "Shoot, I wish you *would* come home one day on the fly."

He dropped her hand gently, then resumed massaging her lower back. "Yeah, but you know that's not gonna happen. The season gears up for real after break."

"Yeah, I know." Mina frowned. "Am I gonna see you at all?"

"Nope. Not until school ends." He pulled her closer so they were face-to-face, practically sharing his stool. "So you know what that means, right?"

Mina pushed his chest and feigned pulling away. "Don't even say something nasty."

His face fell in exaggerated offense. "I wasn't."

"Yes, you were," Mina said, chuckling. She gave up her weak resistance, resumed their face-to-face stance, and put on her best wary tone. "What? What does that mean, Brian?"

"It means I only have a couple days to tap that . . ." He patted her butt then.

He burst out laughing and tugged at Mina as she pulled away, playing mad.

"See, I knew you were gonna say something rude," she said, untangling herself.

He grabbed at her, trying to pull her back, but she quickly slipped out of his grip and stood beside his stool.

"Just for that, I'm making you wait," she said, even as her body grew warm thinking about being alone with him.

"Don't be like that, Toughie," he said, faking sadness.

He swiveled in the stool so she was standing between his legs and wrapped his arms around her. She instinctively put her face up to his for the kiss she knew was coming and lost herself in it. Her hands stroked the back of his neck. Right as her body screamed "uncle," she pulled back, smiling.

"Still making you wait," she teased seductively before walking off to join the girls at the Pac-Man game.

"You so wrong for that," Brian yelled after her.

Mina blew him a kiss.

"Brian, you must have lost your touch," Jacinta said. "I thought y'all would have *been* gone."

"Your girl on that tease tip," Brian said. He watched the rowdy game of Madden for a few seconds before standing up and stretching his long legs. He walked over to the more subdued Pac-Man game, bear-hugging Mina from behind. They swayed lightly, side to side.

"Shoot, from what she told me, I'm surprised she didn't jump you when we picked her up from work tonight," Jacinta said, her grin sly. She moved away before Mina's smack could connect.

"Don't be telling all my business," Mina scolded.

"Actually, Brian, Mina told *me* that she's ready to take the pact with me," Lizzie said. She winked at Mina and they laughed.

Brian snorted. "Abstinence pact?" he hollered over the rising noise. "Todd, you still not handling your business, son?"

A round of bawdy teasing broke out as the guys gave Todd a hard time for complying with Lizzie's year-long virginity pact. Todd took it in stride. The only evidence that he was embarrassed were his hands, first the right, then the left, pushing through his unruly hair.

"She's the boss," Todd said, his blue eyes gleaming playfully.

"Okay, boss," JZ said, never taking his eyes off the plasma screen. "Liz, you my girl and all, but Todd a better dude than me. I would have stepped on you long ago."

"Thanks a lot, Jay," Lizzie said, scowling.

"Hmm . . . Greg's not saying nothing," Jacinta said. "Which means either Kelly broke the pact and gave him some or—"

"Or that Greg works out a lot to distract himself," Greg said. His hand covered Kelly's on the game's joystick as he helped her dodge the colorful ghosts hot on her trail.

Kelly smiled, embarrassed, refusing to join the public discussion of her sex life or lack thereof. She and Lizzie had taken the pact together before she and Greg started dating. She wasn't about to share that, as cool as she was with the pact, she was having a harder time than Lizzie being casual about it.

Todd ran over from the sofa, his hand up for a high five.

"Dude, that's what I'm saying," Todd said. He and Greg exchanged a pound. He yelled over to JZ, "See, Greg knows what it's like to live like a monk. I condition like twice a day so I won't go serial killer."

The clique cracked up at Todd's animated grimace.

"*That's* why you're looking so buff," Mina said.

Brian kneed the back of her leg lightly. "Oh, so you be checking him out?"

"Hells yes," Mina said. She lifted her head for a kiss and Brian leaned over, planting one on her. "Seriously, though. I was like, dang, T is getting huge."

With all the action at the back of the room, JZ and Michael put the game on hold and joined them.

"Ay, I just thought about something," JZ said. He put his arm around Lizzie. "Liz, keep your stuff on lock because I think it's helping T's game."

"I *know* it's helping my game," Todd said, his eyes an exaggerated pool of sadness.

Lizzie put her arms around his waist. "So I improved your game? Cool." She stood on her tiptoes and laid an affectionate peck on Todd's lips.

"Son, you mad aggressive on the court lately. I never connected it with your dry spell, though," JZ said, marveling at the thought. "Maybe I should try that." He laughed loud and hard. "Sike."

The sound of Lil Wayne penetrated the clique's laughter. Jacinta pulled her cell phone out of her pocket and the ring tone grew louder, shushing the group.

"Hey," she said into the phone, walking away.

Conversation resumed about Todd's newfound energy and aggression until Jacinta returned and announced, "I'm getting ready to roll, y'all."

JZ's eyebrow rose. "Where you dipping to?"

"That was Raheem," Jacinta said, pushing the cell back into her pocket. "He over at my aunt's house, so I told him to pick me up. Girlfriend duty calls."

Mina caught the hardening of JZ's stare despite how quickly it came and went. Her stomach rolled at the tension she felt in the fleeting glare and she attempted to joke it off. "Jay, looks like you gotta call one of your little jump offs tonight."

"Who said I wasn't gonna do that anyway?" JZ said, smirking. "I was just waiting for all y'all couples to bounce."

"Geez, are you kicking us out?" Lizzie said.

"Well, you know what they say?" A broad grin spread across JZ's face. "You don't have to go home but you gotta get the hell out of here."

Brain dapped him up. "I know that's right." He squired Mina toward the stairs. "Let's dip."

Kelly, Greg, Lizzie, and Todd followed behind them in the midst of a chorus of good-byes.

"That's messed up about you, Jay," Mina said, over her shoulder.

He saluted her. Just as she and Brian hit the stairs, she heard Jacinta say, "You gonna walk me out, big head?"

JZ's voice came back strong, "For what? You'n know your way out all of a sudden?"

Catching Feelings

" 'Cause first we were chillin', now I'm catchin' feelings."
—Day 26, "Exclusive"

Once everyone left, JZ sat back on the sofa, picked up his game controller, and waved it toward Michael.

"We gon' finish this game, son?"

Michael looked up from raiding the juice bar's fridge. He took a gulp of juice before answering. "I thought you were ready to call one of your side chicks."

JZ forced as much enthusiasm into his voice as he could. "I am, after we finish."

"You sure, kid?" Michael sauntered over and stood behind the sofa. "I don't want to block your game."

JZ grinned. "Naw. The shortie I plan on calling one of those rebel chicks. She'll sneak out no matter what time I ring her up."

He and Michael exchanged a fist pound. Michael walked around the sofa and took his seat on the left side of the large leather sectional. He picked up his controller and JZ unpaused the game. They played in silence for five minutes.

JZ's eyes were on the screen but his mind wasn't. Michael scored on him in no time.

"I can't believe you fell for that fake," Michael said, giddy with victory.

JZ groaned. "I know. And your punk ass just did that same move, two plays ago."

Their duo of laughter was small in comparison to the fullness of the clique's constant chatter, which had filled the room minutes before. Only the canned cheering of the game's crowd and the analyst's voice announcing that JZ's quarterback "seems confused" broke up the silence.

"He dissed you, son," Michael said, enjoying every minute of the whipping he was giving.

JZ cursed when Michael's team intercepted the ball. He hit the controller against the sofa and sat up, determined to focus.

"Hold up," Michael said. He pushed the button to call a time-out, freezing the game. "Gotta go. I finish this whipping in a minute." He walked toward the bathroom, teasing JZ the entire time.

"I be ready for you, punk," JZ said, with more bravado than he felt. When he heard the bathroom door shut, he flicked his phone out of his pocket and texted Jacinta.

Thas messed up about u . . . ur man call n u go runnin' I see how it is

His heart raced. He hoped Jacinta would take it for his normal joking, but couldn't help wanting her to know she was foul for mad dipping like that. He knew Raheem was home, but had figured he was hanging with his boy Angel for the night. That's what really had him angry, he convinced himself. Being caught off-guard was the issue, not the fact that Cinny had to leave, just *how* she'd left.

He eagerly read Jacinta's response.

U know how it is . . . don't trip ☺

He scoffed, typing back angrily.

I ain't rummin over this . . . jus sayin, I ain't know he had u in check like dat

He grinned.
Checkmate.
If there was one thing Jacinta hated, it was anyone thinking they had control over her. Her message back was simple.

Knucka please! He don't.

JZ eyed the bathroom when he heard water running. He typed back quickly.

Coulda fooled me. But w/e. have fun

He sneered at the message. His chest tightened as he wrote "have fun." He'd never meant something less.
He scowled down at Cinny's response.

Raheem says hey

JZ's fingers glided over the keyboard so fast he had to backtrack to delete his mistakes twice.

What he telling me hey for?!

He glared at the phone, unable to take his eyes off it even as Michael made his way across the room, already bragging about finishing up JZ's punishment. A smile broke across JZ's face as the response lit up his phone.

Duh cuz he think I'm talking 2 Mina. ttyl

That's right, I got your girl even when she right there beside you, JZ thought, sending mad telepathy to Raheem.

He put the phone away and settled back into the sofa, relaxed now.

"Come on, so I can beat you down, kid," he said, grinning.

"Man, please. You down by fourteen. You ain't catching *this* kid with that sorry QB," Michael said.

"Watch me. I'm ready go on a roll," JZ said.

He thought about Jacinta sneaking and lying to text with him. He was winning tonight, no doubt, even if it was only a small victory.

"I'm on a roll," he said again, his smile a mile long.

The Next Level

"Take me to New York, I'd love to see L.A."
—Estelle, "American Boy"

There were a few things Michael assumed he'd never see in his lifetime.

A fly pair of sweatpants. Wearing them signaled giving up, in his opinion. The things simply weren't made to be worn outside a gym.

Snow in July.

JZ being sprung.

All bets were safe on the first two remaining as elusive as an endangered animal in the rain forest. But he couldn't have been more wrong about that last one, because JZ was definitely sprung, gone, totally open over Jacinta.

He'd known JZ was texting Jacinta once everyone left last night.

First of all, JZ was mad that Jacinta dipped in the first place. He'd gotten that squinty eyed hurt look on his face, then he'd dogged Jacinta out by not walking her to the door—classic Jay.

Second, whenever it was Cinny texting or calling, the ring tone was always a pimplicious song like, "Playa's Rock" or "Sexual Eruption." Michael guessed that long ago, but had it confirmed when he'd mistakenly seen it was Cinny calling one day when JZ left his phone on the sofa.

Sprung.

JZ.

He'd wanted to give JZ grief about it, the other night, but JZ was working so hard to cover it up, Michael wasn't so sure he'd see the humor in it. He settled for whupping up good on JZ in three Madden rematches.

The losses alone were sign enough JZ was preoccupied about something.

Michael shook his head and laughed softly into the silence of the Bay Dra-da theatre troupe's sewing room, a gracious name for the dimly lit oversized supply closet the crew used for designing and fitting. Two sewing machines stood side by side, just far enough so people sewing wouldn't crack elbows, flush against a drafting table strewn with Michael's designs. Luckily, he was there alone. No more than three people could fit into the room at any given time and even then you risked someone poking your eye out if they moved too fast.

Forgetting about JZ's text creeping, he relished the quiet of the empty school—loving the access being in the theatre troupe gave him.

The holiday break was just what Michael needed. It gave him time to work on his latest design without the interruption of classes or someone bumping him as he sewed. Time he should have taken advantage of instead of hanging with the clique all weekend, but it had been a while since he'd let them dominate his weekend. It felt kind of nice.

Yawning, he stepped away from the headless mannequin, finally giving it his full attention. He took another step and another until he was almost out the door of the tiny room.

Distance wasn't enough.

He squinted at the formal baby-doll minidress, working unsuccessfully to convince his tired brain that the dress was as fabulous as the original sketch. Just a few weeks ago, it had been only a mass of shimmering pink and green tulle and an ambitious creation in Michael's mind. Now, a sequined sweetheart bodice glittered above the wisps of tulle, hugging what would be cleavage if the mannequin had any.

He hated it. The green was too . . . green, like a bag of frozen peas.

He loved it. The soft pink streaks within the green tulle and iridescent pink sequins peeked out just enough. Anyone thinking the dress was only green would be pleasantly caught off guard by the pastel highlights

A slightly electric buzzing in his veins coursed up and down his arms as he alternated between caressing the dress with his eyes and pelting it with darts of loathing. He stepped forward an inch, his hands itching to rip every seam and start from scratch. But his eye for fashion, knowing a good thing when he saw it, wouldn't let him step any closer. He remained frozen near the door of the sewing room thinking how the dress would shimmer under real lighting. Sudden affection for the piece stopped the tingling in his hands and something like hope peeked around the dark cloud above his head.

"Another MJ creation, like it or not," he said to the empty, dark cave.

He stuck his tongue out at the dress, immediately feeling bad. It wasn't the dress's fault he was having a fashion fit. The troupe's latest production was. He'd spent the last few weeks before break bored out of his mind, hemming and sewing costumes for the upcoming production of *High School Musical*.

His eyes rolled. *How original, a high school production of* High School Musical.

It was the first time since he'd gotten the gig as assistant costume designer that he hated the costumes, since they were simply regular clothing—nothing daring or unique, only straight modern-day American school teen. Mr. Collins, the troupe's director, hated Michael's idea of adding a futuristic twist to the production so he'd have at least *some* challenge.

So he'd been stuck feeling like a child laborer in a third-world country making huge numbers of polos and reconstructing denim so it looked more washed or worn. Today was the first real time he'd had to work on his own creation in months. He sent a telepathic apology to the dress and went about compiling his sketches from the messy drafting table.

"Michael, it's gorgeous," Madame Jessamay's voice said from beside him.

Startled, he held his breath to keep his thumping heart in check. He'd almost forgotten he wasn't in the school totally alone—the troupe was in the auditorium, on the other end of the building, rehearsing.

Madame, a French teacher and head costumer, breezed into the room and beelined to the dress. Layers of satiny material flowed around her feet as if there were a fan up her long skirt.

Michael had never seen her wear anything else, no matter the season, in the two years he'd worked as her assistant. The skirts were always colorful, usually silk or cotton. When Madame Jessamay stopped, the skirts kept right on shifting and swaying like they had a life of their own. In contrast, she wore what Michael suspected was a leotard underneath. Never a shirt or blouse, but a simple one-piece stretch top, cut right to her not so ample cleavage. If she wasn't a dancer in her former life, she wanted to be, because she was always dressed as if on her way to audition. All she had to do was drop her skirts and bam, hit a plié.

Madame Jessamay's hands hovered over the blingy bodice of his baby-doll dress before moving on and delicately fingering the tulle. She picked at it gingerly and peeked underneath at the dress's simple green satin body, the only (and most important) thing standing between the wearer and a long night of itching. She nodded as she hmm'ed and clucked, music to Michael's ears.

He ventured as far into the room beside her as he could without invading Madame's space and was still a few inches too close when she whipped around, a huge grin on her face. He stepped out of the way of her billowing skirt.

"You're quite a talent, no?" Madame Jessamay's eyebrow rose, and Michael grinned.

He loved the way she used the term *no* to mean *yes,* more music to his ears and confused heart. The dislike he'd felt for the dress minutes before was all but gone in Madame's praise. Like a junkie needing a fix, her assurance arrived right on time. Michael hated that he needed it. This lack of confidence in his work was new, a monster growing by leaps and bounds the closer he got to senior year and the realization that being the assistant costume designer at Bay Dra-da could honestly and depressingly be the height of his career if he didn't figure out where his life after Del Rio Bay High was going.

Madame Jessamay sat in the high-backed chair at the drafting table and gestured to the only other seat in the room. "Sit, Michel," she said, lapsing into the French version of his name, like she often did as if forgetting they were not in her class.

Used to it, he obeyed.

Madame Jessamay had a commanding presence. Part of it was the billowing skirts. Another part was her heavy French accent, which made it seem as if she was expecting—never asking but demanding—your compliance. As if it was the most natural thing in the world for everyone to do her bidding. Michael took Spanish and was glad for it. He'd heard Madame was a taskmaster and didn't doubt it.

Although she'd always been nurturing with Michael, he'd seen her slice people down in the hallways with a look, usually followed by a tongue-lashing that ended with a terse *no* to indicate absolutely *yes,* the person was in the wrong. It was a side of her he gladly experienced only as a witness from the sidelines. He aimed to please Madame Jessamay and not just because he was a little intimidated by her. Michael adored her, maybe even worshipped her a little—something he'd never admit to anyone, not even Mina.

He sat in the small chair, looking up at Madame expectantly.

Her eyes glanced over his head at the baby-doll dress and another jolt of panic zigzagged up Michael's arm as he convinced himself

Madame had found a major blunder while inspecting it. Up close she wasn't as impressed, and the boom after the praise was coming in five, four, three, two . . . He forced his dark chocolate face to go blank as he waited, breath hitched.

"You know how good you are, don't you, Michel?" Her head shook side to side in a tiny tremor. "No. No, you don't." She frowned, first at the dress, then at Michael. "Your body language is that of some-one worried, no? Why?"

Michael resisted the urge to shrug. They weren't in French class, but Madame treated everyone as if she were teaching a lesson. He'd learned long ago that shrugging, saying "I don't know," or otherwise feigning ignorance were sure ways to incur her wrath. Instead, he took a second and thought about his future, or rather how hazy his future seemed compared to the clique's. Mina, Lizzie, JZ, Kelly, Todd, even Jacinta—the one person Michael had assumed wasn't a whit interested in higher education—were thinking college. They talked about it constantly. His silence during the conversations was deafening. Sometimes it was so loud, Mina would catch herself ram-bling on about this school or that, smile at Michael, and throw him a bone by invoking the line, "And you're gonna be doing big things in NYC, by then, Mike. Getting your *Project Runway* on."

It was an afterthought though. *He* was an afterthought.

He loved the clique to death. He and Mina went back to pre-school. He and JZ to kindergarten. He and Lizzie to fifth grade. And though he'd only been friends with Kelly and Jacinta since freshman year, they were all tight now in some way. Still, he'd cut back on major clique outings an ice age ago. Getting with them at Rio's Ria for pizza, a few trips to the mall to help Mina outfit her wardrobe, gaming with JZ now and then, and the occasional impromptu pool party only peppered his time. Most times Michael was hanging with Rob, a dancer with the Players, Del Rio Bay's theatre troupe, or work-ing on a design—his own or Bay Dra-da's—here, at home, or at the large workroom at the Players.

Sewing and sketching designs was an escape he welcomed from the drudgery of classes and, if he were being honest, the clique's dating woes. When he needed a good dose of drama, he found his way back to them, happy to throw himself in the middle and offer drive-by advice. It worked for him, at first. But now, four months into their junior year, the clock to graduation was ticking so loud he felt like screaming to drown it out. Hanging with the clique only made it more obvious he had no idea what direction he was headed once he grabbed the diploma out of Mr. Patmore's hand.

If talk of who Mina was crushing after or who JZ was hooking up with dominated their freshman year, scholarships, GPAs, and should I/shouldn't I apply were all the rage now, not completely erasing talk of hookups and breakups, but edging them to the periphery of their daily discussion.

Seemed like when talk of the future came up, everyone else had an idea, if not an outright plan. Michael not only didn't have a plan, he didn't have a clue. All he knew was he didn't want to go to college, not even one specializing in fashion. When he walked off that stage seventeen months from now, his long affair with institutional education was over, period. His grandmother didn't like the fact much and his older sisters, who she called in for nagging reinforcement, weren't crazy about it either—but Michael's mind was made up.

And that was the problem. He knew what he didn't want to do, but not what he did.

His mind raced from one blank spot to another in an attempt to identify "his purpose" while Madame Jessamay stared down at him, calm and patient. Shrugs and ignorance she disliked, thoughtful pondering she was cool with. In her warm green eyes, Michael saw the opportunity to tell the truth to someone who might possibly understand.

His breath unraveled within a soft hiss. He pinched the crease of his khakis between his thumb and forefinger, sharpening it before crossing his right leg over his left, and admitted what haunted his mind more and more often. "I'm good enough to make costumes for a high school theatre group, but then what?"

He shuddered inside at Madame's wide-eyed surprise and fumbled ahead. "No disrespect, Madame. I know Bay Dra-da has one of the best troupes in the state. But . . . you know, designing for y'all and designing for . . ." He squinted, struggling to articulate himself. Unable to stop the reflex, he shrugged and ignored Madame's pinched-face disapproval. "I don't know. Somebody like Versace or even Ralph Lauren. It's not like I'm *that* good."

Madame chuckled. "You are humble, Michel. That's what I love about you. I don't know what Versace or Ralph Lauren or any other company might want in a young designer." This time she shrugged and winked to bring Michael into the inside joke, before turning serious once more. "But I know the talent you have could take you far."

The lilt of Madame's accent soothed Michael. There was something musical in her words, the way "humble" was "umble," "Lauren" was "Lah-wren" and "designer" was "dee-zign-air." His brain finally got around to piecing together what she'd said instead of how she'd said it, and a shy smile played on his lips.

"You know Madame Zora, no?" Madame Jessamay said.

Michael nodded, knowing the question needed no verbal answer. Of course he knew Madame Zora. She was Madame Jessamay's best friend—if that's what grown women still called themselves—and the costumer for the Players. She was a former model/graduate of some fancy fashion school in Paris. She had a scar that ran from her eye to the corner of her mouth, a nasty gift courtesy of an overzealous fan at a fashion show that ended her modeling career and sent her on a soul-searching journey ending in Del Rio Bay.

Whenever Michael was around her, and the madames weren't looking, he stared at the scar, fascinated by the price she'd paid for beauty. It was only a faint, dark line now, but one that would cost magazines a mint to airbrush, were she still a model. It also stood out like a Glow Stick in the night when she was angry, embarrassed, or excited—a raised, odd seam in the middle of her crimson cheeks.

With Madame Jessamay's blessing, Michael had assisted Madame Zora on a few outfits over the summer. And when things were particularly busy at Bay Dra-da and the sewing room didn't allow for chaotic alterations, Zora let them use her workroom. So yes, he knew Madame Zora. He looked on, curious, as Madame Jessamay continued.

"Zora sits on the admissions committee of the Carter School." She nodded in affirmation as she asked, "You've heard of it, no?"

Michael did. His boy Rob was a student there.

"It's the school of performing arts in DC," he said.

"Yes, that is the one." Madame waved, as if already mentally past the point. "Every year, Zora asks me to nominate Bay Dra-da's most promising students. The Carter School's music and dramatics programs are the best in the country. But so few of the parents here, in Del Rio Bay, are interested in the life of a struggling artiste for their child, no?" She and Michael chuckled an insider's laugh. Her hand waved dismissively again. "Dramatics, it is okay for school, but not profession, some parents say. Zora, she's so angry that I never have good candidates to pass. She thinks I'm holding out on her, afraid of angering Mr. Collins by sending his best talent to Washington." She snickered. "But maybe there is hope yet."

Madame scooted off the stool. She walked over to the dress, touched the ruched bow under the bodice, and turned to face Michael. "The Carter School has a program for aspiring designers. It is new. A . . ." Madame's eyes rolled to the right as she worked for the proper word. "A trial," she said, eyes shining. She walked over and stood by Michael's chair. "The school is not yet sure fashion design is an art per se, not by their definition anyway. But Zora is a persuasive person and one of the school's patrons. So they are willing to take her word that a program of this nature could benefit them.

Zora, she's impressed with your work. It is your work that convinced her that such a program for students so young would be a good thing."

Michael listened, enthralled. His eyes locked with Madame Jessamay to glean the meaning behind her words.

"Applications for the first year are being accepted now until late February. It's an intense, three-part process. An application, interview, and runway review." Madame smiled at the gleam in Michael's eye. She rushed on, spurred by his obvious interest. "If you were accepted, you would begin the semester in the summer." She laughed at his frown, waving away his concern. "Yes, yes, it's blasphemy to take away a young person's summer, no? But this is a once in a lifetime opportunity, Michel. For the trial, the program seeks only high school seniors with a serious interest in fashion. You'll work with some of today's top labels and be mentored by fashion insiders. It's worth giving up six weeks, no?"

Michael nodded, not quite sure if he agreed completely. This was his last high school summer they were talking about. The Carter School was a performing arts school, but it was still a school. Classes were classes no matter how you dressed them up. The thought of trekking to Washington, DC,—a forty minute metro ride away— every day while the clique swam, ate pizza, and chilled on Cimarra Beach, made him feel even more isolated than he felt when they inevitably coupled off for the night.

Sequestering himself in his basement bedroom—the manpartment, Mina called it—to doodle a new creation or piece one together while his friends canoodled at the movies or snuck in a hookup while the parents were out was one thing. Mandatory classes and sewing on demand while summer passed him by was another. He only half heard the rest of Madame's excited tale and was sure he'd promised to think about it over the holidays. He was sure he'd said it even though by then he hadn't meant it.

Ay Mon, No Worries

"Don't worry about a thing."
—Bob Marley, "Three Little Birds"

The sound of Bob Marley drifted through Seventh Heaven's, making Mina drowsy. Still, she found herself mouthing the words, "let's get together and feel alright," right along with the song. It was old-school reggae hour and Q'uan, Seventh Heaven's other DJ, was lost in the groove of his favorite song, eyes closed, swaying like a human leaf being blown by the song's melodic wind.

Mina bounced along with it, her knees bending up and down slowly, in time to the music, as she waited for her customers, a mother-daughter duo, to make up their minds between a pink cord mini on clearance and a full-priced khaki cargo skirt. They'd been battling over it for six minutes and twenty seconds; Mina knew because she'd eyed the clock on the register. And in her opinion, the khaki cargo was going to remain in the store. Mama Bear was adamant that it was too expensive.

She held a grin at bay as Sara walked by twirling her finger by her head to indicate the mother-daughter debate was crazy. As the back and forth raged on, Mina continued her slow bop. She'd never liked the song much until she'd realized Q'uan played it without fail as the last song of his old-school hour. Which meant their shift was coming to an end in exactly thirty minutes.

Today had been a good day. Between straightening racks and

working the register, she'd been jumping since arriving at nine. The store buzzed with a steady flow of shoppers catching the after-holiday sales.

Everyone and their sister had gotten a Seventh Heaven gift card for Christmas and decided to use it today, during her shift. At least being busy made her shift fly by. Her time with Brian was slipping through her fingers at warp speed. They had only this weekend and New Year's Eve, five lousy days, and then he was back to Durham.

No matter how hard she lost herself in the moments they were together, it seemed like either curfew or time for her to head to work stared her in the face, whisking her away just as they'd gotten comfortable. She'd worked Christmas Eve, and Christmas night was a blur of them exchanging gifts before they both split to their respective family dinners. If she didn't think her parents (and Cheryl, her manager) would straight kill her, she'd go MIA on the job until Brian left for school on Tuesday.

"Miss, when will this skirt go on sale?" the mother asked, her frustrated, pinched face pulling Mina back into Seventh Heaven's. The daughter was equally as battle-weary and tears streaked her face. Apparently Mom had drawn "first blood" while Mina was daydreaming.

"I can't say for sure," Mina said, in her best customer-friendly voice, smile frozen in place. "That skirt just came in yesterday. So probably not for a few weeks."

"Well, fifty dollars for a skirt you can't wear for another three months is insane," the mother said, turning her nose up at the offending item. She gestured to the mass of clothes at the register. "Tina, you already have over two hundred dollars' worth of clothes, right here."

"Mom, it's my money," the girl whined. "Aunt Cindy said I could buy what I wanted with it."

Mina admired the girl's tenacity. She pegged her at about eleven years old, five years younger than the ideal Seventh Heaven's customer. If she'd been in the girl's place, her mom wouldn't even be in Seventh Heaven's much less arguing about which skirt she could have.

You go, girl, Mina thought, rooting for the daughter to win, despite the odds. The mother's eyebrows were knitted so tightly they were one, and her jaw was rigid. She was digging in for that final ladle of "you can't have it because." Mina could feel it.

I don't think you're going to win this one, baby girl.

Mina's heart leapt as the music switched from the slow drag of Bob Marley to a foot stomping Elephant Man track. Q'uan was trying to kill a sister switching tempos that fast, but she tapped her foot in time, happy to be one minute closer to her shift's end.

"Aunt Cindy isn't the one who has to explain to your father why you're wearing a thin cargo skirt in the middle of winter that cost fifty dollars," the mother said. She plucked the skirt out of her daughter's hand and gave it to Mina. "We won't be buying this."

Mina sent condolences to the girl with her eyes as she placed the skirt on the rack behind her.

"Just the cord skirt, these jeans, and these tee shirts?" Mina asked, gathering the clothes off the counter without waiting for an answer. Her hands automatically went about unhooking hangers, patting down the skirt for sensor tags, and folding the dozen tee shirts. She'd scanned the items in no time and just as she was reciting the total, Jacinta, Lizzie, and Kelly came in.

The pouty tween reluctantly handed over the plastic gift card. Mina ran the card through the register and watched as her friends scattered throughout the store, each shopping different areas. Sara and Kelly jabbered near the new shipment of skinny jeans. Mina tore her eyes away as the customer's receipt zipped out of the machine.

"You still have twenty-four dollars." She handed the card back, passing the overstuffed bag across the counter to the girl. "If you wait about three weeks, the skirt will probably cost about that on sale."

"Thanks. I'll be back," the girl said, giving her mother a serious "try and stop me" look.

The mother's eyes rolled.

Mina smiled as the mom started her guilt trip. "Don't even think of asking for another piece of clothing until March."

"March?" the girl exclaimed, trailing after her mom with the heavy shopping bag.

"Have a nice day," Mina called after them.

The mom gave Mina a hurried wave as she lectured on out the front.

Mina cleared around the register, cluttered with tags and hangers, glad to be working the day shift. She had a good weekend on tap— all evening to kick it with Brian and the clique, a sleepover at Kelly's, and then to the DRB Varsity basketball tournament on Saturday.

It had been a long time since they'd all been together for an entire weekend. Mina's insides were jittery with excitement.

She scanned the area, making sure it was neat once more. A few customers milled about, browsing. Mina determined that none were likely to be checking out anytime soon, so she joined Lizzie and Jacinta at the tee shirt counter. Kelly and Sara wandered over, solidifying their obvious chat circle.

"I'm starving. Are the guys getting to Rio's Ria first and ordering the pizza?" Mina said, cocking her elbow on Jacinta's shoulder.

"They're supposed to," Lizzie said. Her eyebrows shrugged. "Customer at one o' clock."

Mina whipped around, smile on the ready. She stepped away from the group and closer to the woman.

"Miss, do you have this in blue?" The woman held up a plaid miniskirt with pleats.

"No. Just the pink plaid and the green plaid," Mina said.

"That's crazy. How in the world is pink a universal color?" The woman stared down the rack with the candy-colored skirts, shaking her head. "I mean, the pink is cute, but I wanted a color that went with the tops my daughter already has."

Mina nodded along, even though she wanted to blurt, "do you want it or not?" Instead she stayed rooted in the aisle while the woman weighed her options, nearly cheering when the woman sighed, handing the skirt over to Mina. "Thanks anyway. She just doesn't have enough to go with these colors."

Mina threw the skirt back on the rack and jumped back into the conversation.

"Who are we talking about?" she said, not caring that she was breaking Seventh Heaven's number one rule, no fraternizing with friends on the clock. She only had ten more minutes anyway.

"Nobody," Sara said. "I was telling them I just sent off my application to College Park."

"When will you know if you get a cheer scholarship?" Mina said, genuinely curious. Even though she wouldn't have to worry about college apps until next fall, she was already narrowing her choices. College Park was among them because cheerleading was considered a Division I sport there and they provided scholarships.

Mina had never seriously considered going to school there until Sara began talking it up, because the competitive squad was separate from the cheerleaders who cheered games. She loved both aspects of cheerleading and was torn about strictly competing. Still, money for school was money for school. She was curious about the University of Maryland, College Park even if lately her college choices fell much closer to Duke, for obvious reasons.

"I probably won't know about the scholarship until spring," Sara said. She absently straightened a few hangers, pushing them so they were exactly two inches apart. "But College Park is cheaper than Florida State, and you know it's all about cost for me and Jess."

"I know your parents are bugging having to pay for two of you at the same time," Jacinta said.

"Totally. Right now they want us both to go to UMCP and commute from home."

There was a collective groan from the girls.

"Just when you think you're getting out—" Mina mimed fishing—"they reel you back in."

The girls' laughter was loud but no competition for Q'uan's super dance hall mix. The walls practically vibrated from the bass.

Spying Cheryl on the floor, Mina scurried a few feet away and organized the miniskirts, making them orderly and color coordinated. The girls scattered. Sara stood nearby, refolding a perfectly folded tee shirt.

A dark-skinned guy walked into the store and made a beeline for Mina. He was wearing a fitted tee and a pair of dark wash jeans snug around his small waist, but casually loose around his thighs. She saw him and he saw her seeing him, so he smiled bright as if they knew one another.

He was good-looking, about five feet six or seven, hair in a low cut. As he got closer Mina saw his arms were much larger and chest broader than she'd expect on someone so thin.

"Hey. You're Mina, Mike's friend, right?" the guy said when he stopped, standing between Mina and Sara.

"Yeah. Hi," Mina said. She gave Sara a confused side glance.

"I'm Rob," he said.

"Ohhh," Mina said. She grinned, embarrassed. "I thought you looked a little familiar."

"Yeah, I saw you looking like, who is this dude acting like he know me." Rob imitated the look on Mina's face. "Mike talks about you all the time. And I've lurked around your Cool Peeps page a few times." He pointed at Mina's promise ring. "The pictures of the ring were cute."

"Thanks. Michael talks about you too," Mina said, though careful not to say "all the time." Because Michael didn't. Usually only a mention here and there, but otherwise, Rob McQueen was merely a name and a few photos posted on his Cool Peeps page. "He said you have a hella crazy schedule. You go to the Carter School, right?"

Rob's eyes lit up as he nodded. "Yeah. My schedule can get crazy, but I think Mike just likes keeping you to himself. I've been wanting to introduce myself since I saw you at the Cove party that time a billion years ago." He gestured to the mall. "I had to get some new kicks and I saw you from in the mall. So I was like, let me go finally meet the diva." He chuckled at Mina's embarrassed smile.

"Okay, that's *Mike's* name for me. I didn't ask to be called that." Mina laughed. Hearing Sara's titter, she remembered her manners. "Oh, sorry. Rob, this is my friend Sara."

Sara said a shy hi, and Rob waved to her as he said, "Girl, nothing's wrong with being a diva. Anyway, I'm glad I finally got to meet the Deev."

"Are you busy tomorrow?" Mina asked.

Rob scowled in concentration. "No. Why?"

"We're all hanging out, having some pizza, then heading to Kelly's to chill. You should come," Mina said. Rob seemed like he'd fit in with the rest of the crazies.

"Now, who is Kelly, again?"

Mina pointed across the store. "Fly little Latina mami, over there. She lives in Folger's Way."

"Umph, Mike be hanging out in Folger's?" Rob's eyebrow shot up. "Boogee much."

He and Mina laughed. Sara chuckled politely.

"Don't get it twisted, it's actually going to be Mike's first time there," Mina said.

"Oh, I was ready to say, I didn't know he rolled with the ballers like that."

Mina put her hand on Rob's shoulder. "We're just gonna be tripping, hanging out. Stop by."

"What? The diva isn't tipping off to be with her man, solo, tomorrow?" Rob said.

Mina scowled. "I need to get on Mike spreading my business. For real, though, me and Brian probably will chill later that night. But Mike would trip if we all coupled off too early."

"Naw, he'd just call me and *we'd* end up chilling," Rob said.

"Well, come meet everyone and see exactly why he needs a break from us," Mina said. Seeing Rob's eyebrow pop, she elbowed him playfully. "Don't trip, I know he be putting us on blast for canoodling."

"Okay, but you didn't hear it from me," Rob said, chuckling.

Mina and Sara laughed so loud that Cheryl looked over.

"We better be quiet," Sara whispered. "I don't think we can convince Cheryl he's buying one of these minis."

They giggled quietly for another second.

Rob stuck his hands in his back pocket and rocked back on his heels. His smile was wide as he cocked his head, giving Mina an easy once over with his eyes. "Well, thanks for the invite, Mina. I think I might dip by."

"Remember, if you miss us at Rio's, go to Folger's and just tell the dude at the gate you're a guest of Kellita Lopez. They'll buzz her."

Rob nodded politely. "All right. Well, later," he said before turning heel and walking out as confident as he'd come in.

Mina and Sara watched Rob until he disappeared around the corner. Kelly, Lizzie, and Jacinta were by their sides immediately.

"You can tell he's a dancer," Mina said.

"Lizzie said that's Mike's friend, Rob," Kelly said.

"That's right, Liz, you're the only one who's met him before," Mina said. "I invited him to hang out tomorrow."

"I've only met him once," Lizzie said, shifting her gaze to Mina. "Are you sure Mike's going to be cool with that? I mean he's never invited Rob over himself."

"Lizzie, I swear, you worry about anything," Jacinta said. "You need to start worrying about the clock ticking on your little virginity pact. Todd is counting down to May like a mug."

Lizzie's green eyes flashed annoyance, but she kept quiet and stared, with the others, at the corridor where Rob had gone.

"He was cute," Kelly said.

"Nice guns," Sara said.

"Nice chest," Mina said.

"He's gay," Jessica said from behind, startling them.

Mina's eyes rolled. "Just because he's a dancer?"

"No." Jessica snorted. "I didn't even know he was a dancer."

"Then why'd you say he was gay?" Sara asked.

"Because he's always out here with your friend . . . the dark-skinned one," Jess said, pointing at Mina.

Mina sucked her teeth. "You mean Michael?"

She'd known Jessica since sixth grade and Jess always acted as if she didn't know Michael's name. It was her way of saying he wasn't important enough to remember. She certainly knew JZ's name just fine.

"Yeah, him," Jess said. She ran her hand over the hangers, ensuring they all went in the same direction. "I've seen them at the food court together and at Abercrombie a few times. They're always out here together. They look like a couple."

"Because they're together in the *mall*?" Mina said, frowning.

Jessica shrugged her shoulder up and down. "Look, I'm only saying they seem more like a couple than two dudes just hanging out. Besides, *isn't* Michael gay?"

"No," Mina said too quickly. She frowned and changed her tone. "No, Mike's not gay. You're stereotyping just because he does the costuming for Bay Dra-da."

Jessica laugh was short and harsh. "Okay, you're giving me way more credit than I deserve. Do you seriously think I knew whatshis-name was with Bay Dra-da?" Her right eyebrow raised in question. "I just thought he was gay because I never heard about him dating anyone and . . . I don't know. I just thought he was."

"Well, he's not," Mina said evenly, working to keep her face blank. If Jess knew she had gotten under her skin, she'd only burrow deeper.

"Well, if he's not, somebody better tell his boyfriend," Jess said, walking away.

Shaken Not Stirred

"I gotta ask myself, what's it gon' be."
—Robin Thicke, "Ask Myself"

"So wait . . . you told Madame Jessamay you'd do it but you didn't mean it?" Rob said, his lip jutted in disapproval. A dark cloud passed over his handsome chocolate face in understanding. "Mike, man, why are you putting your friends before yourself? That's crazy."

Michael pretended to be too focused on the baby-doll dress to answer, double checking for hidden pins even though he knew Rob was waiting for a response. Rob worked under Madame Zora, both as a member of the Players and a student at the Carter. Madame Zora was Madame Jessamay times ten, so dude knew a little bit about commanding answers and patiently waiting for them.

Michael busied himself searching for pins he knew weren't there, doing anything to avoid the questioning expression in Rob's eyes. His basement bedroom was huge, the full length of the house, but Rob's inquisition made the room feel like the troupe's tiny sewing room. Stumbling over the small raised platform, Michael muttered to himself more about being on the hot seat than his stumped toe.

Pretending to check the dress's fold, he slyly checked his watch. It was six-thirty. He needed to wrap this up, get Rob on his way and meet the clique at Rio's. But Rob remained stoic, on the other side of the platform, his dissatisfaction radiating from his crossed arms to the upturned scowl.

"For real," Rob said, his eyebrow inching ever higher. He crossed the short distance between them and stood shoulder to shoulder with Michael, invading his space, boldly asserting his point. "Do you know how many people would be, like, creaming themselves if Zora had started a program based on *their* talent?"

"Don't hate 'cause your jealous," Michael said, attempting to lighten the mood.

Rob rolled his eyes. "Hells yes I'm jealous." He folded his arms, making his well-sculpted biceps pop. "I have to try out for my spot this year and Zora's practically handing you a scholarship."

Michael frowned. "Hardly. I still have to apply."

"Dude, she went to the school's board of trustees and asked them to start a fashion program 'cause of your designs." He shook his head, as if the whole idea were too outrageous to comprehend. "For real, what are the odds they'd turn you down?"

Refusing to look up, Michael shrugged. His neck burned from a mix of embarrassment and excitement. The way Rob framed it, he was the world's biggest idiot for even uttering he wasn't down for applying. Michael had already explained to Rob that it wasn't that easy, but Rob wouldn't let it go.

Michael envied how openly passionate Rob was about theatre. Michael loved fashion as much, but he couldn't go around rhapsodizing about it 24/7 in the halls of DRB High or even around the clique . . . especially not around the clique, JZ specifically.

It wasn't a big deal, really. Michael had a life outside of Bay Drada. He couldn't help it if Rob couldn't say the same.

Still, his seesawing doubts forced his hands to move faster for the phantom pins.

"When your peeps at college, what are you gonna do?" Rob pretended to flip through the pages of a huge book. His eyes mocked wistful reflection. "Reminisce over your portfolio in between your shifts at Subway?"

Michael sidestepped Rob and squatted, checking the dress's hem for the fifth time. The haughty hitch in Rob's voice grated like nails on chalkboard.

Normally, Michael was equally as balls-to-the-walls honest with people. He just wasn't in the mood for it tonight, even though Rob was his boy.

It was his job to be straight with Michael. And dude never slept on that job, not once in the three years they'd been friends. They'd been tight ever since Michael ran his very first errand for Madame, dropping a package of patterns to Madame Zora, just a few weeks after getting the gig with Bay Dra-da. He'd been wandering the Player's cavernous auditorium for ten minutes when Rob took mercy on him and walked him to Zora's office.

It was the first time Michael had met another African American dude, his age, in Del Rio Bay into theatre. It had been like discovering a long-lost family member, and they'd clicked immediately. They didn't disagree often, but when they did Michael received a good, old-fashioned heap of his own medicine in Rob's practical scolding.

Unable to stall any longer, Michael stood up. He scowled, snapping his answer to hide the fear clouding his mind.

"Trust, I'm not putting anybody else first." He elbowed Rob not so gently in the chest and smiled weakly. "And you'll be the first person trying to get the hookup during my Subway shift. So don't trip." He shrugged with a nonchalance he didn't feel. "I told you I don't want to spend my summer running back and forth to DC." He took a deep breath and found the courage to face Rob's angry disdain, infusing commanding annoyance into his words. "And I don't want to spend my senior year at another high school. That's wack."

"Why? You'd already know me, Maribel and Ferdinand." Rob's face hardened waiting for Michael to challenge. When Mike kept silent, Rob traced the shape of the finished baby-doll dress, barely touching it. His voice was all awe and respect. "Even if you didn't know anybody, you got mad talent. It's straight madness to waste it. You turning this down is like . . . it's like a model being discovered on the streets and telling Tyra Banks, no thanks, I don't want be on your show because I don't wanna miss my prom."

Michael snickered and Rob joined in. There was a moment of comfortable silence as Michael basked in Rob's subtle compliment until the indignation returned in Rob's voice.

"You worrying about leaving DRB High, but let you tell it, your friends wouldn't put off their life for you. That's for sure."

Michael had no response for that. What could he say? Yes, they would? He knew better. Obviously he'd complained to Rob about being the odd man out one time too many. It was a truth he didn't want to hear, not like that would shut up Rob.

He was caught off-guard when Rob's voice took on a light paternal lilt. "Mike, it's your decision but I bet if you get all your designs together in a portfolio and see just how tight your work is, you'll change your mind and want to apply to the Carter."

"Maybe," Michael said, playing down the excitement the thought of his arsenal of designs brought on.

Rob's shoulders hitched. "So just do that. If you still ain't down once you see 'em all laid out, then you ain't down. You know?"

As if assured the decision had been made, Rob stretched his lean, muscular body to the ceiling, then leaned to the right, stretching his left arm in a graceful arc.

"Oh, I met Mina the other day."

"Word?" Michael said.

"Yup. She cool peoples," Rob said. He did a deep knee bend, lowering and raising his body fluidly as if rhythmic movement was the only way he knew to move. "She invited me to hang with y'all tonight."

"Oh yeah?" Michael said, working to keep his tone neutral. "Thought you had studio time booked tonight?" He darted over to the table holding his material, unwilling to let Rob see the mixture of surprise and anxiety on his face. He wasn't ready for Rob to meet JZ. Truth be told, never was too soon.

"I do," Rob said. He hesitated a moment before going on, his voice probing. "I don't know, I still might stop through. . . . I mean, 'cause Mina might take offense if I didn't." He chuckled. "I might be breaking one of her friend rules you always talking about, right?"

Michael's mouth provided an answer—"Yeah, she's a little loopy when it comes to rules of engagement"—even as his mind scrambled for a way to prevent Rob from stopping by.

His hands automatically went through the motions of straightening pins, scraps of material, cushions, and miscellaneous sewing supplies. His constant talk about the clique to Rob was finally coming back to haunt him. Although Rob teased him, questioning if the clique actually existed outside of Michael's mind, tonight was the closest he'd ever come to confirming Michael's suspicion that he wanted to meet the friends Michael spent as much time boasting about as venting.

Rob didn't have a single friend in Del Rio Bay not associated with the Players. He brushed it off when the topic arose, but Michael suspected Rob was still plenty bitter about growing up friendless in a neighborhood overrun with other guys his age.

"I can see why she's your girl, though," Rob said, grabbing his jacket off a nearby mannequin. "Cute. Nice. Just like I figured she'd be."

There was no mistaking the longing in his voice, but Michael kept his answer neutrally witty. "I'll let her know you approve." He stood woodenly by the table, nothing else to put away.

"You do that," Rob said, his usual pragmatic tone back. He put his fist out for a pound. "Deuces, brother. I gotta get back over the bridge and burn this studio time."

Saved by the dance, Michael thought, tapping his fist against Rob's, his grin a mile wide. "All right. Later, kid."

Rob paused at the stairway. "Hey, where does that girl Kelly live again?"

"Folger's Way," Michael said cautiously, his grin faltering.

Rob's eyebrows scrunched in concentration, then eased with recognition. "Oh, right." He shrugged his jacket to his ears. "See you."

When Worlds Collide

"It's good to be crazy, ain't it baby."
—Ne-Yo ft. Jay-Z, "Crazy"

Michael sent invisible waves across the table to Mina. He was pissed at her. It baffled him that it never occurred to her that there was a reason it had been three years and he hadn't bothered to invite Rob out with the clique. He stared a hole through her, waiting for her to see him glaring. She was oblivious as she and Brian whispered, dipping in and out of the rest of the table's chorus.

The door to Rio's Ria opened and Michael cracked his neck looking up, hoping and getting his wish that it wasn't Rob.

His heart pattered erratically.

Even as he breathed a sigh of relief, guilt throttled him, making his temples pulsate. It made him sick that he didn't want Rob to show up tonight. But it was what it was. Mina believed in that fairy tale ending, let's all be friends stuff. He didn't. Some people simply weren't compatible. And JZ and Rob wouldn't be. Michael knew it with a certainty that made the pounding in his head boom double time.

JZ was leading man confident, certain laughter would follow at his every witty remark and that people would agree with him as long as he flashed his charisma. Rob was master dancer arrogant, matter-of-fact about his point of view, never doubtful that his way was the obvious "right" path.

They were actually more alike than different, but JZ would never notice, much less ever admit it. Talk about clash of the titans.

Michael willingly played the straight man to JZ's Joker, his role sealed after eleven years of friendship. He rolled with JZ's macho flow without ever giving in to it. On the flip side, he and Rob were on more equal footing. Their similar opinionated personalities meshed surprisingly well, giving their relatively new friendship an old-couple's comfort.

Michael slipped comfortably into either skin when he was with his two best guy friends, but until now lived blissfully ignorant of what life would be like if the two ever crossed paths.

He had no doubt Rob would see his easygoing, low-key attitude around JZ as too side-kickish. And JZ would see his and Rob's comfortable bond as girly. Not that it would take much for JZ to go there. Just knowing Rob was a dancer, the kind who saw beyond hip-hop dancing, would be enough for JZ to discount Rob as soft.

Michael rubbed his throbbing temples. His eyes focused on Lizzie's mouth moving and he slowly emerged from his fog in time to realize she was asking him for his part of the check. The clique was making moves to leave. He'd zoned out of the conversation almost from the start and now they were ready to roll.

Relief washed over him. Rob hadn't shown.

Kelly's nabe was gated. Michael couldn't see Rob showing up in a strange neighborhood with a guard at the gate. His heart did a happy flip.

There was the usual minor confusion as they all chipped in to pay for the food. As he placed a five on the table, Mina's eyes finally connected with his.

His eyebrows furrowed. "We need to talk," he mouthed.

She frowned, but nodded. As everyone streamed to the door, Mina hung back until Michael was by her side. They lagged behind.

"What's up, baby boy?" Mina linked arms with him.

Michael slid his arm out. "Uh-uh. I'm mad at you, Mina."

She stopped just short of the door, looking as if she were having a tough time processing the words. "Why?"

Michael walked into the pizza place's small foyer and leaned against the wall, his arms folded, his expression disapproving. He wasn't that mad anymore, now that Rob hadn't shown, but he had to give Mina the proper amount of grief.

She stood in front of him, chucked his elbow. "What did I do?" She was too sincere for Michael to hold on to his pretend anger.

"Deev, why didn't you tell me you invited Rob?"

Mina's eyes rolled. "Who told you? I wanted it to be a surprise. He's a sweetie. I—"

Michael put his hand up to stem the flow of her words. "He told me. Look, don't take this wrong, but Rob is like . . . he's who I kick it with to get away from y'all."

Mina pouted. "Gee, thanks, Michael."

He grinned. "I told you don't take it wrong."

Michael linked arms and led Mina to the door. It was full dark in the early winter evening. The clique's voices rang above the steady stream of traffic on Main Street. They were already fifteen yards ahead, but Michael purposely strolled, enjoying the few minutes he had Mina to himself.

"You know how Cinny always talking about keeping her life in the Cove from straight mashing her life in the Woods?" He draped his arm around Mina's shoulder as she nodded. "It's kind of like that." He grinned down at her, his smile shining in the dark, and bumped her hip with his. "Plus, Rob is like my parallel world JZ. No one knows what happens when parallel worlds meet. One of 'em might dissolve into a million pieces."

He was relieved when Mina threw her head back and laughed.

"I know, right?" she said. "Maybe if we're lucky just JZ's mouth will dissolve."

Michael's laugh carried in the night's breeze. "You not right."

Their steps sped up, in sync, as they neared Folger's Way, a large enclave of mini mansions set off the main road.

"I'm sorry I asked him to pop over," Mina said, squeezing his waist for emphasis. "I honestly thought you never had him over because, like his schedule was so crazy you always said. I just figured the time had never been right. When I saw him at the mall, I thought it was a sign."

Michael chuckled. "You and your signs."

"Don't sleep on my signs, Mike. For real, most times they're seriously on target."

Michael left it alone. He knew Mina believed in signs like some people believed in God. When it was a "good" sign, she swore by it. When it was "bad," she fretted like nobody's business, driving everybody crazy until her world righted itself.

"He didn't show up so maybe that's a good sign," Mina said, rambling on happily.

"More likely a sign that he ended up getting some extra studio time."

Mina stopped abruptly. "Oh, and how come you never mentioned that his body is like woah?"

Michael tugged her along. "'Cause you have a boyfriend. What purpose would mentioning that serve except to have you window shopping in a store you can't afford?"

Mina wriggled free of his hold and gave him a shove. "That is so wrong, Mike."

They tripped off one another, dissing back and forth until they were only a few feet from catching up to the clique, huddled near the electric eye that would grant them access through the gate. They all stood under the only streetlight near the entrance, a lit mass within a huge pocket of darkness.

"Come on, they must be waiting for us," Michael said, his steps quickening.

The huddle separated as they approached.

Michael tripped over Mina's foot as Kelly said, "There he is. Mike, Rob is here."

Rob's right eyebrow arched. "What's up, Mike?" A big, warm smile spread across his face. "Hi, Mina."

"Hey, Rob. I'm glad you made it," Mina said.

The extra cheer in Mina's voice hurt Michael's ears. He was likely the only one who knew Mina inside out enough to get that high-pitched tremor in her voice was anxiety. She threw Michael a quick, nervous glance of apology before joining the circle next to Brian, whose arm automatically went around her shoulders.

Oh yeah, sure, you *have somewhere to hide,* Michael thought, resisting the urge to grimace.

Rob had shown up. So which sign is this? Michael wanted to ask. Instead, he stepped into the huddle's center and exchanged a half-hearted pound with Rob, his mouth too dry to respond.

"Did you meet everybody?" Mina asked, making up for Michael's absent manners.

"Yeah." Rob gestured to the guard booth, to their left. "Good thing Kelly recognized me from the mall. I think the rent-a-cop was ready to call the real cops on me. I've been here under this light for about ten minutes, hoping y'all hadn't gone through yet." He smiled apologetically. "Sorry, Kelly, I had forgot your last name. I didn't want to look dumb at the gate trying to guess at it. I ain't never been to a nabe where I had to give a blood test and background check."

The clique's laughter echoed off the naked trees surrounding the neighborhood's entrance.

"I know, right," Jacinta said. "Wait till you go through the gate. Kelly's neighborhood is spooky quiet."

Rob's eyebrow jumped. "Shoot, even more quiet than it is out here?"

"Yes," Jacinta said.

"Where do you live, man?" Greg said.

"The hood. I live in Del Rio's Crossing," Rob said. He questioned Jacinta. "You're from the Cove, right?"

"Uh-huh." Jacinta played mad, rolling her eyes at Michael. "I see Mike spreads all our business, proper-like."

"Girl, please, like people can't see you from the Cove," JZ said. He grabbed Jacinta's wrist in a light hold just as she went to smack him. "Just jokes, baby girl. Just jokes. We know you hood fab and proud."

As the chatter increased and grew more casual, Michael relaxed. He shifted his weight so he was perfectly wedged between Mina and Kelly, closing the huddle completely. He scanned the circle, watching everyone's body language, as if to ensure himself everything was going well.

Todd was joking, as usual.

Jacinta was saucy, as usual.

JZ was sarcastic, as usual.

Mina was playing hostess, giving Rob's resume to everyone as if she was the one who'd known him for years—taking over, as usual.

Rob, sandwiched between Todd and Jacinta, chatted easily, fielding the clique's questions about attending the Carter and his tight schedule.

A breeze stirred and the circle tightened as everyone fought to ignore the chill swirling around them.

Mention of Rob's neighborhood, the only other low-income housing in Del Rio Bay besides the Cove, arose again, and Jacinta, glad to have someone in the circle from the side of Del Rio Bay she hailed from, blessed everyone about their boogee ways. "Don't mind them, Rob," she said. "Until they met me none of them had ever even been to our side of the DRB."

"Man, please," JZ said, sucking his teeth. "Me and Mike used to ball on the Cove's courts all the time."

As much as Jacinta deserved the chance to no longer be the sole hood rep, Michael couldn't resist calling her out. "Okay, Cinny, don't even pull the 'I'm so hood thing' on us." He folded his arms. "You definitely a burb chick, now. The point of no return was your A.M. swims with JZ this summer."

A loud chorus of "oohs" broke out. Michael's grin was wide in his dark chocolate face. He laughed aloud when Jacinta had no comeback.

JZ reached across the tight circle and gave him a pound. "Son, you got her good on that one."

"Whose side are you on, JZ?" Jacinta said, hands on her hips.

"My boy's side." JZ folded his arms tight across his chest, towering over her, a smile on his handsome face. "You know you as boogee as Mina and them now. Don't even try it. I'm waiting for you to start wearing your hair in a ponytail."

"Man, whatever," Jacinta said, waving him and Michael off. She absently ran her hands through her straight chestnut hair. It had been a processed blond, short, curly style when she'd first moved to the Woods. Now it was cut in layers and nearly to her shoulders. She wore it pulled off her face, flipped at the ends, the upturned curls defying gravity.

Michael liked her hair long. It softened her honey-complexioned face.

"Hey, what's wrong with a ponytail?" Mina said from beside him. She hugged up against Brian as she fussed at JZ. "Shoot, you try having to do your hair every morning. It gets played out."

Todd interrupted as the other girls joined Mina's mock outrage, ganging up on JZ. "Seriously, I think the guard's ready to call the po-po on us." He waved mechanically at the guard, emerging from the small hut. "Kelly, hurry, flash your credentials."

"Not the credentials, though," Brian said.

"See, I knew it," Rob said. He wedged himself deeper within the safety of the clique, settling in shoulder to shoulder with Jacinta. "Do I need my passport?"

"Hell to the yes," Jacinta said, making them all laugh again. "Or at least have your hood pass ready, so they'll let you back into Del Rio's

Crossing. When you hang on this side too long they turn you into one of them."

"And you love every second of it," JZ said, draping an arm over Jacinta's shoulder.

She shrugged him off playfully.

Kelly left the group and met the guard halfway. He smiled when he saw her face and saluted the clique, politely.

Todd put his arms up, as if holding off questions from a mob. "Okay, people, everything's cool. RoboCop gave us the go-ahead." He peered into the darkness toward the road. "Hey, who's that?"

Everyone turned and stared at a car pulling up next to them at the curb. The passenger window came down as Kelly returned to the circle.

"Ay, Cinny, come here," Raheem said, his face a shadow in the early evening dusk. His voice greeted the clique. "What's up, y'all?"

There were muttered hellos as Jacinta broke the circle and approached the car. She leaned over, resting on the window's ledge, her head inside the car.

"Is one of those dudes her boyfriend?" Rob whispered, when they'd closed the circle.

"Yeah, the one who called her," Michael said.

"Do you know them?" Mina said.

"I thought you were from Del Rio's Crossing, not the Cove," Lizzie said.

"I know the dude driving, though," Rob said. "Hustler named Angel. I heard he already supplying half the campus with drugs up at TU."

"He's still dealing at school?" Mina said. "I figured he'd stop."

"I'm surprised, 'cause college kids *never* do drugs," Brian said, openly mocking Mina. He pinned her arms down in a hug so she couldn't retaliate. "Just kidding, Toughie."

"Shoot, he probably have more customers now than before," Rob said.

"Dude, how do you know all this?" Todd said. His hands skittered through his locks restlessly before settling around Lizzie's waist.

Rob shrugged. "Everybody know Angel and his uncle. They're Colombian dealers."

"He's Puerto Rican," Kelly blurted. Her eyes fluttered as everyone looked her way. "I mean . . . maybe they get their drugs from Colombia"—she shrugged—"but he's Puerto Rican."

"How do you know where they get their drugs?" Greg said, scowling.

Kelly tucked her hair behind her ear and shifted from her right foot to her left. "I don't."

"G, you know your girl just reppin' for her people," JZ said. He beamed at Kelly as he called out, party-style, "Puerto Rico. Ho-oh."

Kelly smiled gratefully and stepped so she and Greg were hip to hip. Her face fell when he shifted his weight away, his eyes intent on Rob as if he didn't feel the tiny bump from Kelly.

"Whatever they are, they pushing mad weight from what I hear," Rob said. "I just thought maybe y'all girl was messing with Angel and didn't know. But she messes with the other dude, so . . ." His shoulders hunched quickly, dismissing the rest.

"Well, I guess that was the hood four-one-one," Michael said, hoping to break the wave of anxiety he felt pulsing from Kelly. There was some teetering, but the cloud that accompanied the arrival of Angel's car showered the group in tension.

Greg's usually smiling face was tight. Not that Michael blamed him. Dude couldn't seem to emerge from Angel's shadow, even though he and Kelly had now been dating longer than she and Angel ever officially had. He also felt bad for Kelly. Even though she'd made sure not to even look Angel's way, the old vibes from her ex had soured the moment anyway.

He started to throw in the towel, ask Rob to walk home with him and call it a night. It wasn't Rob's fault he didn't know that Angel was a sore subject, but he'd opened a can of worms for sure.

The light banter they'd all been exchanging seconds ago fell as silent as the night.

Kelly, standing next to Michael, shifted uncomfortably, then cleared her throat. "Are we ready?"

"Aren't we going to wait for Cinny?" Lizzie said. She stood on her toes, looking over the top of the circle at Jacinta's backside wiggling in the gloom.

"Man, for what?" JZ said. He raised his voice, turning his head in the direction of Jacinta's back. "She need come on or get her ass left."

"I know I wouldn't walk through here alone. It's mad quiet," Rob said. He shrugged his jacket closer to his ears and snugged his hands in his pockets as he looked around the dark street. "I know the burbs supposed to be safer. But seriously, it's crazy quiet here."

"Told you," Jacinta said, as she stepped back into the circle.

As if Jacinta's voice were a starting gun for a race, Kelly quick-stepped to the gate and the others followed.

"Oh, so you still hanging?" JZ said. He sauntered a step ahead of Jacinta. "I figured you was gon' dash with your boy."

"And if I did, you'd just be texting me all night." Jacinta grinned up at him. "So I figured I might as well stay here."

"She got you there, kid," Michael said.

The raucous laughter of the clique echoed in the silent night, quickly breaking up the somber mood.

JZ vs. JZ

"Shorty made me smile when ain't a damn thing funny."
—Lloyd ft. Lil Wayne, "Girls Around the World"

JZ joked along, taking Jacinta's ribbing in stride.

He lobbed his retorts through barely clenched teeth, even throwing in a few about Brian being whipped and Todd's case of blue balls so it wouldn't look like he was singling Jacinta out in his "friendly" wrath. He flopped his hood onto his head, sunk his hands into the pockets, and sauntered in the middle of the pack's fast pace.

"Are we there yet?" Michael said, whining good-naturedly.

"Told you we should have drove," Brian said. He stopped, stooped down, and hefted Mina onto his back, trotting to catch up with the others. "Y'all know when we go to walk back home later, it's gonna be freezing like a mug."

"I can give you guys a ride, if you want," Kelly said.

"And who's riding on the roof?" JZ said. "Only a few of us can fit in that M-class."

A minor debate broke out about the return trip to their separate communities as Kelly's brick-front colonial house came into view.

Jacinta tugged the arm of JZ's hoodie. "Jay, let me get on your back, please."

He frowned at her, barely resisting the impulse to snatch away. "Nope," he said, lengthening his stride and leaving her back a few steps.

"Wannabe player," she called after him playfully.

His chest heaved. He fought the urge to call her a trick. Even in his anger, he knew it would cross the line. They play-fought all the time, not quite as often as he and Mina, but a lot. Still, *trick* would be hurtful and way outside the flirting of their light jokes and dissing.

Raheem's random appearance tonight had thrown him. It was as if dude could read his mind. As soon as JZ was comfortable, tripping with Jacinta, certain he had her to himself for the night, Raheem either called or showed up, a subtle reminder that no matter how much time JZ might spend with Cinny, she wasn't his.

His nostrils flared and he quickened his step, nearly outpacing Kelly when they reached the house.

The clique bunched up in the spacious foyer, quieting their chatter respectfully until Kelly reminded them her grandmother had taken Kevin, Kelly's twelve-year-old brother, to a skate party. The talk then rose among the girls, who had been coming to Kelly's regularly for years. Soon it was bouncing off the high ceilings.

JZ kept his eyes straight, ignoring Jacinta as she whisked by him, elbowing him playfully in the back. He quietly observed, waiting for Kelly to lead them to the theatre, as the rest of the guys spoke in lower tones, taking in the spiral staircase, elevator, and general luxe vastness of the house.

In JZ's opinion, Kelly's soft-spoken demeanor didn't match the house's grand vibe. When he first met Kelly he'd been instantly attracted to her caramel complexion, tiny build, and long, thick hair, which always fell in soft waves around her face.

It had only been a momentary crush.

He'd squashed the feelings, partly because Mina was squeamish about him dating "her" friends, and mostly because Kelly started dating Angel. Through her and Angel's short but rocky time together, Kelly proved to JZ that she was soft-spoken, but not to be trifled with. She cut Angel to the quick after he made her hide his drugs during a routine traffic stop in O.C., winning major respect points in JZ's mind.

He'd never say it to Mina, because she'd take it wrong, but Kelly was a serious down-ass chick, handling her business even when it wasn't the popular thing to do. Mina was his girl, but she cared what people thought and that got her in trouble.

As Kelly led them away from the brightly lit foyer, JZ followed automatically, trailing last in line. The noise level increased as talk of which movies to watch circulated. JZ kept mum, happy with the general consensus—no chick or dick flicks. It was quickly decided they'd watch two horror films, a strange compromise between the two. As they entered the theatre, a windowless, dark-chocolate room with fifteen rows of plump reclining leather seats leading to a tiny projection room in the back, the debate on which slasher flicks raged on.

"Help yourself to the popcorn, soda, and candy," Kelly said, over the hub-bub. She gestured to a mini version of a cinema's concession area before walking the fifteen stairs and disappearing into the projection room.

JZ stood at the bottom of the stairway, taking inventory of the seating while his friends stockpiled snacks. He pretended to check messages, waiting for each of them to sit before deciding where to go.

Mina and Brian chose two aisle seats in the third row; Lizzie and Todd sat in the seats across the aisle from them; Greg sat two rows above them in the middle.

Michael took an aisle seat in the fifth row.

His friend Rob sat in the seat directly below it, so JZ took the seat behind Michael, in the sixth row. He leaned back in the comfortable seat, stretching his left leg in the aisle, resting it on the step.

Michael turned in his seat, toward JZ. He chewed away at popcorn, talking with his mouth full. "Ay, you know who has a theatre room like this?"

"Who dat?" JZ said. He sunk in the seat another inch.

"Jimmy B."

"That's right. I haven't seen him in a minute," JZ said, glad for the distraction of the conversation.

"His sister is in Bay Dra-da," Michael said. "She had a wrap party at her house, in the spring, and we watched a tape of the production in their theatre."

"Word?" JZ said halfheartedly, tuning out the second Michael mentioned Bay Dra-da. He slouched another inch, his leg overhanging the step, and pulled at the hoodie so his head disappeared in it. He leaned his head back on the seat's head-rest and closed his eyes.

He heard Michael talking with Rob and tried not to feel so replaceable. If Rob wanted to talk that theatre junk, cool. But it was the one thing he didn't even pretend to care about when it came to him and Michael's friendship. It wasn't anything he'd ever told Michael, it was just unspoken, guy-style.

Jacinta's voice made him peep an eye open.

" 'Scuse me," she said, standing on the step next to Michael's seat, hands on her hips.

Her jeans lovingly hugged her curves, forcing JZ's eye to the way her small waist exploded into phat thighs and strong calves. He'd spent a lot of time correcting her form, during their summer swim lessons, so he knew every inch of her curves, well. Before he could stop them, visions of Cinny in her two-piece danced across his mind.

He closed his eye again, ignoring her and forcing the image away, only to peep at her again when she cleared her throat.

She frowned and he scowled back. "What?" he said, closing his eye and resting his clasped hands on his stomach.

She rolled her eyes. "Move, so I can get in."

JZ sucked his teeth, but pulled himself upright. Jacinta squeezed by, her butt in JZ's face torturing him for a fleeting second before she plopped in the seat beside him.

"You all right?" Jacinta said.

Heart pumping as if he'd already had a good scare, no horror flick necessary, he snorted coolly. "Yeah. Why?"

" 'Cause you ain't get no popcorn or nothing." She chuckled. "I've never seen you not hungry."

He shrugged. "I'll get some later."

Like always, his anger melted the more Jacinta talked. He had to give her props. Even when he was acting total fool on her, she went on as if it was all swazy. It was one of the reasons he dug Cinny. One of the reasons she had him wondering how things would be if they made it exclusive.

He jerked the hoodie tighter and slouched in the seat, mad at himself for thinking like a sucker. Here it was Friday night and he was sitting next to a chick who had a boyfriend.

Wack.

There were a dozen, probably more, shorties within walking distance of Kelly's he could be with who could sweeten up his night, properly. To prove it, he took his cell phone out and texted Erica, a sophomore chick who'd made it more than obvious all he had to do was call and she'd be down for whatever.

"Uh-uh, don't be texting no chicken heads all night," Jacinta said, reaching for his phone. "I don't feel like seeing your phone flashing a million times."

"Man, whatever." JZ raised it out of her reach. A flood of warmth in his chest betrayed him. He was secretly pleased that Jacinta cared about him calling another girl. Still he kept his guard up. "I might dip instead of chilling with y'all all night long."

"You're foul, Jay." Jacinta folded her arms against her chest. "You can do your little creep-creep later. Everybody know Erica all on your tip."

JZ grinned. "You're all in my business." He stuck the cell in his hoodie pocket, as it vibrated, ignoring Erica's reply.

Jacinta's eyes rolled. She held her hand up to JZ's face. "Only 'cause me and her have gym together and she always asking about you, making it my business."

"And what you tell her?" JZ imitated a girl's voice. "Jason is the man, girl. Everybody want him, so stand in line."

"Umm-hmm, something like that," Jacinta said. She scowled, as if concentrating, then her eyes lit up suddenly. "Only I said . . . Jay is a mo, girl, a male ho, so don't even let him put his mack down."

JZ sucked his teeth. "Man, go head with that. I can't help it if the girls love them some JZ."

Jacinta shooed him. "Whatever, Mo, do you." She hollered toward the projection room, "Today, Kelly."

"For real," Mina echoed from the lower row.

"We want a movie. We want it now," Todd chanted.

Lizzie and Mina joined in.

Greg stood up, swinging an invisible sword at the chanters to fend off an attack. "I got your back, Kelly," he said. "If it gets nasty, lock yourself in the room. I'll hold 'em off till your grandmother comes home."

On cue, the movie previews popped on the screen, quieting the friendly riot. The sound overpowered the room, blaring from every corner.

Greg and Kelly sat down and everyone was quiet for the first time all evening.

Jacinta leaned in, whispering loud to be heard above the preview's racket, "What are we watching anyway?"

"Either *Saw Two Hundred* or *Prom Night*," JZ said.

Jacinta laughed. "Not two hundred though."

She rested her elbow on their shared arm rest, nudging JZ's aside.

"Dag, so what, you gon' take up the whole spot?" he said.

Jacinta frowned. "Use the other one."

"You use the other one," JZ said, narrowing his eyes for effect.

Jacinta held fast to her spot.

He hissed dramatically, shifted, and placed his left elbow on the outer armrest. Seconds later, her hand guided his right elbow to the armrest, so they were sharing. The last of his annoyance and frustration shattered with the gentle gesture. Thoughts of hooking up with Erica fled, gone in the comfortable ease and the way Jacinta boldly kept it real with him.

He wanted to put his arm around her, but settled for their elbows touching.

Jacinta stuck her tongue out at him. "See, I can be nice even when you being King Asshole."

JZ propped himself up an inch, so his mouth was level with Jacinta's ear. He spoke normal, since no one could hear them over the movie's screaming.

"Why I gotta be an asshole?"

Jacinta's lips pursed. She pulled her head away for a second and gave him a look as if to assess if he was serious. She shook her head as she leaned in to answer in his ear.

"Don't even trip and deny it. You get pissy every time Raheem dips by."

JZ was glad the shadows of the movie made it dark enough so she couldn't see his openmouthed surprise. He put his game face back on and played nonchalant. His lips grazed her ear as he answered, "Nah, that's your boy, so I ain't rummin. Besides, I know you be thinking of me when you with him anyway." He licked her ear, lightly, then pulled back and faced the screen. He glanced at her from the corner of his eye.

A shot of warmth went straight through him when he saw the grin on her face, answer enough.

A few minutes later, she leaned in again. JZ cocked his head toward her mouth.

"What do you think of Rob?" she said.

"Uh-huh, changing the subject 'cause you don't want to admit I got you sprung."

Jacinta rolled her eyes. "More like I got *you* sprung. But whatever.

For real, what do you think? You glad to finally meet the theatre, JZ, or you jealous?"

"Girl, please." JZ's eyes narrowed. "You rummin for real. How I look jealous of some dude?" His knees wagged, the only proof that the question (or answer to it) indeed bothered him, then he hunched his shoulders. "I mean, he seem all right." He dangled his hand. "A little too proper-acting, but you know . . . I don't need roll with him. So it's swazy."

Jacinta nudged his elbow, teasing. "Shoot, he's from Del Rio's Crossing, so trust he know how, knuck."

"Okay, he's a *dancer*." JZ's eyes rolled. "What kind of knucking he doing? A pop/lock contest?" His limbs popped in an exaggerated, erratic freestyle.

Jacinta shoved him but muffled her laugh behind her hand.

JZ smiled, chuckling low and deep in his chest.

"All right, hold it down back there," Michael said, turning to give them the movie "shhh." "Or do I need to separate y'all two?"

JZ nodded his head at Jacinta. "That's her, kid." He shoved Jacinta and raised his voice. "Be quiet, Cinny, dag. People trying to watch the movie."

When Michael turned back around, Jacinta leaned in a final time, whispering, "You all kinds of wrong for that."

JZ's smile was sincere. "Naw, I guess he's all right, though." He shoved her knee playfully, stroking her thigh as he withdrew his hand. "Want some popcorn?"

" 'Bout time you asked," Jacinta said. "And some M&M's too, please."

He frowned. "What I look like, your slave?"

"Yah, trick, yah," Jacinta sang. She pretended to crack a whip at him.

"I got your yah," JZ muttered. "See who ain't getting any M&M's."

"Just joking, baby boy," Jacinta said, smiling her sweetest.

She patted his thigh, sending energy to JZ's groin. He stood up abruptly, willing the surge to travel down his legs and to his feet, toes, anywhere but his groin. The sudden position change worked. But as he walked down the stairs toward the snack counter, the memory of Jacinta's ear on the tip of his tongue and the smile it produced on her face sent the energy surging again.

It was going to be a long night.

Clash of the Titans

"So poof—vamoose son-of-a-b#$%&."
—Jay-Z, "Izzo (H.O.V.A.)"

Michael stood on Kelly's front lawn with Rob and JZ in the crisp night air, waiting for the couples to say their good-byes. The cold air scorched his lungs each time he sucked in too much. He'd known they were walking tonight and still hadn't prepared. With a mix of envy and annoyance, he watched Rob wrap a gray wool scarf around his neck until it reached his mouth and pluck a pair of leather gloves from his coat pocket.

By the time they began trekking down Kelly's long driveway, Michael's hands were chilled to the tips. Icy dew shimmered on the black tar, glimmering against the motion lights shining from either side of the drive. JZ, Brian, and Todd cruised in the lead. Greg walked solo in the middle, carefully picking his way to avoid black ice; Michael and Rob behind him, pacing their steps so as not to step on Greg's heels. Michael blew in his hands, relishing the momentary relief his warm breath brought to his frigid digits.

Talk of JZ's New Year's Eve party quickly took center stage.

"Ay, Brian, since New Year's Eve your last night in town"—JZ's eyebrows arched—"are you and Mina even coming to the party?" Chunks of cold smoke punctuated his devilish chuckle.

"We'll be there . . . not long though," Brian said, a smile in his voice. He exchanged a pound with JZ. "But you know Mina, son. We'll definitely be there."

"For real, she not missing an upper bash," Michael said, raising his voice to be heard in the back. "Not even for you, B."

"Ain't that messed up?" Brian looked over his shoulder, his scowl playing to the guy's light Mina-bashing. "It's our last night together until spring probably . . . but if it's a party, you know her face gotta be up in the place."

The guy's voices, animated and loud, floated through the limbs of the naked trees, falling short of reaching the houses well off the road. The banter fueled their pace and the neighborhood's entrance was within view in minutes.

JZ glanced back at Rob. "Stop through if you want. You can bring somebody too, if you flow like that."

"Thanks," Rob said. He smushed his scarf under his chin. "Is it a couples-only thing?"

"Might as well be," Michael said. He was secretly pleased that JZ had extended the offer.

"It ain't no couple thing," JZ said, righteously indignant. "Bringing a date to a party is like bringing your own water to a pool." He laughed at his own joke as he talked on. "Why bother?"

Rob's elbow tapped Michael's as he thought aloud. "I could bring Maribel."

Michael nodded approval. "Yeah, she'd be down. And she knows me and Lizzie, so she would probably flow."

"Whatever," JZ said, interrupting. "Like I said, bring somebody if you want. Just don't bring a whole bunch of dudes."

Michael scowled. "Why would he?"

JZ flashed Michael a look of annoyed confusion. "You know how people roll in mob deep, and I don't want to end up with a bunch of hardheads at the party. I rather there be more shorties there." He feigned brushing off his shoulder. "Because the kid ain't in no couple."

Todd cackled. "Does Tonya know that?"

"I didn't invite Tonya," JZ said. A trail of cold smoke exited his nose as he snorted. "Erica trying get on. So I invited her." He rubbed his hands together with glee. "The kid knows how to play it. A sophomore all up in an upper class party. Shoot, you know how grateful she gon' be?"

He made an obscene gesture, setting off snickering.

"Dude, for real, I'm gonna need you to stop bragging about all your conquests," Todd said. "It's like living across from a playground but being grounded or something. I can watch you play but I can never come out."

The guys' laughter exploded in the night, just as they reached the guard's booth. The guard looked up, momentarily jolted by the noise, saluted them, and went back to looking at a tiny screen in front of him. The group tightened their circle, walking swifter and talking louder once out of Folger's Way and on the main road leading to their respective neighborhoods.

"Just save all that tension for the game tomorrow," JZ said. "Poly trying to act like they can ball this year. We need some of that new aggressive Todd, throwing bows."

Todd rolled his eyes. "No problem there."

"So, Jay, you letting Cinny bring Raheem?" Michael said, meaning it partly as a joke and getting the expected offense from JZ.

"Letting?" JZ sniffed. "Cinny can do what she wants." He cleared his throat, shrugging as he casually added, "But he supposed to be heading back to DC early. So I think she's riding solo. I don't know."

"And you just happen to know this?" Todd said. He knocked shoulders with JZ. "I wish you and Cinny would just do it already."

"Yeah, I saw y'all all cozy tonight," Brian said. "You and Cinny like that now? On that creep tip."

"No," JZ said quickly. He frowned. "That's Todd always fantasizing about people sexing 'cause he's not getting none."

"Aww, see, that's wrong," Todd said, managing to look wounded.

"Just for that, I'm not sharing the profits from that sex tape of you and Tonya I've been selling on the web."

"Naw, player, you gotta split the cheese with me, 'cause that joint probably making you rich." JZ gave Todd some dap as he belly laughed. "Shortie is wi-zild."

"For real, y'all made a tape?" Brian said, properly skeptical. They all knew anything was possible with JZ when he was wilding out about girls.

JZ and Todd exchanged a look.

"Naw, I didn't," JZ admitted. "But I was telling T I should have. Man, y'all wouldn't believe this chick." He bucked as if taming a rodeo horse. "I was like buck wild, in that joint."

The guy's cracked up, laughing. Their footsteps slowed, then stopped when they reached a four-way intersection. Greg's neighborhood was to the right, Todd's to the left, the Woods straight ahead. They huddled around JZ as he regaled them with Tales of Tonya.

Knowing JZ could go on for hours, if they let him, Michael interrupted a few minutes into the gory details. "I'm gonna dip because I'm gonna borrow my grandmother's car and drive Rob home."

Content to let JZ's hot details warm them in the cold, Brian, Greg, and Todd exchanged a pound with Michael and a fist knock with Rob before huddling back together. The hoots and catcalls of the guys followed Rob and Michael down Main Street a few blocks until their footsteps were the only sound, loud and hollow on the sleepy street. Stoplights blinked, easily accommodating the half dozen or so cars that rolled by, flashing into the windows of empty storefronts and restaurants.

"Dang, what time everything shut down over here?" Rob said, craning his neck at the long block of ghost town businesses.

"Except for the eating joints, everything be closed by seven," Michael said.

"Except coming by your place, this is my first time over here this late." Rob glanced side to side as if still expecting people to emerge from the darkened buildings.

Michael nodded. "I didn't think you were coming tonight."

"I wasn't at first. But Mina was so nice . . ." Rob glanced at Michael. "She's as crazy cool as you described her."

"The Deev's my girl," Michael said. His face lit up. Without realizing it, he slowed his steps as he looked over at Rob. "What did you think about . . . everyone else?"

"They all seem cool . . . crazy, definitely." Rob chuckled. "Especially that dude Todd. He got a joke for everything."

Michael nodded, hoping Rob would go on with his reflections. He wanted to know what Rob thought of JZ, but couldn't bring his tongue to say the words. It felt gossip-y and backstabbing to ask one of his closest friends what he thought about the other. At least JZ would think so. Michael had no doubt Mina would openly dish without any prodding, not only on what she thought about Rob but what she thought anyone else thought about him.

Michael had mad respect for the way Mina melded her longtime friendship with Lizzie with her relatively new one with Jacinta and Kelly. All nice and good for her, but he couldn't see himself kicking it so easily with both Rob and JZ on the regular.

JZ was too JZ—loud and playfully sarcastic edging toward arrogance. Especially lately, his sarcasm had a bitterness that jolted Michael. A few times JZ had said things to Jacinta that Michael thought for sure was going to get JZ knocked in the head, but Jacinta had let it roll. Apparently, it was all a part of their new play/flirt relationship. To Michael it felt like things between the two would explode the second one of them no longer thought their light barbs were funny anymore.

He hoped he wasn't there if it did.

Rob's voice reached out of the cold, snapping him to attention.

"At least I can finally go back and tell Maribel and Ferdinand that your clique exists."

Michael laughed low in his throat. "Running bets about whether they're my imaginary friends or not?"

"Naw, I knew Mina was real," Rob said, his eyes glinting. "I thought you made up everybody else, though."

They crossed into the Woods. Trees loomed, large and bare on both sides of the street, in an ominous welcome. Only the street-lights, glowing orbs of safety every fifteen feet, broke up the darkness ahead just enough to keep it from being eerie. For Michael it was home, familiar, but he felt Rob's arm brush against him as his friend stepped closer.

Michael smiled. Del Rio's Crossing was second only to Pirates Cove in being not only one of the poorest, but also one of the tough-est neighborhoods. As a dude who studied ballet, modern dance, and tap, Rob had had his fair share of harassment from his nabe's peers. But for some reason, the quiet dark of the burbs unsettled him. Michael didn't get it and was about to severely joke Rob about it until Rob spoke up first.

"Ay, so you gon' get your portfolio together?"

"Yeah." Michael's lips pursed as he shrugged away the tingle of pride creeping in. "But I'm not pressed."

He felt Rob's eyes on him and took longer than necessary to zip his already zipped jacket to the neck so he wouldn't have to look over.

"You don't need to be pressed, but bring your A game," Rob said, offense bristling. "Madame told me she already has a hundred applicants. Just because Del Rio Bay don't recognize, doesn't mean people from other schools are sleeping on this. Trust, if you trying to make it in the arts, the Carter is the place to be."

"I haven't heard that a million times in the last week," Michael said, working to keep his tone good-natured. He didn't want to ruin the night arguing about it. He was only putting the portfolio to-gether because he'd need it for his Plan B.

He hadn't shared it with Rob yet but Plan B, fuzzy as it was, was his plan to head to New York after graduation and get a designing job with one of the hundreds of productions. Do the urban starving artist thing. The idea had started forming sometime between Madame announcing the Carter auditions and Rob's not-so-subtle pressure.

Madame had a lot of contacts; surely she'd share his talents with a few and get him on somewhere. He'd worry about minor details like where he'd live later.

As great as the Carter opportunity was, Michael was certain it was merely a sign, there when he needed it most to open his eyes to some of the things he could do post-graduation. Now his mind was brimming with thoughts of New York and the possibility of finding a new mentor, like Madame, there.

Yes, I've had a Mina moment, he thought, satisfied with where the sign guided him but reluctant to truth up to Rob about any of it.

Rob didn't understand. Couldn't understand. He'd been going to the Carter since seventh grade. Del Rio's Crossing was where he lived, but he was barely there between classes, rehearsals, and finding reasons to hang out in DC or with other members of the Players.

Rob had admitted that if it weren't for Michael's friendship, he'd spend even less time in the DRB. As much as that stroked Michael's ego, the fact was, he had more of a life to leave behind than Rob had when he'd entered the Carter—something Michael tried to play down, to save Rob's feelings.

The clique had their issues, but it was nights like this when they all had a good time that convinced Michael that doing his last year at a new school around strangers wasn't the move.

The terse cluck of Rob's tongue brought him back from dreams of New York City.

"Your skills are fierce, but there will be plenty of others just as talented, I bet," Rob said, rearranging his scarf to cover his mouth.

"What's up?!" JZ's voice blared from behind.

Rob's feet scurried to the safety of the nearest streetlight until he realized it was JZ and Brian.

"Oh, shit," Rob cursed, relief flooding his eyes. "Man, I ain't gonna lie, you scared me. It's way too many trees around here."

"Only thing in the Woods is deer, kid," JZ said, laughing.

"Man, you a fool," Michael said, playing it cool as his heart thumped against his chest.

"Told you they didn't hear us coming," JZ said.

"We weren't even sneaking up on y'all," Brian said.

"How y'all catch up with us?" Michael said.

"Jogged a little bit," JZ said, falling in step behind them.

There was a moment of awkward silence until they reached the crest of the neighborhood's hill where JZ and Brian would take the right and Michael and Rob would keep straight. They stood under the streetlight in a four-square.

"So, man, how you like the Carter?" JZ said, surprising Michael with his curiosity. "I heard y'all don't take regular classes. That must be sweet."

"No, we still take regular classes," Rob said. "But most of my core classes I finish this year. So next year, it'll be all my majors."

"What's your major?" Brian said. He squinted. "I thought you only did majors in college."

"No, we choose one by sophomore year." Rob moved the scarf away from his mouth. His voice was animated, happy to share. "Mine is dance, classical and modern. I minor in dramatics."

Michael tensed as JZ, smirking, asked, "So what, y'all be dancing down the halls and in the cafeteria like *High School Musical*?"

If Rob took offense at the stereotype, he hid it well, rolling good-naturedly along. "Yup, all the time. Now that Mike has a chance to go to the Carter, he'll see for himself." He chuckled. "The nondance majors are the ones you see standing on the tables singing in the *HSM* numbers."

JZ frowned at Michael. "What would you go to the Carter for?" His face eased into a smile, as he joked. "So, what, you're really a rapper or singer trying get that label deal? You been holding out on us, Money Mike?"

Michael shook his head, but couldn't form the words fast enough. Rob happily supplied answers.

"It's a new program for fashion design," Rob said, happy to trump Michael's prowess for him. "Mike could be like a trailblazer, for real."

"Is it like an after-school thing for credit?" Brian said, genuinely curious.

"No. He'd have to transfer to the Carter for his senior year," Rob said.

"Man, that's crazy," JZ said. He looked from Michael to Rob, as if questioning if they understood how little sense it made, then proceeded to tell them when neither stepped up to agree. "Mike, for real, why would you go to another school your last year? That's like . . . being the star player of a team and then being benched during the most important half of the game."

Michael's heart raced as a scowl spread across Rob's face. He wanted to reply, step in before one of them said something he wouldn't be able to fix, but the words were caged in his chest, unable to free themselves.

"Man, it ain't like that at all." Rob hastily tucked his scarf under his chin. He looked JZ in the eye, unflinching. "It's like you being scouted and asked to play pro right out of high school. Are you saying you'd turn the Lakers down if they wanted to make you their next Kobe?"

JZ snorted, his eyes hardening at the challenge. "They not offering him a job, they offering him a slot at a school. How is that the same?"

"He could get into a good fashion school or maybe even get a job with a designer. That's how," Rob said with a mix of offense and snootiness. "Everybody can't make it by bouncing a ball, man."

Michael felt it coming, knew JZ was ready to say something worthy of causing a brawl. He forced out the words, now stuck in his throat, projecting them so loud, he startled the guys. "I'm not going." He repeated it, more for himself than them. *"I'm not going to the Carter."*

His chest rose and fell, laboring from the effort. Puffs of cold smoke gathered in front of his mouth before dissolving. JZ, Rob, and Brian stared at him.

Anger poured from Rob's eyes, burning a hole through Michael.

Michael looked away from the stinging glare, unable to face the truth of his cowardice in it. Instead he faced the smug victory in JZ's face, felt the fist-pumping triumph surging from JZ in invisible waves.

If JZ felt he'd won, he wouldn't go on the offensive.

The tension in Michael's chest gave way to relief.

Relief that he'd averted a war between his friends.

Relief that the night was over once and for all.

Relief that for JZ, this would be forgotten in the morning. He'd won, so this would be a hazy, extraneous memory tied to Michael's "hobby" they never discussed.

He'd smooth things over with Rob on the ride to Del Rio's Crossing or tomorrow or the day after. If it took a few days, that was okay; he didn't have to see Rob everyday like he did JZ.

He and JZ were boys from way back. Like it or not, he had to play to that loyalty, right now. And the truth was he didn't disagree with JZ. Switching schools his last year made about as much sense to him as deciding to start school from scratch, after thirteen years, by going to college.

Some things just aren't for everybody, he told himself.

He wasn't knocking college or the Carter; they just weren't for him.

He'd have to make Rob understand that somehow.

Hot Duke Boys

"I'ma fly girl and I like those . . . hot boyz."
—Missy Elliott, "Hot Boyz"

The thick scent of perspiration and socks worn one day too many coated the gym. If anyone noticed or cared, their protests were lost in the crowd's excited hum and the canned music blaring from the speakers.

The Blue Devils were wiping up the floor with Poly, a team from Baltimore City. Normally one of the state's best teams, Poly was struggling to keep the Blue Devils in check, and the overwhelmingly DRB High crowd was feeding off the usually stellar team's struggles.

Mina stood among her squad mates, huddled on the sideline, their bubbling conversation overflowing with talk of the game, crush-worthiness of the Poly boys, and of JZ's New Year's Eve party. Caught up in the babble, Mina eyed the time clock—five more minutes left—then stole a glance Brian's way.

"Don't worry, girl, he's still there," Kelis said, elbowing Mina's side.

"I was looking at the time clock." Mina blew out an exaggerated sigh. "You know Coach Em will have a fit if we're not back in the cheer line at exactly thirty seconds left."

"Uh-huh, sure, that's what you were looking at. . . ." Kelis darted

her eyes toward the clock, then to Brian's seat thirty yards in the opposite direction, to show how far the two were apart.

She and Mina laughed. They were tentative friends and even that
wasn't the right definition. They'd been squad mates since recreation
cheerleading, but their constant quest to be top cheerleader made
for a tense, fragile friendship. They shared cheerleading in common
and not much else, unless you counted the time they shared Craig,
which Mina didn't.

He'd been Mina's boyfriend at the time. Kelis had kissed him. He
and Mina had broken up. End of story.

Mina didn't harbor much fire for the old grudge anymore, and
Kelis had never seen it as a source of contention in the first place.
She was eerily casual about those kinds of things in a way Mina refused to understand. Bottom line, she was way over Craig, who'd
graduated the same year as Brian, and Kelis had been dating Beau, a
senior on the football team, since the fiasco.

In small doses, she and Kelis peacefully coexisted.

"I don't blame you though." Kelis smoothed a stray hair, tucking
it behind her ear. She openly ogled Brian, who sat in a front row
bleacher surrounded by fellow Blue Devil alumni. "He fine as ever.
It's like whatever they have in the water at Duke is agreeing with
him, for real."

Mina nodded slightly, bypassing a formal answer. What was she
going to say, "Gee thanks for scoping out my BF"?

Knowing Kelis, Mina figured she should probably be grateful
that Kelis wasn't actively gunning for Brian, just for sport.

Kelis and Beau's relationship was shaky, due to his constant cheating and her propensity to flirt, but they'd lasted this long. Mina had
no reason to believe it wouldn't go the distance until he graduated.
Still, she didn't trust Kelis as far she could see her when it came to
Brian. But showing fear or insecurity around Kelis wasn't too bright.

Mina peeked Brian's way again. He laughed at something Stefan, a former teammate of his, said, but not hard enough that he missed the Poly cheerleaders walking by, heading to the visitor sideline.

Jealousy tapped Mina's chest, knocking her blood pressure up a notch as Brian's eyes appraised a few of the cheerleaders head to toe. His eye lingered on the last cheerleader, a tiny-waisted light-skinned chick with brown hair to her shoulders. Her phat butt swayed in the pleated skirt, tick-tocking side to side as she moved past the Blue Devil alums.

Grilling her down, Stefan said something to Brian and they knocked fists before laughing uproariously.

Kelis turned toward Mina, nearly face to face, cutting them off from the rest of the squad's chatter. Her brown eyes were wide and slightly too far apart in her light brown face, but Kelis wasn't unattractive by any definition, and she knew it. She carried herself with a level of confidence that came from years of people feeding her compliments about her firm build, thick brownish-black hair, and rosebud lips. It came off as flirtatious bossiness when she was around guys and as tempered patience with her female peers.

Kelis got on her nerves, but still Mina envied the ease with which she went about everything. It was as if nothing bothered her, a trait Mina would have given her right arm to have at the moment.

"I don't know how you do it," Kelis said, shaking her head.

Mina scowled. "Do what?"

"You must be cool with him seeing other people while he's at school. Right?"

Mina worked to keep her face blank. But her heart thumped in time to the music playing overhead. She took her time answering, unsure where Kelis was going with it but needing to know.

"He's three hundred miles away. I can't control what he does," Mina said, not believing a word of it but proud of herself for pulling it off.

Kelis's right eyebrow steepled. "Hmm . . . I always figured you'd be the clingy type, Mina—no harm." She smiled a condescending smirk that whispered that she knew good and well Mina *was* the clingy type. "I tell you what, though, that's better than sitting home stuffing your face with cookies and ice cream worrying 'bout what he's doing. Shoot, Beau already said that either we're breaking up when he goes to college next year or I better be cool with him doing what he wants." Her laugh was shrill. "I was like, dude, please, like you're not doing what you want now. He's a trip." Her shoulders hitched in time to the music.

Mina's mind raced alongside the club mix playing as she tried to get Kelis back on track. "Well, me and Brian didn't sit and talk it out like that," she said, choosing her words carefully, hoping they prompted Kelis to reveal more. "But you know, three hundred miles is no joke."

"I know, right. You know what I say, girl? Shoot, get yours." She bumped shoulders with Mina as if they'd solidly agreed. "Still, I know you gotta be tripping over some of the stuff on that message board." She scowled at Mina's confused squint, then smacked her hand over her mouth in mock horror. "My bad. You didn't know about the site, did you?"

"What site?" Mina said, keeping the high-pitch anxiety to a minimum.

"Uh-oh, I didn't mean to out him," Kelis said, looking over Mina's shoulder toward Brian's bleacher seat.

"Out what?" Mina said, hearing the panic in her voice. She looked up at the clock. Time counted down swiftly. Kelis had one more minute to spill. She swallowed and calmed her speeding thoughts as the squad spread out around her, gently herding her along the sideline back to her cheer spot. "What site?"

Checking the time herself, Kelis spoke hurriedly, lingering by Mina. "It's this forum called Hot Duke Boys, and Brian is the featured hottie of the month, girl. The site is tripping. It has a message board and chat section for all the groupies. The juiciest bits are from girls at the school posting about stuff that happens on campus—the hottest guys on the yard and who they've hooked up with." Her words sped up as the buzzer toned. "Look, if you really are cool with him doing whatever when he's at school, it's nothing to trip about. I think some of the girls are lying anyway." Her voice rose over the announcer, welcoming everyone to the second half of the game. "Let me go before Coach trips."

She walked to her end of the cheer line, leaving Mina open-mouthed.

The words *Hot Duke Boys* rang in her ears the rest of the night. Nothing would blast the words from her mind—not the joking of the clique while at Rio's Ria after the game or Todd and JZ's overzealous happiness at the 94–78 win over Poly.

Hours later, the clique gone their separate ways and her curfew hovering, she and Brian sat cozy on the sofa in the sunroom of her house. He snuck long, laborious pecks at her neck, threatening to leave a mark, in between peeking toward the door on parent alert.

"They're knocked out asleep," Mina said, anticipating his usual question about her parent's whereabouts.

Brian scooped her closer to him. He laughed a TV villain cackle. "So I got their baby girl all to myself, helpless, huh?"

His lips nibbled at her neck, then ears, feeling their way around her face until they landed on her lips. She kissed back halfheartedly even as her face and body warmed, enjoying the attention.

Brian drew back, squinting at her through the shadows flickering from the television.

"What's up? You okay?"

Mina nodded.

Brian slid his arms under Mina's butt and lifted her onto his lap. "Okay, here's the deal. I have"—he stared up at the ceiling, pretending to calculate—"about fifty-five hours before I gotta book it back to school. We could spend the time violating every rule your parents ever made." He smiled devilishly, then scowled in contrition. "Or we could share our feelings. I'm sure you know which one *I* want do, but you're taking some of the fun out of it by not enjoying it. So . . ." He looked Mina in the eye, serious. "What's wrong? You've been quiet since after the game."

Mina wriggled her way off his lap. She sat cross-legged, facing him. "You ever heard of Hot Duke Boys?"

A shadow flickered across his face. Mina wasn't sure if it was emotion or the television. She willed herself to remain quiet, heart galloping, as she waited for his answer.

He shrugged dismissively. "Yeah. It's like a fan forum. Why?"

Mina was unable to articulate her questions without whining. She played it close, keeping her answer simple. "I just heard about it and wondered if you had."

He peered at her. "You ever been to it?"

Mina shook her head no and was sure Brian relaxed as he said, "I mean, I don't know what else to say but that it's a fan site."

"I heard it's more like a groupie site," she said, biting back an accusation.

Brian laughed. "Yeah, that's about right too."

She hated how often she needed a lifeline, but clung to his laughter like a person adrift at sea would hold on to a plank of wood. His voice, casual, relaxed her and she listened unguarded. She was doing this more and more, holding on to every little word, sign, and quirk that Brian was being faithful.

"It's like a wiki. Anybody can add information to it." He shrugged. "A lot of the stuff on there is true. But not all of it." His fingers raked through his curls, fluffing the hair to perfect disarray, as he chuckled. "It was kind of cool to be on there at first. Seriously, it's also a little scary to have your business out there like that. But I don't buy into the hype." He glanced at her, sideways, teasing. "What? You worried about the competition?"

Mina peered through the flickering shadows. "Should I be?"

He cracked his knuckles. "You do you, toughie," he said, sliding down an inch on the sofa, putting some distance between them. "But I can't do nothing about what other people are saying about me."

A tense moment of silence hung in the air until Mina leaned in, her face inches from his. He took the hint and kissed her, soft on the lips. Before closing her eyes, she saw him give her a hungry look and lick his lips.

His hands went to her hips, pulling her flush against him, and she willingly climbed back onto his lap. He might be Hot Duke Boy #1 on the groupie site, but based on his roaming hands and hungry lips, he was *her* groupie tonight.

It wasn't until the next afternoon—exhausted from flip-flopping the desk, bed, and shelves in her bedroom—when she sat at the PC for a well-earned break that idle curiosity about the site set in.

She was still high from the night before. She and Brian had smothered themselves in one another, wrapped in mushy exchanges of how much they'd missed one another and how much more they would once he returned to school.

Hot Duke Boys who?

Yet her fingers scampered across the keyboard, typing the term into Google.

A spread of ten pages popped up. She waded through five pages of links about the Dukes of Hazzard and various other dukes—including Duke Ellington, some swing band, and an inexplicable link to something about hot pink boy toys—and was ready to call it quits.

I'll just get the link from Kelis, she thought—and then her eyes stopped on a description:

Groupie Love's the go-to source when you're trying to find your guy.

A message from Jacinta popped up before she could click the link.

CinnyBon: 'sup GF?
BubbliMi: jus finished remodeling my room
CinnyBon: ummm . . . yeah somebody is b-o-r-e-d
BubbliMi: ::raising my hand:: ever heard of Hot Duke Boys?
CinnyBon: nope. What is it?
BubbliMi: some sort of fan site. Kelis told me about it, said Brian was all the rage on it. So I wuz gonna check it
CinnyBon: lord somebody ready get their feelings hurt up in here. Y bother Mi?

Mina flushed, but Jacinta's scorn didn't dissuade her. She clicked on the link and drew in a breath. Groupie Love was right. The site wasn't just a Duke thing, by a long shot. She scanned the endless list of categories: Purdue University, Georgetown, UCLA, USC, Michigan, Duke University, and just about every other NCAA Division I school was listed. It was an entire world dedicated to girls (and guys, she supposed) obsessed with high-profile students.

She clicked on Duke University and was taken immediately to the Hot Duke Boys page. Every conceivable stat on a person was listed—favorite color and food, screen names, even the best times to find the guy in the dining hall or library.

Just as Kelis mentioned, Brian was featured Hottie of the Month. His face smiled at her from a glittery blinged-out frame.

She zipped off a message to Jacinta with the link.

BubbliMi: Ok u've gotta see this.

She cruised the site, waiting for Jacinta's response.
According to the About Us page, Groupie Love was maintained

by two chicks who went by the obviously fake monikers Monica Love 'Em Up and Heather Head-lee. Their avatars implied they were white, busty, and thick-lipped. The site's mission was "to make it easy for fans to be in the right place, at the right time, with the right information to meet their favorite player."

Brian's "friend" stat indicated he already had fifteen thousand girls interested. Mina shuddered. The season was still early.

Her head bobbed at Jacinta's reply.

CinnyBon: WTF?! Is that site for real?
BubbliMi: yeah. I asked Brian about it and he said he knew about it. I guess all the players do.
CinnyBon: I'm checking the Georgetown page to see if Raheem getting as much love as Brian. Imma be mad if he not hottie of the month!
BubbliMi: LOL Ok not mad though
CinnyBon: I'm just saying, if he not popular that reflects on MY game.
BubbliMi: Shoot if he's not maybe we can trade BFs. it's too much pressure 2 b with the cutie of the month.
CinnyBon: Anytime!

Mina was glad to joke with Jacinta about it, but reviewing the intimate details of Brian's life at school, including what parties or events he'd been sighted at since attending Duke, was unsettling. Drawn to the chat section, but afraid to see what groupies might be saying about him, she minimized the page and turned her attention back to Jacinta.

BubbliMi: that's enough of that
CinnyBon: what's the big deal? He had groupies at DRB high 2.

Mina nodded at the PC as she typed back.

BubbliMi: I know . . . but I was there to like stop them at the pass. hee hee
CinnyBon: i hear u. but u know if he is dipping on u, it's not like u ever gon' find out Mi. Not tryna b cold, just saying.

Mina gnawed at her fingernail, agreeing with Jacinta in theory but unable to completely convince herself to let the issue go so easily.

BubbliMi: ok don't get mad but . . .
CinnyBon: go ahead
BubbliMi: i hear u. but ur saying that cuz u and JZ got a serious side thing going. if Raheem knew don't u think he'd be pissed?
CinnyBon: 1st of all me and Jay just tripping, flirting—no hooking up or anything. Ya heard?
BubbliMi: LOL yeah, yeah but remember I see how *ahem* close y'all be sometimes. even if u haven't hooked up don't sit there and say if Raheem walked in on one of ur "moments" u wouldn't be caught dirty
CinnyBon: LOL tru dat. still what he doesn't know and what I don't know about what he does is what it is
BubbliMi: so ur saying I should just . . . what? b happy when we're 2gether and not care when we're not?
CinnyBon: u gotta do what's best 4 u Mina. but yeah something like that. jus saying, out of sight . . .

Mina typed back reluctantly with a sigh.

BubbliMi: out of mind.

It was hands down one of her least favorite phrases lately.

Happy New Year

"Love must be a drug to make me feel this way."
—Chrisette Michele, "Love Is You"

Mina sat on a stool at the counter in Brian's kitchen, staring down the clock on the microwave. JZ's New Year's Eve bash was forty-five minutes in. She swore she heard faint strains of Vic's mixes, but knew that was her imagination. Brian's and JZ's houses were the only two in the heavily wooded cul-de-sac, but even JZ's parents, liberal as they were giving JZ what he wanted, weren't going to let Vic's speakers blow the roof off their house.

Mina checked the clock again and wondered who might already be across the street. She and Brian were beyond fashionably late. But the party was a marathon. They had all night. No idea what JZ's parents were thinking letting him have it from seven until one A.M. But it left her and Brian plenty of time to dip in and out at their leisure. If his parents ever left.

Mina crossed her legs primly, tugging at her miniskirt to ensure no cheek peeked out, and watched as Brian's mother, a former model with the body and carriage to back it up, transferred a lip gloss, mascara, powder, and her license into an evening bag. She walked from the counter to the sink with a confident ease, neckline straight, movement purposeful, as if she might face a camera at every turn.

"Bri, you all packed?" she asked, for the fourth time. She smoothed a stray hair back into her intricate chignon, as she fretted. "I hate that

Daddy and I aren't driving you to the airport. I keep thinking you're going to forget something."

"I'm cool, Ma," Brian said. He stood by Mina's stool, calm, used to his mother's last minute nit-picking. He headed off her next question by rolling off his itinerary. "The car's picking me up at ten-thirty tomorrow morning and you and Pop are going to meet me at the airport at eleven-thirty. I'm all set."

Mrs. James's eyes smiled, reminding Mina of Brian. "Okay, that means you don't want me to ask anymore, right?"

"Now see, I didn't say that," Brian said, his own smile devilish.

Mrs. James raised a perfectly waxed eyebrow. "But that's what he meant, didn't he, Mina?"

"Uh-huh, probably," Mina said, giggling as Brian slyly wiggled his finger up the side of her skirt before tracing it down her thigh to her knee. She swatted him away as Mrs. James asked him to check on what was taking his father so long. Brian was up the stairs in a flash, leaving his mom and Mina to gab.

Mrs. James was a fun person to be around. She had stories to share about her modeling days and life as an NBA baller wife. Often, she playfully commiserated with Mina about the hardships they bore as women attracted to guys with fans. She never seemed aware that she likely had fans of her own and that Mina was the only ordinary one in their midst.

Their bond was genuine and Mina cherished it, but as Brian's mom lamented how little of Brian she'd seen during the break, she silently wished for the Jameses to speed up their preparation and move on to their star-studded, overnight party at the St. Regis in DC. Any other time Mina would anxiously prod Brian's mom for details about the who, what, and where of her glam evening.

Not tonight.

All she wanted was for them to say their byes, so she'd get Brian to herself for a few hours on his last night in town.

Sorry, Mrs. James, but he's mine tonight, Mina thought, feeling a sliver of guilt but not much more. The Jameses got to travel to any of Brian's games they wanted; she couldn't. Also, she and Brian had spent their fair share of nights, over the break, hanging out with his parents playing games or having dinner. So tonight was her night.

Her knee started an impatient jump as Brian and his dad barreled down the stairs, each carrying a matching Louis Vuitton suitcase.

"So you're all set for tomorrow," Mr. James said. He took the smaller piece of luggage from Brian and retracted its handle.

Mina hid her smile at Brian's rolled eyes, sure she was the only one who caught the frazzled undertone of his patient reply.

"Yup, *all set.*" Brian opened the front door and the distant thumping of bass floated inside. "Have a good time. I'll see y'all at the airport."

Brian's father looked across the yard in the darkness. "Oh, we're making you all miss your party." He ushered his wife to the door. "Come on, babe. I can take a hint. Have fun tonight."

"If we ever get there," Brian said. "Good night."

He and his dad embraced, one hand in a grip, the other pounding the back. Then his father grabbed the handle of the suitcase and lifted the other.

"Have fun," Mina called out, a little too cheerfully.

Brian's mom spun on her heels and headed back into the house. Brian hung his head, sighing dramatically. "Ma, what?"

She rushed past him, scowling, and gave Mina a hug. "Happy New Year, Mina. I probably won't see you for a while." She kissed Mina on the cheek, zipped back to the door, and gave Brian a peck on the lips. "All right, all right, we're gone."

"Happy New Year," Mina called after her, a lump lodged in her throat.

Brian stood at the door, watching them until the car's rear lights disappeared up the road. He cocked his head toward JZ's house and nodded to the heavy bass for a few seconds before closing the door. He locked the door, then blocked it with his body, grinning. He wiggled his finger at Mina, beckoning her over. She obeyed and walked into his open arms, burying her face in his chest. She hugged him so tight, he frowned down at her.

"What's wrong?"

"Your mom said Happy New Year to me," Mina said, unable to ward off the tears flooding her eyes.

"Okay, and that . . . offends you?" Brian said, teasing. "Is it against your religion?"

Mina chuckled at the confusion in his voice, even as the tears kept flowing. She kept her face buried, feeling silly for crying and not wanting Brian to see her. If she looked into his eyes, brown and smiling, she'd start bawling. She knew it.

His fingers pushed gently at her shoulders in an attempt to pry her off. She held on, refusing to lift her face until his tone turned concerned.

"Seriously, what's wrong?"

Mina swiped at the tears and sniffed them into submission before looking up. "Nothing. I mean, she said she probably won't see me for a while and . . ." A rebel tear plunked down her cheek and the words got caught in her throat. She unsuccessfully forced the whining out of her voice. "I'm saying, it's like I realized I'm not going to see you until April or May."

She dropped her head back onto Brian's chest. He held her tight for a few seconds until she pulled away, laughing and sniffling.

Brian's eyebrows smushed together. "Toughie, either you're losing your mind or I got you seriously sprung. . . ." He shook his head. "You're all to pieces."

"First of all, don't even play like you don't have me sprung. That's old news," Mina said, hands on her hips. She placed her hand in his, grinning when he closed his hand around hers. "I'm laughing because you totally missed your lines. You were supposed to say, Mina, it doesn't matter if we don't see each other for a year, you always gonna be my girl."

Brian hit a switch and the lights in the kitchen and foyer dimmed, cloaking the first floor in shadowy darkness.

"My bad. Somebody forgot to give me the script," he said, intertwining their fingers as he led her up the darkened stairway.

Mina's fingers gently massaged Brian's knuckles.

"Then I was going to say, 'Always?' And then you would say"— her voice deepened in an attempt to imitate his voice—"Always, Toughie. You know how I do."

Their laughter echoed through the hallway of the empty house.

When they reached Brian's room, he put his arms around her and she snuggled against him, looking up at his face in the darkness until her eyes adjusted enough to see his looking into hers. His voice was husky as he lowered it, speaking directly to her.

"So what's my line now?"

She stared dumbfounded, too caught up in his presence, unsure of her next line much less his, and let Brian's kisses lead them to the next scene. She could have played out the whole night there, at his house, in his room, talking, kissing, whatever, but ninety minutes later they were in JZ's packed family room. JZ's special dark blue "party" lights cast an ethereal glow, lighting the room while dimming it enough to give the partiers semi-anonymity. Streaks from a strobe light popped like tiny lightning flashes.

People were everywhere—clustered around the pool table and arcade games, spilling out the door leading to the basketball court, up against walls, crowded around the juice bar, packed on the sectional, and gyrating in the space large enough to serve as a dance floor.

Mina vibed with the energy, letting it put her in the mood. She would have been fine rolling into the party at eleven-thirty, in time for a festive group Happy New Year, but Brian insisted she was playing mind games by saying there was no hurry. He swore he'd hear it later if she missed any of the party's juicy bits.

He wasn't fooling anybody. He was the one who wanted to be in the mix.

No sooner had they hit the bottom step of JZ's family room, Brian was swarmed and loving every minute of it. Everyone wanted to talk to him, about college, playing ball, or just catch up with him, see how he was doing. His fingers slowly slipped from Mina's waist as his old Varsity teammates whisked him away. He gave her an apologetic look over his shoulder and she dismissed him with a casual wave.

Might as well get used to him being gone, she thought, craning her neck over the dancing crowd to find the clique.

Switch!

"The way she rock that, got the boy in love."
—The Dream, "I Love Your Girl"

Erica's butt was hypnotizing. It had a mind of its own.

JZ stared at it, lost in the way it moved, first beckoning him with a slow wind, grinding against his groin in an intoxicating circle, then pulling away as it shook up and down in a vicious, painful-looking booty pop that forced him to keep his distance or risk injury.

Slow wind.

Booty pop.

Slow wind.

Booty pop.

He kept up with the rhythm, pressing his hands against her hips during the wind to get the full effect, then letting go during the pops, waiting anxiously for the storm to calm again.

He closed his eyes as Erica backed up, blessing him with another slow wind, this one huge swirls swiping deliciously from his naval to his thighs.

Shortie was gon' mess around and get fu—

"Having fun?" Mina said, blasting him from his thoughts of a private after-party.

She and Jacinta stood beside him, grinning while they snuck disapproving glances Erica's way.

Mina's tone was mother-hen perfect. "Hey, Erica." Her eyebrow went up a notch, just in case Erica missed the vibes sent by her "tsk, tsk" hello.

"Hey, y'all," Erica said, undeterred.

JZ took a step back as the booty pop started its violent shake.

Mina and Jacinta gave each other a look. Mina turned her head and giggled.

Jacinta scowled. "Umph, girl, chicks get paid top dollar for moves like that at the Flaxson. You better get you some." JZ couldn't help laughing along with Mina as Jacinta lectured on sarcastically about Erica's future career in pole dancing. "And you doing all this for free?" Her arms folded and she leveled JZ with a critical eye. "Jay, you wrong. Lace her with a few dollar bills. She working hard."

"Jealous?" JZ asked, flashing a smile. He grabbed Mina and Jacinta by the arm, pulling them toward him. "Come on, y'all know you want make a JZ sandwich."

Mina pulled back, swatting. "Okay, eww."

"Oh, my bad, Mi. I know you do your dirt in the dark," JZ said. "Don't hate on my girl working it." JZ smacked playfully at Erica's bouncing butt and she responded with a special wiggle-pop that would have made the girls at the Flaxson proud.

Mina nodded toward Erica, "Uh-uh, I don't even do *that* in the dark."

JZ laughed. "Then I feel bad for Brian." He held on to Jacinta's elbow, trying to force her to rock along. "Come on, Cinny, show me what you got. You know you want to."

Jacinta remained close enough to become an awkward still partner in the dance triangle. She snorted. "Yeah, cause I've *always* wanted to give you a lap dance in front of the whole world. Anyway . . ." She sucked her teeth and her gaze was intent for a full second, sending additional messages JZ didn't understand, before she said, "I just wanted you to know I brought Raheem."

Erica smashed up against him, grinding double time to get his attention. JZ kept time with her as he pulled Jacinta to him by her arm, leaned toward her ear, and raised his voice over the music. "Did I say you could bring your man?"

He chuckled when Jacinta thrust her hand in his face.

"I'm not asking permission. I'm letting you know so there won't be drama," Jacinta said. "And no, he didn't bring Angel. So don't ask."

JZ scanned the room for Raheem. "Where is he?"

"Talking to Brian 'nem." Jacinta pointed in the direction of the pool table. "You know Raheem and Stefan boys now since they both go to GU."

"Weren't you trying get on with Stefan, one time?" JZ's brows furrowed in mock concentration. "Now they're boys. Ain't that a bitch? Messing up your creep-creep, for real."

"Wrong," Jacinta said, casually shaking his hand off her elbow. "I said Stefan was fine. That was it. Don't get it twisted, Mo."

"You gon' stop with all that mo' shit," JZ said, shoving her playfully.

He glanced over the dancing crowd at Raheem, immediately gleaning two things. One, Raheem had cut his braids off and was sporting a Caesar cut, and two, he looked more comfortable than JZ had ever seen him on this side of the DRB without a basketball in his hand.

He didn't mind Jacinta had brought Raheem tonight. Erica was a good distraction. Something was going to pop off between them tonight. If all the booty shaking and grinding wasn't message enough, Erica's flash of jealousy anytime any girl tried dancing with JZ was. He hoped she knew that if she wasn't willing to share him tonight, then she had best plan to be on the clock all night.

She was enough to keep his mind off Cinny. He just wished Raheem didn't seem so comfortable on JZ's turf.

At the very least, dude should have his guard up, stepping into

Blue Devil's territory by his lonely. Instead, he blended in with Ste- fan, Brian, and David—laughing, exchanging dap as if they were all old friends.

Jealousy tightened JZ's chest. This was his house, the side of Del Rio Bay where he reigned supreme. *Kid, better recognize,* he thought as a dance hall mix vibrated the ceiling.

Erica whooped, "That's my song."

"I'll be back, Shortie," JZ said, still eyeing Raheem, mind brim- ming with bravado. He wasn't going to be ignorant. He and Ra- heem had mostly been cool. But seeing Raheem so chill tonight juiced him up.

He nudged Mina and Jacinta. "Come on, let me go speak to your man."

Erica pouted. "But this is my jam."

"Just start dancing," Jacinta said, the sarcasm in her voice quilted with sincerity. "Trust, you won't be by yourself for long."

"Jason, don't *leave me* hanging," Erica said, the warning hollow as he walked on without a second glance.

"Oh my God, Jay, you're corrupting that poor girl," Mina said, when they'd cleared the dance floor. "I thought she was ready do you, right there."

JZ laughed. "Shoot, if she down she down."

"Down, dirty, desperate. She's all those," Jacinta said. "Please get your shots before you run up in that."

"She's not that bad, Cinny," JZ said, amused that Jacinta was so judgmental. If he closed his eyes, he would swear it was Mina talk- ing. His long stride led them through the thick crowd. He spoke over his shoulder, quickly closing the distance to Raheem. "Don't be mad 'cause she's eager to please the kid, unless you want take her place."

He chuckled to himself as Jacinta started to say something, then cut herself off as they reached the pool table. JZ extended his fist for a pound a full foot before they reached Raheem, deep in conversation with Brian.

"What's up, son?" JZ said, laying the buddy-buddy on thick.

He and Raheem knocked fists softly.

"Ain't nothing, kid. I see you bringing in the new year proper-like." Raheem nodded toward the DJ table. "Vic got it banging up in here."

JZ's head shook up and down. "That's how I do."

Jacinta stood guard between them, feigning disinterest in their conversation but with no one to talk to as Brian and Mina huddled up. JZ felt the unspoken warning her stance gave off—back straight, head cocked slightly toward JZ as if on the ready for him to pop some nonsense she'd have to smooth over.

"How y'all look this year?" JZ said, playing to the area he and Raheem shared a passion for. They'd battled on the hardwood for the last two years, Raheem's Trojans besting JZ's Blue Devils four times out of six—a record JZ was determined to better when they met again in college, eventually.

Raheem ran his hands over his low cut, then leaned against the wall near the cue stick cupboard, legs splayed. "We looking good, son. You know I'm swinging for Final Four."

"Right, that's how you gotta think," JZ said. "It's all about going to the dance."

He and Raheem's hands gripped, slid apart, then gripped again at the finger tips in a quick shake of agreement.

"I heard y'all whupped on Poly the other night," Raheem said. "Sam-Well beat Northern Del Rio like ninety to forty-five, son."

He nudged Jacinta's side, an intimate signal she understood. She rested flush against him, facing JZ, Raheem's hands wrapped around her waist in a light hug.

JZ's stomach twisted in a jealous clench. He cleared his throat, forcing his eyes away from Raheem stroking Jacinta's arm. "Yeah, I heard they tore it up." He cracked his knuckles, anxious to get back to Erica and her hypnotic butt even as he kept up his end of the discussion. "Poly was light weight. It's gonna be us and Sam-Well at States this year. We banging for that championship."

"Word. But Sam . . ." Raheem paused, as Jacinta wriggled free.

JZ and Raheem stared at her, stamping her left foot on the floor.

"Sorry, my foot was going to sleep," she said, stamping a few more times before coming to rest, arms folded, near Raheem but not against him.

"Anyway, son, just wanted to holler at you." JZ put his hand out. As he and Raheem gripped hands again, he smirked at Jacinta over Raheem's shoulder. "Thanks for stopping through."

"I was supposed to be in DC tonight." Raheem tickled Jacinta's side. "But I ain't want hear wifey's mouth about leaving her hanging on New Year's Eve."

"Yeah, I hear that," JZ said, fake smile frozen at the corner of his mouth. "Trust, we don't want hear her mouth about it either."

"Whatever, Jay," Jacinta said, eyes rolling.

"Naw, we would have taken care of her," JZ said. His eyes locked on Jacinta's. He fed off the caution flashing in them. "I always take care of *my* girls." He hollered over to the pool table, "I got next," as he walked away, grinning.

He laced Jacinta with the same impish smile when she stepped to him a few hours later, catching him in the back room, a large supply closet, where his parents kept the sodas, juices, and waters for the bar. He fought the laughter rising in his chest at the look on her face. She was hot and chomping at the bit to lay into him. It didn't take a mind reader to know it.

He threw his hands up in surrender as she steamrolled into the stockroom, closing the door halfway behind her, finger stabbing him in the chest.

"You not right, Jay."

"What did I do?" He feigned offense. "See how you do me?"

Jacinta's lips pursed. "How I do *you?*"

"I went out of my way to dap Raheem up for stopping by and look at you bringing drama."

"Oh my God, you are so foul," Jacinta said, the fire already dying in her voice at his silly grin. "For real, why did you have to say that mess about taking care of your girls? All Raheem keep saying now is, what that mean, Cinny? Since when you his girl?"

"You want me explain to him what I meant?" JZ's shoulders shook in a silent chuckle as he worked to keep a straight face. "Mina's my girl too. And Kelly and Lizzie. It's all swazy."

"You're not even slick." Jacinta smacked his arm. "I just had to get through one night, one more night with him. We haven't argued once all break. We—"

"Woah." JZ put his hands over his ears. "I don't want hear about what y'all did over break. My ears too pure for that."

Jacinta's small hands pummeled him, playfully battering his arms and chest. He reached out, caught them, then twisted her around, pinning her up against him so her own arms were a straitjacket.

"I was just playing," he said, resting his chin on her head. "For real, for real."

"Uh-uh, playing nothing," Jacinta grumbled.

"So, what, he mad at you?"

"No . . . I mean, probably. He's playing like he not mad but he is. . . . He'll be all right till we leave, then he's gonna trip." She swayed lightly in JZ's hold to the music surrounding the room, rocking against him, setting his mind racing to places he knew he couldn't go.

I'mma let go, he thought to himself, but found himself moving with her to the midtempo mix thumping the walls of the stockroom.

"Just tell him nothing up between us," JZ said, unsuccessfully willing his arms to release her.

Jacinta sighed. "Been there, done that, over it."

Okay, now . . . now I'mma let go, he said to himself, but aloud asked, "So tell me again why you still with dude if all y'all do is fuss like a ol' married couple."

Jacinta was quiet for a beat. Her answer was matter-of-fact. "It is what it is, Jay. I feel like . . . out of sight, out of mind, at this point." She shrugged. "He probably doing a little sumpun, sumpun at school. But, I'm his girl, for now."

JZ snorted. "Yeah, well, you don't act like you somebody's girl-friend sometimes."

Her arms wiggled under JZ's grip as she laughed. "Who have who pinned down?"

"But you not trying get away either."

JZ lifted the pressure from her arms as proof. His body melded into Cinny's when her shoulder and back relaxed into him. She spoke loud enough to be heard over the music, but in a low, uncer-tain voice that made JZ want to protect her.

"Me and Raheem's stuff is on this complicated tip. He—"

"Ay, you don't have to explain." JZ unpinned Cinny but kept his arms draped around her nonchalantly, so his lean, hard stomach rested against her soft curves. "You know what they say, right?"

He waited until Jacinta looked upside down at him, then grinned.

"You do you, I'mma do me."

She grinned back, teeth shining. "Yeah, but you *wish* I would do you."

He snorted. "Girl, please."

"My bad. I got you all wrong?"

"Yup, dead wrong."

"Then you better tell that to him," Jacinta said, bouncing her butt, one good time against JZ's groin.

"Man, whatever." He thrust against her, once, mocking her ges-ture, playing down the embarrassment heating his face. "Your ass is phat, most definitely, and you *are* all up on me. And, real talk, it's not like I'm gay." He put his arms up, surrendering her once and for all.

"You know how me and you roll. . . . I know your game and you know mine."

Jacinta stepped away and turned to face him. A smile played at the corner of her mouth, as if she were reading JZ's mind and knew he was lying.

"Exactly. I wouldn't want cramp your game since so many girls trying to be with Jason Zimms." She flicked imaginary dust off his collar on each side, then folded her arms against her chest, teasing him with the things she wasn't saying, like whether she was down with being one of those girls. He leaned his head back, so he was looking down at her in his best "whatever" nod, as she said, "Go 'head back to your little sophomore freak, now that you've made sure the rest of *my* night is busted."

"My bad." JZ chuckled. "For real, tell Raheem I was just clowning. I don't want to be the cause of you ringing in a new year with your boy all pissed."

"Uh-huh." A smirk played behind Jacinta's exaggerated eye roll. JZ stared at her lips, unable to take his eyes off how lush they were as she fussed good-naturedly. "So foul, blocking my game on New—"

Before she could finish, he pulled her to him. His lips went over hers and when she responded, kissing back, he eased his arms around her, pressing her against him so hard they rocked back, thumping against a shelf of straws and cups.

His fingers wandered over her curves, probing under her tee shirt, creeping toward her bra, caressing it until he stopped, as quickly as he started.

Jacinta stepped back, dazed, her eyes darting to the half-open door of the stockroom, then back to him, silently questioning what had just happened.

Chest heaving, JZ pushed against the shelf to stand upright. Straws and red plastic cups rained down to the floor. He swallowed hard, savoring the lingering taste on his tongue of whatever mint Jacinta had recently eaten.

sound system was so pristine it seemed as if a live band were playing. Suddenly, the beat transitioned from a traditional ballet tune to classical smothered within a contemporary bass line, and Rob, possessed by the music, went from a dizzying round of pirouettes to a funky krump, his arms and legs contorting, fighting off an invisible army of attackers.

A ballet remix, Michael thought, nodding his head along in time to both the music and Rob's angry gyrations. By the time Rob finished serving his imaginary foes, Michael's chest heaved as if he'd been the one dancing. He breathed slowly through his nose, calming himself from the raucous performance, stood up and made his way to the stage where Rob paced back and forth, silently analyzing his recital.

Rob's right eyebrow shot up when Michael, standing at the bottom of the stairs, stage left, called his name.

"Ay, what's up, man?" Rob said, chest heaving a mile a minute. He padded to the back of the stage and grabbed a hand towel and bottled water off the floor. His face disappeared behind the towel, as he mopped away the sweat.

"Nothing." Michael proceeded up the stairs and stood at the stage's edge as if needing an invitation to go further. "I had to drop off a costume Madame Zora asked me to tailor. Upstairs is crazy packed. Auditions?"

"Yeah," Rob said, dejected. He plopped down on the edge of the stage, his feet dangling dangerously over the ledge leading to the orchestra pit.

"Oh, was that the piece you auditioning with?"

"Nope." Rob sipped from the water bottle. "I'm not trying out."

"Word?" Michael's eyebrows rose. He eased beside Rob onto the stage floor, his back against the stair's railing. "You're missing a production? That's gotta be a first. How long you been with the Players?"

"Six years." The pride in Rob's voice rang out into the empty auditorium. "Never missed an audition and never missed a production . . . until now."

"Why now?"

"Going through masters review at the Carter." Rob arched his back and peered toward the darkened ceiling. He rolled his neck, then stretched his arms as he continued. "It's mandatory for all second-semester fourth-year students. I could probably still do the Players' production. I'd just have to give up something." He smirked. "Yanno, like sleep and eating."

Michael laughed, lowering his voice when the echo sounded back boastfully. "Oh, just not sleeping or eating? That ain't no big."

Rob smiled. "Yeah. But masters ain't no joke. It's an eight-week review and the final week is all auditions so they know what level classes to place you in for the fifth year." He stood abruptly. "I need to be at the top of my game. The spring production's just the sacrifice I gotta make, so I don't slip and end up in the special ed dance classes."

He and Michael's low-key laughter rang back softly. There was an awkward silence when the echo died. Rob draped the hand towel around his neck and sat, poised.

Michael cleared his throat. He glanced about the vast stage, hesitant to go on. It was the first time he'd spoken to Rob since their awkward ride to his house Friday night. He teetered between apologizing and simply acting as if nothing were wrong.

Chickening out, he chose the latter. "Your dance piece is tight, son. You gonna rip master's auditions."

A ripple of doubt waved across Rob's face. "Thanks. I hope so." He swiped at the sweat dripping from his arm, glancing at Michael sideways. "So how was the party Monday night?"

Michael fidgeted against the railing, as if trying to reach an itch. "It was all right."

Rob took a gulp of bottled water, then wiped his chin with his arm. A small grin played at the corner of his mouth. "You know

Maribel was hot that I didn't go. Once I told her I was going, she definitely wanted to roll through."

Michael started to ask why he didn't come, but instead kept it low-key. "Oh yeah?"

Rob nodded. "A friend of hers used to mess with JZ." His eyes rolled. "Keep in mind, dude totally played her. But she still must have given him a good review, 'cause Maribel was pressed to meet him." He shook his head, laughing. "She kept saying she wanted to see if he was as cute as his pic. I'm like Mar, day-um, where's the loyalty to your girl? He dogged her out, hello."

Michael chuckled politely, conscience now of how loud they were inside. And he didn't want to act overly relieved that Rob had unofficially called bygones. "That sounds like JZ," he said. "Kid is like butter with chicks, for real."

"The thing is, I was going to dip by the party but Madame asked me to fill in for Melias." He dabbed at his brow with the towel. "I didn't get out of the performance until eleven-thirty. Mar still wanted to go but I was through."

So happy to see Rob's absence wasn't his fault, Michael admitted it, his grin sheepish.

"Real talk, I thought you were icing me 'cause of what I said Friday night about not auditioning."

Rob shrugged. He stood up, walked to the back of the stage, and placed his water and towel on the floor, raising his voice to be heard. "Naw, I'm not tripping. It's your future, Sean Gianni." He walked over to Michael, his fist extended for a pound. "We cool through whatever."

Michael grinned. If Rob was calling him by the nickname he'd given Michael when they'd first met, a mixture of Sean John and Gianni Versace—two designers whose work Rob thought Michael's style resembled—then they were definitely cool again. He knocked fists with Rob, satisfied that his friendships were in order without any casualties.

High from that satisfaction and still infected with the way Rob performed, Michael sat in the Del Rio Bay auditorium the next day, staring at the Carter application through the room's dimness, an off-key version of "Start of Something New" assaulting his ears. By the time he'd registered the blissful silence when the music halted momentarily, Lizzie was in the seat beside him plucking the paper from his fingers.

"Oh my God, is this an app for the Carter?" Lizzie's green eyes gleamed as she looked from the paper to Michael. She gushed on as Michael nodded. "Are you thinking of going? For which major? Their art major?"

Michael told her about the new program, speaking in the usual hushed reverence reserved for rehearsals. The last thing he needed was Mr. Collins peering through the darkness from the stage, evil-eying him for disrupting his henpecking disguised as stage directions to the Bay Dra-da cast. A dance number broke into full effect, showering the auditorium in sound, just as he finished.

Lizzie stared wide-eyed at the paper. She held it gingerly in her fingers, as if the paper were made of fragile parchment.

"So you're thinking of going?" She scowled, rushing on before he had a chance to say anything. "Mike, you've gotta go. God, I'd kill to attend the Carter. But you know my 'rents." She nagged in a nasally passage that sounded nothing like either of her parents, making Michael laugh. "Elizabeth, we're glad you have an appreciation for the arts, but school is school and theatre is an extracurricular activity." She reluctantly handed the paper over to Michael and slumped in the seat.

Michael tweaked her shoulder. "It's all right. Either you'll end up like Julia Stiles—Columbia graduate actress—or the Olsen twins—NYU dropouts slash actresses."

He and Lizzie laughed freely within the cover of loud music and dancing.

"It's definitely going to be Columbia actress then." Lizzie shook her head, her eyes gazing at the application on Michael's lap. "My parents would kill me if I dropped out of school for acting." She plucked the application off his lap, reviewing it as she spoke. "Oooh, did you see this?" She poked her finger at a line on the program's fact sheet. "There's housing for the summer students. How cool is that? You could live in DC, on your own, all summer while you go." Her grin exploded. "Oh my God, that's so starving-artist. I'm glad we're good friends because I know you'll understand when I say I'm so jealous." Her eyebrows wriggled playfully. "Not like push you down the stairs so I can take your place on stage jealous . . . happy for you jealous."

They laughed, long and hard, trading jokes about theatre-cides, "accidents" befalling leading guys and girls right before showtime, before lapsing into silence. Lizzie's attention returned to the application. Michael gazed at the stage.

Mr. Collins's voice, thin and proper, rang bass-less in the auditorium and the music stopped instantly. High-strung and persnickety, he was hands-down one of the least liked teachers in the school among anyone taking advanced math. But here, in the auditorium, the students respected him. Persnickety and high-strung translated to innovative and often well-hailed productions.

The students on stage hung on to Mr. Collins's every word, anxious to get it right, anxious to please both him and their own thirst for success in the spotlight.

Michael couldn't blame them. Because of Mr. Collins, Madame Jessamay, and Bay Dra-da, he'd found his place at school. Before joining the troupe's crew, he'd assumed he was doomed to go through high school feeling like a fish out of water as the clique became increasingly busy with their own schedules.

Until then, his designs had been secret from everyone except Mina because he'd been too afraid JZ would find his stash of drawings and give him grief for sketching girl's clothing.

I was only thirteen though, he thought to himself, justifying his reluctance to crow about his talent. He shifted in the chair as the old feeling, the icy fear of discovery, wrapped itself around his heart.

His head ticked slowly side to side as he spoke. "But I'm still doing it."

Lizzie, practically vibrating beside him with excitement, tore her attention away from the application. "Still doing what?"

"Holding back."

Lizzie frowned. "Umm, are you gonna tell me what you're talking about or is playing Twenty Questions part of the fun?"

Michael's smile was tiny, but genuine. He plucked the application from Lizzie's grip and shook it gently at her. "This. I want to audition, but I'm also kirkin' out about it." He talked through Lizzie's confused gape. "Liz, when Mr. Collins reviewed my designs the first time, I was a wreck. Having people judge my designs is still like . . . woah. I'm not used to it."

"Now you know how I feel every audition." The giggle in her throat died when she saw the worry crease on Michael's brow. She rubbed his shoulder. "But Mr. Collins loved your designs, Mike. Who wouldn't?"

"Thanks." He shrugged. "I'm just saying, there's a part of me that's scared to put myself out there. Rob said there's already over a hundred candidates. If they're applying, they must have the talent."

Lizzie laughed. "Have you never watched reality TV or Bay Dra-da auditions?"

Michael chuckled along. "True."

He'd sat through enough theatre auditions to know that plenty of people showed up without an ounce of talent. But this wasn't a Bay Dra-da audition, which he reminded her. "Lizzie, people come from all over to attend the Carter. Trust, they're gonna have some level of talent."

"Mike, you have more than 'some level' of talent." Her eyes

rolled. "I should be recording this. Next time you go on lecturing me and Mina about something, I can remind you of a time you weren't Mr. Know-It-All."

"Shoot, don't trip." Michael's eyebrow popped in mock disapproval. "I do know it all." He knocked shoulders with Lizzie. "But if you must keep score, go ahead and mark this as the *first* time I didn't have all the answers."

Lizzie looked toward the stage as her group was called. She stood up. "It's only because you're thinking about the answer." Lizzie's smile was gentle, apologetic, as if talking to a toddler. "If you just did what your heart wanted, I bet you wouldn't be questioning what to do."

"Oh, so what?" Michael grinned. "You gunning for my job as clique guru?"

Lizzie backpedaled up the aisle. "Uh-uh. *That* job you can have."

Her laughter was lost in the hundredth run-through of "Bop to the Top."

"I can do this!"

"And I'm here helplessly in love."
—Black Eyed Peas, "Don't Phunk With My Heart"

Twenty-nine.

Thirty.

Thirty-one seconds.

There's my boo-boo, Mina thought, a huge smile brightening her face as Brian's image rolled across the television screen for a few fleeting seconds. He was handsome in the dark blue Duke uniform, calf muscles flexing as he ran up the court. The camera even captured the glistening of his thick black curls, damp with sweat.

High-definition was the shiggity.

The picture faded into a commercial with big-busted girl-women in tiny tee shirts, and a sly murmur of approval made its way between JZ, Todd, and Greg.

Mina let their crude boob jokes and Jacinta, Kelly, and Lizzie's disapproval of them buzz over her head as she restarted the clock on her countdown to the next appearance of Brian's face on screen.

He'd gotten a lot of playing time, so far. Mina had been rewarded with a camera shot of him every thirty to ninety seconds.

The next best thing to being with Brian was watching him on television. At least that's what Mina told herself. The Duke game popped back on the screen. She stared intently, trying to ignore the snug seating arrangement on the large sectional sofa. Squeezed between JZ and Kelly, she was surrounded by couples to her left and right.

She'd imagined that having a Duke viewing party would be better than watching the game solo. *Color me wrong on that one,* she thought.

Instead of gossiping with her girls about the cute players and catching up on the latest DRB dirt, Kelly and Lizzie were in low-voiced discussions with Todd and Greg. They threw Mina a bone every now and then, responding if she said something to them but otherwise lost in their own conversations. She'd stopped bothering twenty minutes ago.

Even Michael, JZ, and Jacinta, her three aces in the hole as the only noncoupled people in the room besides her, had fallen through.

Michael sat in the easy chair, at the end of the sofa, actually into the game.

And JZ was hogging Jacinta. Anytime Mina tried talking to her, JZ, being silly and rude like a kid trying to get his mother's attention, interrupted.

Not that she's hating it all that much, Mina thought, sneaking a glance at Jacinta tucked under JZ's wing.

Mina wriggled, making a breath of space on her quarter of the cushion. JZ spoke up and her arm vibrated from his loud voice, because they were sitting so close together.

"Man, this game sorry." His arm dipped from around the sofa to Cinny's shoulder as he analyzed the game. "Florida State's basketball team ain't no match for Duke. Look how slow their point guard is and the defense not strong enough."

"FSU balling better than I've seen 'em do before. You gotta give 'em that," Greg said.

"And Duke not invincible," Michael said, glad anytime there was actually conversation about the game. He rocked his chair back so the footrest popped up.

JZ scowled. "Sorry-ass Florida State fan." His eyes, wide, skated toward the door in search of Mina's parents.

Mina laughed. "That's what you get, Big Mouth. But they left ten minutes ago." She shook her head up at him, nagging in close range. "You didn't notice 'cause you were all up in Cinny's grill."

JZ palmed her face, pushing it gently out of his own.

"Ay, first of all, I like FSU's *football* team," Michael corrected, interrupting Mina and JZ's duel. "Now let me hear you talk smack during football season, punk."

Todd and Greg laughed, co-signing.

JZ joined in. "You know I don't mess with Duke during football season," he said.

"That's what I thought," Michael said, snickering.

"Shhh," Mina said. With some effort, she popped off the sofa, holding her hands up for silence. The camera followed Brian down the court. Clapping, she sang her support. "Go, Brian. Go, Brian. Two points. Two points."

"Girl, sit down," JZ said, nudging the back of her thigh with his foot.

She swiped at him, refusing to sit until the camera angle changed to a wide shot of the Duke players running back up the court.

"Are you gonna stand up every time?" JZ scowled. "I'm gon' miss half the game."

"You said it was a sorry game, anyway," Jacinta said coyly. Her eyes twinkled at JZ in a flirtatious wink. She put her hand up for some dap and Mina tapped it with her own.

"It is." JZ sniffed with indignation. "But if y'all gon' make a brother come out and watch basketball, at least let me see the game."

"We could turn to the Georgetown game," Mina said with a sly smile.

JZ rolled his eyes. "They're not even playing today."

"Lucky for you," Mina said.

JZ bumped hips with her. "Man, whatever."

"Ow." Mina smacked his arm. "Stop, boy."

JZ kept it up, bumping hips, smushing Mina even more between him and Kelly.

"It's not enough room for you and your phat booty, Mi," JZ said, an innocent grin on his face. "You're practically on Kelly's lap." He leaned on her, his shoulder pinning her between him, the sofa, and Kelly.

Kelly pushed back, trying to help Mina out, but was no match for JZ's strength.

Mina pushed at JZ's strong arms, finally squeezing her way out. She stood up, giving him the evil eye "You're ignorant."

She squatted to sit back down and JZ moved quickly to fill the spot, stopping her mid-sit.

"Come on, Jay, stop playing." She pouted.

"It's too crowded on the sofa," he said. "Sit on the ottoman."

"Here, sit on this side," Jacinta said, making room.

JZ threw his body across Jacinta's lap, his long arms stretched out to take up the tiny space meant for Mina.

"I see I need separate y'all two as usual," Michael said, shaking his head at their antics. "Come on, Mi, sit with me." He scooted over, leaving a sliver of space for Mina to squeeze in. She settled in and stuck her tongue out at JZ.

In answer, he spread his legs and arms out in the new open space her absence left, grinning devilishly. "Ahhh, that's better," he said.

Todd and Greg's exclamation over a play saved Mina from more taunting.

"Oooh, dude, did you see that?" Todd said. He and Greg high-fived. "Jay, watch the replay, dude. The shot was sick."

"Did you make me miss Brian making a shot?" Mina asked, threatening.

JZ waved her off, his attention on the game.

The noise level went up as he and the guys analyzed the highlight.

"Brian on fire, ain't he?" Michael said.

"Uh-huh. Fifteen points, four assists, eight rebounds," Mina said.

"Dang, I didn't know you were watching that close!" Michael's head snapped back as he eyed her, surprised. "Got his stats and everything."

Mina's voice rose and she eyed her girlfriends pointedly. "Shoot, not like I have anybody to talk to."

But her words and Michael's laughter were lost as the guys' voices grew more animated and the buzzing of the girls' mixed in as they began their own conversations. Within seconds, there were several different conversations going on at once on the sofa, an island of couples.

"Oh sure, now they talk among themselves," Mina said, rolling her eyes in feigned offense. "Nobody wanted to say a word when I was over there."

Michael's eyebrow steepled. "Like you wouldn't be all hugged up with Brian if he was here."

Mina scowled in mock disagreement before smiling wide. "You know I would."

"Leave 'em alone. You're just stuck with me tonight."

Mina patted his thigh. "That's swazy too." She fidgeted until she faced Michael, her hip corked into the crevice of the easy chair, their faces only a foot apart. "You never asked me what I thought about Rob. Scared I didn't like him?"

"Shoot, I figured you would have turned in your report already. But go ahead." His eyes probed hers, brightening when she gave a thumbs-up.

"I like him. He rolled like he'd been chilling with us forever." Her voice rose, high-pitched with excitement. "You know I love anybody who can hang tight with the clique. Oh my God, but if he doesn't remind me of you, I don't know who he reminds me of."

Michael's chest shook as he chuckled under his breath.

"Uh-huh, you know exactly what I mean." Mina's laughter mixed with the growing noise of the clique. "He was cracking on stuff and people like he'd known us forever. I was tripping off how straightforward he is."

"Yeah, that's just him though." Michael nodded toward their rowdy friends. "What did they think?"

"Everybody said he was cool." Mina leaned in and pressed against Michael's shoulder. "So that means you can stop hiding him and invite him over more often."

"I don't know about all that," Michael said with a gentle shoulder nudge. "I told you, he's who I chill with to get away from y'all."

"Yeah, yeah." Mina rolled her eyes, then lowered her voice. "Jess thinks he's gay. She called him your boyfriend. But you know that's just Jess, always think she knows people's business." Mina pretended not to see the disapproval in Michael's knitted brow. She rambled on to fill the awkward pause. "It's official, though. I like him. If I ever need to replace you, I'll give him a call." She wriggled her shoulder against him to get a laugh, but Michael's return smile was weak.

"When did Jess say all this?" Michael said finally.

Mina's breath streamed in an internal sigh as she gathered her answer. She'd only brought up Jess's side remark because she thought Michael would dismiss it as Jess being her usual Queen Bee–self, their shared dislike for her mutual. She hadn't expected Michael to actually be concerned about the offhand comment. But his eyes, small in his face, were a mix of concern and what Mina was sure was fear. She put as much nonchalance in her voice as she could muster.

"The day he came and introduced himself to me." Mina waved it off. "Man, forget Jess. I told her—"

"Was Jay there when she said it?"

"No," Mina said, understanding. She was relieved when Michael's eyes brightened and the worry knits disappeared from his forehead. She touched his leg, gently. "I know JZ can be a real tail about your design skills. But he's still your boy, Mike. If he'd been there he would have defended you."

Michael snorted. "I don't need defending." His eyes wandered to JZ, bouncing between low-talking to Jacinta and loud-talking about the game. "I just know if he'd heard Jessica say that, he'd be like, 'Man, Mike, I told you people was gonna start tripping 'cause you designing girls' clothes.'"

Michael's laugh was uneasy.

Mina kept mum about the fact that Jessica claimed not to know about his fashion skills. Instead, she rolled her eyes. "That's 'cause Jay don't know what to say out of his mouth sometimes."

"And *that's* why I was worried about what he might say when he met Rob," Michael said. He cocked his head and glanced at Mina. "Rob *is* gay, you know?"

Mina swallowed, nodding vigorously in confirmation even though she had no idea if Rob was gay, straight, or ambidextrous. She hadn't known much of anything about the dude until recently. He definitely had a way about him that was a little on the feminine side. But so did Michael and . . . well, Mina had never questioned if Michael was gay and had no plans to assume it.

She felt as if she'd walked into a trap when Michael stared into her eyes as if he were reading her mind, and probed. "You did? How?"

"I . . . I mean, I didn't know." Mina licked her lips, forcing moisture onto her tongue. "I just meant, no I'm not surprised. I . . ."

Michael's tongue clucked as he exhaled. "So JZ not the only one who assumes then?"

Mina felt the disappointment radiating off him in thick waves. Her throat clenched with embarrassment, but she spoke low near his ear, defending herself vehemently. "It's not that I assumed. I mean you were the one who asked the question like you assumed I assumed."

Michael chuckled without humor. He spoke in the same low, intense voice, his lips inches from Mina's ear. "Because I figured every-body would assume it anyway. And that's why I ain't wanna bring Rob around JZ." His hoarse whisper, meant only for Mina's ears, seemed loud even in the noisy sunroom. "The whole night, I kept thinking Jay was going to tell some stupid homo joke, just to test Rob and see how he reacted." He shook his head. "You know what's messed up about that?" He paused long enough for Mina to shake her head no. "I don't even know whose side I would have been on."

Mina scowled. "Well, Jay didn't say anything about it to me or the girls. Even if he thought it, he's not gonna bring it up unless some-one else does." She attempted to assure Michael despite not quite believing herself. "No one's judging Rob."

"Or me?" Michael shot back. "Just because nobody said anything doesn't mean they not wondering or judging. Right?" He cocked his head, appraising Mina. "What about you? Are you wondering if Rob is my boyfriend, Deev?"

The question lit Mina's face on fire. It didn't help that Michael's warm breath closed in their tight quarters even more. She pulled her head back an inch, to get a better look at his face. It was tight with anxiety and as close to panic as she'd ever seen Michael, belying the icy fury in his voice.

"I'm not wondering anything, Mike," she said, her own voice contradicting the pure terror she felt at fighting this battle alone. Relief softened the hard creases in Michael's face and Mina let the breath she'd been holding out slowly between her teeth. She scooted her hand underneath his hand, sliding her fingers in between his, de-bating for a second how to go on, before adding, "You said Rob was your friend and I believe you. But if it's more than that, that's swazy too. For real."

Her heart beat crazily in her chest, waiting. She had no idea what she'd do if Michael revealed he was gay, right here, right now.

In their silence, the clique's noise volume hit its peak. The game forgotten, Mina's eyes skittered between looking at Michael and looking just beyond him at the sliding glass doors. She prayed she'd have the right reaction—whatever that was—yet knowing instinctively that it was whatever didn't set off any alarms and bring JZ over with his joking sarcasm.

As if conjured up by her thoughts, JZ's voice, sing-songy in its demand, climbed over the chaotic buzz. "Ay, what y'all two girls over there gossiping about?"

Never missing a beat, his eyes on Mina, Michael threw up the middle finger at JZ, cutting tension JZ wasn't aware existed.

Mina laughed and rolled her eyes in JZ's general direction, doing her part to act normal. But it was hollow.

Finally, Michael's fingers curled gently around hers, squeezing enough to make her look up squarely at him. His voice was low and steady and his eyes probed hers, searching for what, Mina didn't know. She swallowed to moisten her dry mouth, as he said, "Look . . . I need a favor."

Psychic Flashes

"There's a piece of me who leaves when you gone."
—Keyshia Cole, "Heaven Sent"

Mina had an itch.

Her fingers tingled, barely able to resist dialing Brian's number so she could scream at him—or his voice mail, didn't matter—"Why haven't you texted me back?"

Fifty-nine minutes and thirty seconds is more than enough time to get a text back, she thought, frowning down at her phone as if it were to blame for its silence.

Any other time she would have made good on her impulse and called him by now, but Michael had her captive on the wide circular riser in the workshop portion of his basement bedroom, altering the sapphire blue prom dress he'd made special for her last year. She dared not ask Mike for a break. Little taskmaster, he'd already busted her for fidgeting and huffily reminded her that this is exactly why she'd never have a career in modeling.

That and the fact that I have zero interest in starving myself for a living, Mina thought, shifting her weight to her left leg.

She jumped, gasping as a tiny prick pin of pain stung her lower left thigh.

"Ouch, Mike, that hurt." Her legs twitched in an impatient dance, almost knocking Michael off the riser. She scowled down at him, behind her on his knees deftly pushing pins into large segments of blue fabric. "I thought you were a professional. That's twice you stuck me, boy."

"Keep still." His hand stung her bare legs. "I am a professional but I'm not used to models with as much booty as you."

She threw darts at him with her eyes. "Okay, if you didn't have tiny, sharp objects in your hand I'd respond to that." She fussed good-naturedly down at him. "When you asked me for a favor, I had hoped it was something easy like not revealing that in reality you are Batman." She chuckled at her own joke, while Lizzie, getting dressed behind a rice-paper screen, burst into a fit of giggling. Encouraged, Mina nagged on, happy for the distraction. "I didn't know it was going to involve Manchurian torture with needles and hours of being a living mannequin."

Michael swatted her leg again. "Yeah, yeah. I appreciate your assistance." He poked her butt with a finger. "Seriously. I keep thinking I'm sinking it into the dress but it's your buns."

"Shoot, what are you talking about?" Mina pinched her tiny waist. "I've lost weight."

Still on his knees, Michael straightened up and squeezed a handful of fabric at Mina's torso. "Who you telling? Look how much of this I need to take in. Seriously, Diva, are you eating at all? Or have you found a way to exist on the fumes of love?"

Mina chuckled half-heartedly and, speaking of love, turned her attention back to her cell phone, making certain to remain stock still to avoid more pricking. She flipped open the phone's clam shell top, willing a message from Brian to pop up on screen.

She checked the time, for the fifth time in five minutes.

It was four P.M. and it was Tuesday.

She mentally ticked off Brian's schedule tattooed in her mind. She didn't need Groupie Love's maniacal detail; she knew his whereabouts back and forth like she knew her own.

He would have had practice early that morning, eaten breakfast, attended most of his classes, and would have just been getting out of biology and heading to a late lunch when she texted him. His second practice was at five P.M. The window was closing for them to talk.

"Love nothing. It's called stress," Lizzie offered, emerging from behind the screen wearing a yellow pin-striped zoot suit. She stood beside Mina on the riser, shoulder to shoulder. "Did you have another 'psychic vision'?"

Lizzie bumped shoulders with her, then gave Michael a tiny "oops sorry," look.

"I'm not saying I'm psychic." Mina sniffed. She'd explained this a million times. "But every now and then . . . I don't know, it's like I get this feeling that something's going on with him."

"When you have 'feelings' that come true, it's psychic." Michael gave her a knowing look from the floor. "For you, it's called paranoia."

"He'll call back, Mi," Lizzie said, confident.

"Why is it taking him so long?" Mina frowned at the phone. "I try to only text or call him when I know he has a few minutes to talk. It's been an hour." She pouted. "Who can't hit somebody back with a text in sixty minutes?"

"Hysterical much?" Michael said, eyebrows peaked in a fatherly reprimand. He nudged Mina's thigh, signaling her to turn and face him. As she turned slowly he stood up, eyeing the dress carefully for any bulges. His fingers ran over the fabric gently, picking and pulling at spots, testing them for give. "There are a million reasons he hasn't hit you back, yet. And I bet none of them have anything do with Hot Duke Boys."

Mina winced in the face of Michael's reassuring smile.

She wanted to believe that so bad. But at the mention of the message board, she fiddled with the phone, debating whether to send Brian another message as Michael went to work on the dress's sides.

Text him and say what? *Why haven't you texted me back?!*

Her heart wanted to trust Brian.

Her mind wanted her not to care.

She hadn't been totally bluffing when she'd said to Kelis that she couldn't control what he did three hundred miles away. It was hard-core reality and, in an effort to avoid being consumed by thoughts of what Brian was doing every second, one she'd believed in whole-heartedly last semester.

I can't control it. I can't control it. I can't control it. She told herself that often and most times it helped her cherish the moments he called, said he loved her and missed her.

The problem was, she realized with painful clarity, that it had been so much easier to believe it when she'd had no clue Brian was officially a Hot Duke Boy or that fifteen thousand plus girls were arming themselves with data that Groupie Love claimed could help snag him. Back then, she'd been equipped with the arrogance that went along with the security of his regular messages and calls.

Now, all she had was Hot Duke Boys and seventy minutes without a return text.

She rolled her eyes at the phone, then looked over toward the stairwell. The sound of thundering steps vibrated until JZ's cinnamon face appeared.

"What's up, party people?" He threw a fist pump Michael's way but avoided going near the work area. He turned the TV on, flipped a switch on the gaming console, and plunked down onto a sofa more than halfway across the room.

Michael returned the fist pump.

"Hey," Lizzie said.

"Hey, Jay," Mina said, reluctantly closing the phone.

JZ looked Mina up and down before returning his attention to the game. "You plan on going to prom again? Or ya'll having some kind of dress-up party?"

"Yeah, it's a dress-up party." Michael snorted. "Come over. I have the perfect dress for you. It'll go just right with your brown eyes."

JZ's eyes rolled. "Don't even play like that, kid."

"Mike's getting his stuff ready for the Carter review," Lizzie said. Her mouth kept moving, but her body instinctively froze as Michael moved from Mina to her with the pins. "Mina and I are his models."

"More than I needed to know," JZ said, his fingers flying fast and furious over the game controller.

"Where's Cinny?" Mina said.

JZ patted the pockets on his jeans. "She's not in there." He shrugged. "No idea."

"Oh my God, the sarcasm is so unnecessary," Mina said.

"I'm saying, how I'm supposed to know where she's at?" As his fingers jammed at the control, JZ's eyes intently penetrated the screen of the TV, before sliding Mina's way in a sarcastic glare. "She's y'all girl, not mine."

"Not the way I hear it." Mina beamed. "What's up with y'all kissing?"

"What?" Michael looked up from pinning Lizzie's pants leg. "Son, you holding out on me?"

"I was just messing with her." JZ scoffed. "Gave her a little New Year's Eve kiss."

"Uh-huh. Little nothing," Mina said. "Somebody is so pressed."

"Cinny spreading my business like butter," JZ grumbled.

"If it wasn't a big deal, then it's cool that she told us," Lizzie said. She gave an impish eyebrow raise. "Right?"

JZ's shoulders rose, then fell in a sluggish heave.

Unable to resist, the trio teased him mercilessly about his undercover feelings for Jacinta even as JZ feigned indifference, twice flipping them the bird for their troubles, causing the teasing to go up a notch.

"Why are you acting like it's so wrong that you like the girl?" Mina said. "She—"

A Keyshia Cole song burst lustily from her phone, stopping

Mina's words cold. She flipped the phone open so hard she rocked its tiny hinges. Her eyes scanned the text from Brian, greedily absorbing every word.

Wassup Toughie? Whatchu doin?

Eager, she texted back, letting the conversation about Jacinta and JZ float over her head. A few words registered, "Raheem" "hot" "Cinny's tripping" "not trying," as she delicately punched the keys, unable to avoid posing the question that had nagged her the last eighty minutes.

Nothing. Modeling 4 mike. Whut took so long 2 hit me back?

She blew out a deep breath, relieved to get the question off her chest, and picked back up on the conversation as if she'd never left it.

"I think Cinny would break it off with Raheem if it wasn't for the fact that he has to come home and then she has to see him," Mina said. "It's not like she can avoid going to the Cove to see her family. She knows they'd just end up back together."

JZ turned away from the game long enough to give her a contorted look of confusion and annoyance. "Sound like dude stalking her to me." He shook his head, muttering to the television. "What part of *breakup* don't he get? The *break* or the *up*?"

"I'm not saying I agree," Mina said, gazing down at the first note from her phone. Her words flowed quickly. "But they've been friends for a long time. She's just trying to figure out how they can break up and still be cool."

JZ's reply—"Maybe they can't. But if she's not trying be with him that way . . . it's wack to keep stringing dude along if she know at some point she gon' finally kick him curbside"—went over Mina's head as she read Brian's response.

I wuz in class, couldn't answr or the prof would trip. Wht kind
of modeling u doin . . . nekkid? ;-)

Mina laughed aloud, grinning harder when Michael said, "All is
right in Mina-land. Must be Brian."
Her fingers flew as she responded to Brian.

O u wld b cool w/me posing nude? I thght u had bio 2–3:15
on Tues?

She looked up in time to see Michael push himself upright. He
stood in front of her and Lizzie, looking over the alterations with a
critical eye.

"Ay, Jay, I need a solid," Michael said. His knees cracked as he did
a deep knee bend. He stretched as if ready to take a run while JZ put
the game on pause and walked over to the middle of the room, stopping at the four-foot-tall white bar table, closer but still just outside
the work area.

JZ sat at one of the table's two silver scoop stools. "What up,
kid?" he said, rising silently above the table as his foot deftly played
with the stool's hydraulic footrest.

"I need to take a video of the outfits I plan on showing for the
runway review," Michael said. He put his hands up to Mina and
Lizzie, signaling them to stay put on the riser, then took a seat at the
other bar stool. "Once I get the outfits all fixed up, can you record it
for me? I'm gonna need Lizzie and Mina to model them from front
and back, to show my whole portfolio."

Mina caught the frown crease in JZ's forehead just before she
looked down and checked on the incoming message.

I kno mike all artsy n shit. So naw he cld paint u nude n I'd b
cool. Jus him tho! I have all new classes, Toughie. My schedule
changed up.

"Ohhh," Mina said under her breath. She'd forgotten it was a new semester.

JZ's voice boomed tense and disapproving, snapping her to the present. "So you seriously doing this Carter thing? I thought you said you wasn't down?" His frown crease deepened, giving his handsome face a menacing appeal.

His tone made Mina's stomach flip. She heard it anytime she tried talking in-depth about Michael's Bay Dra–da work to JZ. His favorite words, "Mi, I don't feel like talking no yang about costumes and fashion design."

She'd only heard JZ use the tone around Michael once and it had ended badly. She typed back quickly,

o I forgot. Still have practice @ 5?

and focused on the live conversation.

"I changed my mind. I'm gonna apply," Michael said. His voice was firm, his dark chocolate face subtly blank as he looked JZ in the eye, silently challenging his obvious disapproval.

Good for you, Mike, Mina thought, happy that Michael stood his ground. She knew better than anyone how hard Michael worked to avoid outright discussing his Bay Dra-da work with JZ. Though Sunday was the closest Michael had ever come to admitting how much he cared about JZ's opinion when it came to his designs and the world costuming introduced him to, Mina always suspected hurt feelings lingered because JZ never uttered a word of praise or acknowledgment that Michael's skills were as special as JZ's athleticism.

JZ and Michael had been her friends since kindergarten and still she didn't totally get their bromance. She'd take JZ's constant teasing over the bizarre golden rule of silence that seemed to be the guy code, any day.

Over the years she worked to break the code and force JZ into a more active supporting role of Mike. Once, she asked JZ how he would feel if Michael suddenly was like, "Son, don't talk football or basketball around me. I'm sick of hearing it." But JZ's answer had been a typical shrug and one-liner avoidance.

"Why would he do that? Mike loves football and basketball . . . it's not like it's just about me."

And that had been that. When he didn't want to talk about something, he was king at cutting a topic short.

As usual, he was unabashedly one-sided about his support. But Michael's dull-eyed stare spoke volumes. He wasn't going to let JZ's low-key taunting stand in his way, this time. The hairs on Mina's arm stood straight up as the tension between the guys mounted.

She forced herself to mediate. "Jay, what's the big deal? Just record the outfits." Her high-pitched chuckle sounded fake even to her. "Not like you don't owe Mike for all the basketball and football games he came to watch you play in."

She hushed her phone as it sang, a momentary burst of sun in the gloom settling over the room, and quickly read the message.

Jus walked in the gym. L8r Toughie. Luv u.

Smiling, she closed the phone. The small flash of defiance in Michael's eyes made her throat dry.

She looked at Lizzie, frozen beside her. They were human replicas of Michael's costume mannequins. They shared a furtive glance before returning their attention straight ahead to the guys, neither of them sure what to say.

JZ inhaled slow and long, as if needing a full lung capacity to speak. He swiveled his chair, facing Michael head-on. Only inches separated them at the tiny round table.

"Son . . . all right, I'm not trying dog out your little design game." He flashed an impish grin usually reserved for his "aw shucks" boy next-door flirting moments, then grew serious so quickly, the grin could have been an illusion. "I'm saying, why are you gonna do your last year at a different school? I don't get that."

"Jay, the Carter is the best school in the state for people majoring in the arts," Lizzie said. "I wish I could go."

JZ scowled. "Yeah, Liz, but you all into that arsty stuff. I—"

"Why my design game got be 'little'?" Michael said, tone still even, defiance glittering madly in his brown eyes.

"Man, I ain't mean it like that." JZ frowned. His chin stiffened in challenge as he leaned as far back as the tiny-backed stool allowed. "I'm saying—"

"Then why you say it like that?" Michael said. His chin jutted, mirroring JZ's insolence with an added touch of defiance.

Mina shot off the riser, closing the few feet to the table in record seconds, pulled toward it by the guys' posturing. She stood between them, as if her presence could stem the tension. She towered a full foot over the table but was nearly dwarfed by Michael and JZ.

"Mike, you know how JZ always tripping." She gave JZ a look, hoped he got the message, then wrapped her arm around Michael's arm. "I don't want you to go either but—"

She jumped as Michael pulled his arm away, nearly smacking her in the jaw.

"See, this is what pisses me off." He looked from Mina to JZ, hurt making his eyes glossy. "We supposed to be down for each other. But it's only swazy when I'm the one in the backseat. When have I ever told one of y'all not to do something just 'cause it's gonna cut into how much time we get to chill?" His lip turned up, as if he smelled something bad. "Shoot, for that matter, when was the last time one of y'all cut back on something you had to do to chill with me instead?"

At the collective silence he snorted, satisfied he'd made his point.

"Mike, you didn't let me finish," Mina said, frustrated that Michael had lumped her with JZ. Her sorrowful brown eyes sent him an apology as she explained. "I was going to say, 'But I'm glad you're getting a chance to do what you like.' "

Lizzie came over, placing herself between Michael and JZ on the opposite side of the tiny table, completing the small huddle. The four of them stood there silent for a second, elbow to elbow.

"Mike, I can video the outfits," Lizzie said. Her eyes skated nervously around the table, looking at each one of her friends, silently pleading that they let this be the solution to end the escalating argument. "When Mina's modeling an outfit, I'll video. And then she can do it for me."

"Look, if this is what you wanna do, son, cool," JZ said angrily. "All I was doing was making you see the other side. But sound like your boy Rob already convinced you." He shrugged so hard, the table tilted with the motion. "We been boys for a long time. How you gon' get mad at me for speaking my peace, but not at him?"

"Rob don't have anything to do with me deciding to apply," Michael said, abruptly stepping down off the chair. He whisked over to the workroom and cleaned up the scattered supplies with a robotic energy.

"Yeah, all right," JZ said. Sarcasm dripped from every word. "Dude popping all that yang about how this the same, like if an NBA scout stepped to me and offered me a contract right out of high school." He snorted. "Man, that shit ain't the same."

"But it is, Jay," Lizzie said.

"Don't even waste your breath, Lizzie," Michael said. He stooped and swept all the stray fabric into a pile with his hand.

"How is that the same?" JZ said, grilling Lizzie with a skeptical eyebrow raise.

Lizzie looked from JZ's cynical stare to Michael, his head bowed as he grabbed the pile of fabric, dumping it in a plastic bin. She cleared her throat and her cheeks burned crimson as she explained.

"Graduating from the Carter would look good to fashion schools," Lizzie said weakly, as if unable or unwilling to argue further.

"Mike already said he not trying go to college. He's said it a million times," JZ said, barely holding back a grunt of satisfaction.

"Well, the Carter might hook him up with some contacts for a job," Mina said. Her elbow shot out and connected with JZ's arm hard enough for him to frown at her. She rolled her eyes at him, hard, and shook her head. She wanted to shake him senseless for not simply letting it go.

All he had to do was say he'd video the stupid outfits and this whole conversation could have been prevented. She sighed silently between her teeth, relieved when JZ dialed his tone back to casual conversation levels.

"All right, I hear y'all. But like I said, that's nothing like going from high school to the pros. I could see if they were like, do this and somebody gon' straight offer Mike a big money deal designing . . . but they're not." He plucked a peanut from a silver bowl at Mina, grinning as if to ask if she were satisfied. "Mike, if going not gonna get you where you somewhere, then why bother, man? That's all I'm saying. Y'all acting like I'm hating. I'm not . . . for real."

Mina peered over her shoulder at Michael, methodically placing everything on shelves. She thought maybe he hadn't heard JZ, but his voice, devoid of any emotion and just loud enough for them to hear, assured her he had.

"It's swazy, son. I know you not hating."

JZ grinned. "See, that's my boy. He know I got his back." JZ reached out and shoved first Mina's, then Lizzie's elbow off the table. "Y'all birds trying to start drama. It ain't even that kind of party."

Mina swung and missed smacking JZ's hand. He stuck his tongue out at her and she returned it, hotter with him than the childish act relayed. Angry that it was easier for JZ to focus on Michael's last words, totally ignoring that the boy couldn't even turn and face them right now.

But she dare not point it out.

JZ was already joking and laughing, teasing Lizzie, thanking her for Todd's latest thirty-point-game winning performance. JZ had moved on. The tension had ebbed, just enough.

But it wasn't over. Mina knew it.

It was like knowing something bad was going to happen but not knowing when, where, or who it was going to happen to.

Shoot, maybe she was psychic after all.

"Say it, girl!"

"She give a new definition to the word curve."
—Akon, "Dangerous"

Jacinta's butt wriggled against JZ as she attempted to wrestle her way free from his crushing, but painless, bear hold. They were a tangled statue, his arms tightened, pinning her crossed arms around her waist. He laughed at her futile attempts to unlock herself.

"All you gotta do is say it and I'll let you go," he said, calm and pleasant as if he were asking if he could take her order. He enjoyed the friction their bodies made, as she struggled, but not enough to alert Jacinta that his motives to bear-hug her were anything more than his usual teasing.

"I'm not saying nothing." Jacinta stopped fidgeting and went limp. "So I guess we gon' stand here just like this forever."

"Is that a challenge?" JZ adjusted his grip to take up her dead weight. " 'Cause you know I can."

"So can I." Jacinta snorted.

"You just like having me all up on you," JZ teased, bumping her from behind.

"Whatever, Mo."

He gripped her elbows and easily lifted Jacinta straight up until her feet dangled a few inches from the ground, as he fussed. "Now, see, why I always gotta be a mo?"

Jacinta laughed. "I don't know. You tell me . . . *Mo*."

He placed her back down and she laughed harder when his right hand tickled her side. Anticipating her attempt to escape, as she tugged away, he twirled her toward him like an amateur ballroom dancer, scooped her up and threw her over his shoulder. He walked over to the sofa, lecturing the whole way.

"Don't hate. How whack would it be if I didn't share myself with the chicks who appreciate me?" He let her body slip over his shoulder until he held only her calves.

Jacinta's feet kicked, uselessly. "Come on, Jay. Put me down."

"Just say it. Come on, it's not like I'm gon' snitch on you for truthing up."

He waited as Jacinta's body quieted, grinning as she considered it.

He let her body dip a few inches deeper, chuckling at her flailing arms.

"You gonna drop me on my head," she said, poking JZ in the back of his legs to no avail. His grip on her was solid.

"The sofa will break your fall." He smacked her on the butt. "I'm waiting."

"Oh my God, you're so foul."

"Say it."

"Just 'cause I say it don't mean I'm gonna mean it."

JZ laughed at the petulance in her voice.

"Say it, girl."

After sucking her teeth for good measure and sighing so hard JZ wondered how she had enough breath to say anything, she sang in a testy chirp, "I like spending time with you more than with Raheem."

She yelped as JZ dropped her abruptly, face first on the sofa.

He laughed. "My B. You all right?"

Jacinta kicked at him. "Lucky for you."

She pushed herself upright and sat cross-legged on the couch. JZ sat beside her with just enough space between them to claim innocence if any of the clique burst in.

He and Jacinta had started off playing the arcade games. But as usual, he'd come around to taunting her about Raheem—something he swore he'd stop doing. He didn't want her thinking she had him sprung or anything. But he couldn't help it. One minute they were chilling, enjoying just kicking it, and then a deep, warm sense of satisfaction would spread across his chest and next thing he knew he was teasing her. Making Jacinta admit that she liked being with him more than either of them admitted was like scoring a much-needed three-pointer at the buzzer.

Sweet.

He batted his eyelashes at her. "Now was that hard?"

Jacinta rolled her eyes, but JZ saw the smile in them. He picked the TV's remote from the floor and pointed it at the screen. Jacinta snatched it from his grasp.

"Uh-uh. For torturing me, I get to watch what I want."

He put his hands up, in surrender. "All right. All right." He slouched down on the cushion, scowling. "No girlie ish, though."

Jacinta laughed. "And what's girlie shhh?"

"The crazy stuff you and Mina be watching. *The Hills Have Eyes on the Runway* or whatever."

Jacinta cracked up and surfed channels. Five minutes into the search, she sighed and turned to music videos.

"TV is booty," she said.

"Shoot, I got plenty of things we could do besides watch TV." JZ raised his eyebrow at her, grinning when she pushed his face away, playfully.

"You wish."

JZ straightened himself up just enough to put another inch between them. "Naw, I just like you to *think* I wish it."

"Really?" she said, in a conversational tone as if she were asking him to confirm some curious trivia. In answer to his "now what you think?" scowl, she uncrossed her legs and knelt on his cushion. The leather sank under her weight, pulling her toward him. Her breast brushed his shoulder before she steadied herself, leaving a breath of space between them.

She lurked inches from JZ's face.

"What's up?" JZ said, keeping his voice steady, even as his body grew warm. He hoped his face was as icy neutral as he intended.

She knelt closer on his cushion, closing the sliver of space. Her chest and stomach pressed against his arm, her lips near his ear. "You tell me, what's up," she said in a low flirty whisper.

He cleared his throat and grimaced when it came out as a strangled choke. "Girl, go 'head." His hands went to her waist and caressed lightly before pushing her away. "You gon' mess around and get tapped."

Jacinta popped right back in position, pressing against him. Her smooth cotton tee shirt was cool against JZ's arm. He resisted the urge to pull her onto his lap.

She moved JZ's hand back to her waist as she talked into his ear. "I thought this was what was up."

Her warm breath sent JZ's body into autopilot. His hand kneaded her waist. In a few seconds he was going to willingly give his brain a fifteen-minute break and let his hands and mouth take over. He closed his eyes, briefly, savoring the pressure of her body.

It took a second for his brain and body to reconcile Jacinta's voice, still hot and flirty, taunting him, "Now *which* one of us is wishing something was up?" She laughed as realization dawned on JZ's face.

His face burned, a mix of wanting Jacinta and embarrassment. He pushed her away, snatching his hand as if it were on fire. "Girl, get out my ear."

She poked at his neck, jabbing and tickling at the same time.

"I played you." She clapped. "You was totally ready to do me."

JZ rolled his eyes. "Trust. If I wanted to do you, it would have been done. For real."

"Yeah, okay," Jacinta said. She plopped back down, cross-legged on her cushion, laughing her head off. She taunted in the new way they had of torturing one another, a sick game of hard-to-get, giving him grief for almost falling for her seduction.

JZ half listened, pretending to suddenly have a great appreciation for the wonders of MTV Jams. His mind raced back and forth over the last few seconds. Already the memory of Jacinta pressed against him, her voice convincingly beckoning him to touch her, and her breath streaming in his ear, were breaking up like wisps of a dream. Only her laugh rang clear in his mind.

Either Cinny was a pro at playing their game or she was an A-1 actress. He didn't believe she would reject him if he came at her the right way.

She ain't that good of an actress, he thought, shaking his head clear.

Two could play that game.

The stakes had just gotten higher in their hand of catch me if you can.

But the next evening he had another game on his mind and it was whipping him better than Cinny. Coach Ewing had been on his back the entire practice.

"Jason, stop hotdogging. I thought you outgrew that bullshit last season."

"Jason, pass the ball. Ain't no scouts here tallying up your stats—pass the ball!"

"Aww, Jesus, what is this? A SportsCenter highlight?"

Sweat poured down JZ's face. Coach Ewing had a real bug up his ass tonight. But JZ dared not show his frustration. It would only rile his coach more, make him nastier. The way Coach was on him, nobody would ever guess that three years ago, the man had literally begged JZ's father to let him play Varsity when JZ's father had been adamant that his son remain on JV for a year.

The three years felt like an eternity away, tonight.

JZ was the star of the team, but Coach Ewing wouldn't let him enjoy it even for a minute. He felt his legs ready to go rubbery and willed them steady as he passed Coach Ewing, whistle clamped between his lips, ready to blow it at the slightest hint that JZ was slowing down. Several players ran past JZ, forcing him to dig in and catch up.

He was the captain of the team; if any of the players reached the foul line before him, he'd have to run an extra lap at the end of practice.

JZ would sprint-crawl before stopping. He had mad respect for Coach. Besides his father, Coach Ewing was the only other man JZ feared. Tall, lean, and broad across the chest, the thirty-something history teacher had an easygoing demeanor that could turn into mouth-frothing anger at mediocrity in a heartbeat.

JZ was no psychologist, but he didn't have to be to know Coach's disdain for weakness had something to do with his own unfulfilled dreams. A former McDonald's All-American player, he'd been a top college prospect until he blew out his knee, junior year. No knee meant no scholarship, and once the big-name schools stopped calling, he ended up at a small HBCU in Tennessee. He reminded his players often that they should take basketball seriously, but be just as serious about a backup plan.

JZ feared Coach Ewing's wrath, but he feared the prospect of becoming Coach Ewing more.

Talent down the drain. That would never be him.

JZ pushed harder, outpacing Todd, sprinting past Dave B., and easily overtaking Carlos to reach the foul line on the last sprint. He put his arms over his head and walked off the lightning bolt piercing his sides and chest, until his breath steadied from panting to just plain heavy.

"Well, ladies, look like your captain doesn't wanna run extra laps today," Coach Ewing said, the smile in his voice genuine.

JZ's heart steadied. He'd done good. Coach was happy . . . finally.

Coach waved the team over. They huddled around him, the heat steaming off their bodies as he lectured. "That's the kind of effort I need to see when we play Sam-Well. Not five of you on the court, but one team handling the ball like they're connected at the hip. One picking up the slack when another struggles." He leveled a look at JZ. "We got an understanding, Jason?"

JZ nodded. He greedily reached for the water bottle Todd handed over and squirted the cool liquid down his throat, never tasting it.

"I hope so. You try stacking your stats over doing what's right to get a W in the column, I'll bench your ass," Coach said, refusing to look away until JZ nodded again. Once he did, Coach put his hand in the huddle, palm down, and waited patiently while the players followed suit, placing their hands on top.

"Blue Devils go, on three," he said. "One, two, three . . ."

"Blue Devils go," the team chanted.

The huddle broke up immediately. The team scrambled to run their mandatory laps, forcing their way through it like a sick child taking medicine. Afterward, the losers of the sprint drill gathered the equipment, while the rest of the team beat it to the locker room.

Todd walked beside JZ. He glanced at the back of JZ's soaked practice jersey, tugging at it slightly, "Dude, did you have a bull's-eye on your back or something? Coach was just like . . . man, on you."

Not like it was the first time, JZ thought bitterly. He pulled the jersey over his head, wincing at the soreness in his arms, and wiped his face with it.

"You know how he gets," he said, not really wanting to dwell on it. Coach didn't play favorites—he was an equal opportunity bitcher—but JZ would be lying if he didn't admit to himself that the closer they got to senior year, the harder Coach was on him. If JZ didn't know better, he'd swear Coach Ewing was jealous because so many Division I schools were actively recruiting him. They were calling Coach Ewing's office daily and flooding him with letters requesting to come out and see JZ play.

JZ was at the foothills of the promised land. Coach Ewing must have been having flashbacks to his own stunted career and JZ was catching hell for it.

It wasn't anything JZ knew for sure, just a feeling.

"Is it me or is Coach seriously dogging you out a lot more lately?" Todd said, blithely summarizing JZ's miserable thoughts.

The team's noise muted around them as everyone hit the showers, leaving Todd and JZ standing at their lockers.

JZ shrugged. He sat on the wooden bench that ran the full length of the locker room and kicked at his sneaker until it worked itself off.

"I'm just saying, you've been the golden child and now . . ." Todd's blue eyes clouded with thought. "I don't know. It's probably that reverse psychology thing—being harder on the favorite." He laughed, unaware that JZ was silent beside him. "Man, whatever it is, remind me not to be his favorite."

"Play like you did today and that won't be a problem," JZ said. "All those bricks you threw tonight."

Todd mimed taking a shot.

"Bonk," JZ said dully, imitating the ball hitting the rim.

"That's wrong." Todd mimed a few more shots as he talked. "Yeah, I was off today, no doubt."

"Why? Did you finally get some?" JZ asked, chuckling.

"Yeah, right," Todd said, rolling his eyes to the ceiling. "But that's probably it. I've reached my peak. Now the no sex is *killing* my game."

"Then you gonna be a no-playing somebody." JZ stepped his right foot on his left and yanked until the sock came off. " 'Cause Lizzie ain't thinking about giving it up."

"Tell me something I don't know," Todd said. He put his fist out for a pound. "Later, dude."

JZ banged his fist against Todd's gently. He sat on the bench until the first wave of guys emerged from the stable of showers, then stood up, stretching, taking his time to the line of open nozzles. He bypassed the empty nozzles and headed to the last one, making it clear to his teammates he wasn't in the mood to talk smack tonight.

He turned the shower on full blast and let the tepid water quell the sticky clamminess that coated his body, scrubbing until the locker room went silent. Finally alone, he rinsed and toweled off. As he threw on jeans and a tee shirt, jazz played softly from the back of the locker room where Coach Ewing's office was located. Many days, JZ would stop by and talk with his coach. They talked about everything—JZ's grades, JZ's parents' expectations, random game highlights, and every now and then, girls. But not tonight.

JZ had eaten enough humble pie tonight. Coach was probably in a better mood; he'd certainly been at the very end of practice. But if he wasn't, JZ would have to stand there, face passive, body language neutral, as Coach went on about JZ stacking his stats or hogging the ball.

Man, fug that, he thought, grabbing his Blue Devils duffel bag and taking the long way around to avoid walking by the office. He trudged out quietly, relieved when he escaped without Coach looking up and sensing his presence.

He squinted in the bright fluorescent shine of the hallway, taking his time going down the long corridor that ran the length of the school's athletic area. He passed doors to the gym, three mini gyms, the girls' locker room and weight room before nearing an open door at the end of the corridor. Hip-hop blared from the room, tinny and bassless like someone was playing it on bad or tiny speakers.

That's my joint, he thought, his head automatically nodding along to the song. He slowed down. He'd never noticed the room before.

Curious, he stopped just short of the doorway and stretched his neck so he could glance inside without being too obvious. His face brightened when he saw Michael inside, hunched over an art drafting table, head nodding to the music.

JZ stood in the doorway. "What up, money?" He laughed when Michael jumped. "My B, Mike. I ain't mean to scare you."

Michael swiveled on the tall stool, chuckling. "No problem. I usually shut the door. But it gets mad claustrophobic in here when I do."

He put his fist out for a pound. JZ was beside him in two strides, connecting his fist in a gentle tap.

"Mad claustrophobic is right," he said, eyeing the cramped room, scowling. "Did this used to be the football team's supply room?"

Michael nodded. He dropped his pencil on the desk, welcoming the interruption.

"That's right." JZ pointed to the back wall. "That area used to be caged in, where Coach kept the balls and stuff. But we haven't used it since freshman year."

"Yeah. Last summer, they gave Madame Jessamay permission to use it as a sewing room, 'cause Ms. Epps went off and wouldn't let us use the Family Life sewing machines regularly."

JZ chuckled. "Ms. Epps always like that. Remember I had to take Family Life that semester? Man, she acted like those sewing machines was made of platinum." He nagged in a high-pitched nasal, "Jason, respect school property. This is a sewing machine, not a weight machine."

Michael nodded. "Uh-huh." He rolled his eyes. "You know I don't have no love for Ms. Epps. She got hot with me because I asked her how come we didn't have more challenging sewing projects." He scoffed. "How I look, fifteen years old making a stuffed animal?"

He and JZ tapped fists again as they laughed.

"I know that's right. I only took it 'cause they messed up my schedule and Coach Ewing couldn't flex no muscle and get it changed." JZ's scowl turned into a smile at the memory. "Only good thing was, the class had so many chicks in it who I never noticed before. I hooked up like a bandit that semester."

"I remember," Michael said, head bobbing up and down. "I figured it was gonna be an easy A for me. But Ms. Epps got all technical on me. Failed my shorts project 'cause I used a different type of stitch than the one she taught."

"Son, that's so foul." JZ howled. "That sounds like her though."

Michael grinned. "When I told her I was applying at the Carter for fashion design her mouth practically fell open. She had the nerve to say"—his voice took on a tight, proper imitation of Ms. Epps— " 'Well, Mr. James, I hope you follow directions better there . . . *if* they accept you. Willingness to be taught is as important as skill.' "

JZ's chuckle was snide. "You should have said, Yeah, be-yotch, I know you pissed 'cause I'm doing what you only wish you could do."

Michael's eyebrow raised at the venom in JZ's voice, but his voice remained neutral. "Yeah. But I needed her recommendation. We gotta have three recommendations from people who have worked directly with us in design and I only had two." He shrugged, grinning. "So I needed the old bird. I'll tell her off if I actually get in."

"That's my boy." JZ put his fist out for another pound. "Get that revenge. I'm with that."

Their one and only shared experience about fashion over, a heavy silence settled between them. JZ shifted from his right foot to the left and adjusted his duffel bag, absently. He glanced down at the sketch Michael had been working on, then shifted his eyes to the expected costume dummy in the corner. The partial outfit on the dummy was the same Michael was playing around with on paper.

JZ was surprised to see how similar the two were. He could see the penciled design taking shape before his eyes, even though it was half-finished. He'd seen plenty of Michael's finished designs but had never seen any of his sketches. Seeing the direct connection gave him an odd sense of pride in Michael's skill.

He fought the warmness in his chest with his usual arrogant wit. "So, son, if this whole thing takes off"—he gestured casually to the dummy, then brushed at his shoulder—"I expect the hookup. I'm gonna need a fly suit for NBA draft day and then I want your shit hot off the sketch. I'm talking hooking me up with that private custom line."

He was relieved and happy when Michael extended his hand for a grip. They gripped hands, ending with a pound to the back, the closest they would ever come to a hug.

"You got that, kid." Michael beamed, his pleasure at JZ's acceptance obvious. "You know your boy gon' look out."

"That's what I'm talking about," JZ said. He cleared his throat. His voice rose, as he talked over the emotion building in his chest. "Do you, cutty. I gotta dip."

He tapped fists with Michael once more and turned heel. He was out of the room in the same two strides that brought him in, and in several more, onto the main corridor leading to the front parking lot. He walked briskly, trying to outpace the mix of emotions threatening to overwhelm him.

You Do You

"Wanna see how it's done? Watch me do me."
—Rocko, "Umma Do Me"

Michael was vibrating. It had been two days since JZ stopped by the sewing room and given, in his own JZ-way, his blessing, and Michael was still soaring. His hands moved a mile a minute over the new sketch he was working on, a fly men's suit—never too early to get started on JZ's draft day gear. He stopped to admire the charcoal gray, pin-striped suit. The jacket had only one button, so Jay could unbutton easily and show the black vest with bold gray stripes, making it contrast crazy with the thin stripes of the dark pants. The thick stripes, at the top, against the tiny ones, on the bottom, forced your eyes to the wearer, head to toe.

JZ would love it. Attention was his addiction.

Playa', you're the straight shiggity, Michael thought, swelling with pride.

A loud, old-fashioned telephone ring blared from his computer, stopping him mid admiration. He turned from the sketch, surprised to see Rob on.

Crazylegs: whut up dog?

Michael pushed the sketch aside, happy to chat.

MikeMan: its ur world, son. Thght u had a masters audition 2nite?

Crazylegs: my time got moved up. done 4 the nite.

MikeMan: u rip it?

Crazylegs: LOL if u say so. Any word frm da board yet?

Rob had been more nervous about the masters review than Michael had ever seen him about any audition. Normally, Rob carried himself as if he assumed he'd get any role. Masters review was only about class placement; Michael couldn't understand his anxiety. His own worries about life at the Carter tickled the back of his mind, as he thought about his portfolio with the school's admissions board.

MikeMan: no word yet. But damn u mkng me nervous. If u shook like this how im gonna keep up there?

Crazylegs: the mod dance major is mad competitive. im not pressed abt making it, pressed abt getting the right instructor! U get the rgt 1 n seriously once u graduate u practically guaranteed da hookup w/certain schools & contacts.

MikeMan: u gon b alright.

Crazylegs: o I got the job done 2nite, trust. Jus' sweating my balls off now.

MikeMan: LOL I hear dat.

Crazylegs: u gon' know what I'm talking 'bout once u do ur live portfolio review

MikeMan: dayum thx dude . . . tht don't make me nervous at all!

Crazylegs: LOL my b. just meant having ur shit on display live is mad nerve wracking. But I get off on the pressure, its all good.

MikeMan: speaking of pressure, finally got one less thing 2 trip abt

Crazylegs: whuts dat?

MikeMan: JZ finally gave me props 4 mine
Crazylegs: thas cool . . . it only took him 3 yrs. Better late than
never huh?

Michael read the message a few times. As low key as Rob's response was, in his mind Michael saw Rob's mouth upturned in distaste. He'd been the one person Michael had been totally honest with when it came to his anger that JZ never acknowledged his design skills. Mina knew, but he always played it down with her. If he hadn't, it would have only stressed her out to know just how hurt he was. She would have tried bringing him and JZ together to talk it over, kiss and make up or whatever. That was her wishful thinking/fantasy land solution, while Michael knew no amount of "talking" would change JZ's mind. That's just how JZ was—stubborn, a little aggressive with his viewpoint. Michael was used to it and letting JZ go with his own flow was why they'd remained friends so long with no drama.

As maddening as the last three years had been, he was willing to call bygones. It was more important that JZ had come around, and though he knew he shouldn't have, he admitted it to Rob.

MikeMan: extly, better late than never. It's swazy. Just glad he accepting that this is me . . . it's what I do.
Crazylegs: yeah he accepting thts what u do but he ain't accepting u

Michael's heart thumped to his throat. He was here again, caught between his two friends, two worlds. He swallowed anger, treading carefully with his words.

MikeMan: accepting what I do/me is the same thng 2 me
Crazylegs: no it ain't, Mike. Save dat bullshit 4 JZ don't spit it 2 me. JZ not accepting u cuz he don't even kno u, son.

Michael stared at the screen, unable to type back. The response standoff went on for five minutes, then Rob blinked first.

Crazylegs: look man, im not tryna dog u out. 4 real. but i can't let u lie 2 urself. Im ur boy. I would b jus as bad as JZ if i ain't b real. da only way u gon' kno if JZ down w/u is if he kno all of u.

It took Michael a second to realize that the tapping in his head was his heartbeat pulsing in his temples. He rubbed the sides of his forehead, wanting to be mad at Rob, wanting to burn the bridge of their friendship so he could stay safely on the side with Mina, JZ, and the rest of the clique. He glanced at the sketch of the suit, caressing it with his eyes.

Didn't matter if JZ went into the NBA tomorrow or five years from now, the suit was hot. JZ would rock it fierce. He fingered the sketch, pushing it away when his throat tightened.

The computer chirped as Rob continued. Michael reluctantly read the messages.

Crazylegs: im not saying its easy, money mike. But u gotta do u, rght?
Crazylegs: come on, man, don't ice me like this. Jus tryna have ur back.
MikeMan: thx, son. I kno u lookin out.
Crazylegs: u at least tell Mina yet?
MikeMan: started 2 last Sunday . . . changed my mind. Lizzie the only one who knows.
Crazylegs: not tryna pressure u. cuz it ain't like admitting u prefer pepperoni 2 sausage

Michael laughed out loud at the analogy. His hands zipped a reply.

MikeMan: it kind of is. ROFL
Crazylegs: LOL mayb sausage was a poor choice of words.
Im sayin I kno its gon' b rough. But I b here 4 u.
MikeMan: I kno. Check it, I know wht u sayin'. I respect it. But
respect tht I gotta do whut I gotta do. In a yr and a half JZ b
on his way and I b on mine. Jus let it lie son. Don't hate cuz im
handling mine different.

Michael's breathing slowed as he waited for, but hoped against,
Rob's wrath. He knew staying in the closet was against everything
Rob believed in. It would crush him if Rob turned his back on him,
for his choice, but it was the chance he was willing to take.

Crazylegs: real talk?
MikeMan: always
Crazylegs: u gon' always feel torn. n honestly if JZ trash y'all
friendship cuz of this y'all was never friends anyway. BUT respect son, do whut u gotta. I ain't mad.

Michael blew his breath out, relieved.

MikeMan: thx
Crazylegs: welcome. Jus focus on rocking the runway Sean Gi-
anni. ur moment in the spotlight coming up. remember u only
as hot as ur last design.
MikeMan: LOL bye hater
Crazylegs: LOL deuces

Michael clicked the message box closed. His hands trembled.
He'd dodged a bullet. Rob had every right to ice him. He'd been
there for Michael for three years, through every doubt, concern,
and struggle as Michael came to terms with the duality of being

gay with an ultrastraight alpha male best friend. Michael owed Rob and himself—maybe even JZ, being honest. Torn was an understatement to describe how he felt lately. But it wasn't new. He'd been conflicted this long, doing it for another 465 days was a cake walk.

Groupie Girlfriend

"Take this, haters."
—Kanye West, "Stronger"

"Rule number one," Mina said, raising her voice to be heard over the clique's buzzing. "This is not couples hour. So break it up right now." She grabbed Lizzie's hand, pulled her up from the sofa in JZ's game room, and walked her to the opposite end of the couch away from Todd.

Lizzie gave Todd a forlorn look and waved.

"What's rule number two?" Kelly asked, removing herself from Greg before being assigned a seat. She sat beside Michael, who'd already been forbidden from sitting anywhere but on the sofa.

Mina double-checked her handy work.

Lizzie on one end of the couch next to Jacinta.

Todd and Greg, lonely, on the opposite end.

JZ in the back of the room, at the pool table, refusing to be told where to sit.

Michael and Kelly in the middle of the sofa.

Satisfied, Mina sat in the middle between Michael and Kelly. "There is no rule number two. Y'all can still talk to your honey boos . . . just from across the sofa."

"Lizzie, catch," Todd said, tossing her a note.

Lizzie opened it, pretending to read the empty paper. "Meet me in the bathroom in five." She winked. "Got it!"

Mina laughed. "T, the only thing that's gonna happen in the bathroom is you leaving miserable."

Everyone laughed, and Todd popped his middle finger up and down at her as if it were a jack-in-the-box.

"Thanks, Mi." His eyes suddenly gleamed with hope. "That's okay. Only three months and four days before the pact expires."

"Not knowing the expiration date down to the day," Jacinta said, snorting.

"Shh, the game's on," Mina said. She turned the sound up on the television.

The room filled with the voice of announcers rolling off stats of the intense Maryland versus Duke rivalry. A sea of red filled the camera as it panned Maryland's packed arena.

"Sold-out game," Michael said.

"Always is, when Duke comes this way," Todd said. "I think the Terps might give 'em a run today."

"Not even," Greg said. "I know rivalries get the blood pumping, but Duke's been on fire."

"God, it's killing me. He's only like thirty minutes away and I can't see him," Mina said, openly wistful.

"It's so weird watching Brian on TV," Lizzie said.

"Speaking of TV . . ." JZ said, from the back of the room, "Mina, if you're going to force us to watch the games with you, at least let people sit where they want." He bent to take a shot. "Besides, this my crib. I'm gon' sit where I want anyway."

"Don't make me hurt you," Mina said over her shoulder. Her head whipped back to the television as the announcer said Brian's name.

"Like you could," JZ retorted, a laugh in his voice. He was behind the sofa in an instant, his forearm around Mina's neck in a hold.

"Stop, Jay," Mina said, smacking at his arm, never taking her eyes off the television.

"Be nice and I'll tell you a secret." His grip relaxed into a snuggly hug draped around her shoulder.

"What secret?" Mina asked.

"Is it that Brian's ranking at Groupie Love went from number twenty-five to top five?" Greg said, his voice all awe and respect.

Kelly shot him a look.

"Not that I ever really look at that site." Greg smiled innocently, before scowling. "Nasty groupies."

Todd dapped him up as they snickered.

"That site is tacky," Lizzie said. "Can you say ripe for a crazy stalker?"

"Not that I see a lot of lacrosse players on it," Jacinta said, teasing. "So Greg don't need worry about no stalkers."

Greg thumbed his nose at her and Kelly muffled a giggle as Jacinta slyly put her hand out for some dap. She tapped it softly, blowing Greg a kiss at the same time to cover up her duplicity.

"Y'all wrong." Greg pouted, playfully. "I could get a stalker."

"Did I miss the fad where having a stalker is in?" Michael said.

Mina smiled, grateful for the moral support. Groupie Love had become one of the clique's new obsessions. The guys admired Brian's rising status on the site, talking about where they might rank once they joined the collegiate athletic arena, while the girls condemned the very notion that a site like it existed.

JZ cupped his hands around his mouth, shouting, "Okay, I guess nobody wants to know my secret."

Mina sighed loudly. There was going to be no watching this game until JZ was heard. She patted his arm as if she were a patient mother trying to appease a toddler. "Okay, Jay. What's your secret, Boo?"

"I know you hate Groupie Love, Mina, and some of the facts on there straight bull." JZ sat on the back of the sofa, addressing his friends. "But some of the information on there is real, especially if you register as a member."

Mina's eyes rolled. "Oh my god, you registered?"

"Yeah, cause we were curious."

"We?" Lizzie said, throwing Todd the evil eye.

He shrugged, his grin sheepish.

"Anyway," JZ said, loudly shushing her. "You get a lot more personal info if you register."

Jacinta scowled. "More personal than their class schedule?"

"Y'all gon' let me finish or what?" JZ said.

The clique answered with silence.

"Okay, yeah, so me, Todd, and Greg registered. If y'all ever go on there, we're Cutieboomd."

He got up and knocked fists with Greg and Todd as they laughed. The girls rolled their eyes, but kept silent. Michael chuckled, shaking his head.

"We're totally Brian James's number-one fan," Todd said, batting his eyes.

"So if he ever tries to hook up with us, Mina, we'll let you know," Greg said.

The guys howled, enjoying their farce. There was another round of hand slapping and fist knocking.

"The secret?" Mina said, her patience thin.

She'd been anxious for this game. Having Brian playing just down the beltway at University of Maryland was as close as she'd get to him until spring. She wanted to actually watch the game. She kept one eye on the game as JZ talked.

"The secret is, there's a password protected section on the site that gives out ultra-secret spots where you can catch sight of some of the guys," JZ said. He smiled when Mina turned around in the seat, curious. "Got your attention now, don't I?"

"So what does that have to do with anything?" Jacinta asked.

"Mina knows," JZ said, staring in her eye for acknowledgment.

She nodded. "You mean you know a spot at College Park we could hit and see Brian today, don't you?" Mina asked, grinning.

JZ smiled in answer.

"You want us to ride up to the Comcast Center now?" Lizzie asked.

Todd jumped up. "Road trip!"

Kelly groaned. "Remember our last road trip?"

"We're just riding up to College Park," JZ said, already standing. "We'll be back by eight o'clock."

"So where's the spot?" Michael asked.

"It's this area of the arena where the visiting guys exit to get on their bus." JZ shrugged. "If nothing else, Mi, you'll get to catch a quick look at Brian. He might be able to talk to you . . . if they win. But if they don't, forget it. Coach will hustle them on the bus."

Mina's head swiveled from the game on television to JZ's excited face.

Jacinta squeezed her knee. "Come on, Princess. Let's go see your man."

JZ headed up the stairs, yelling to his parents. "Ma, can I take the truck? We're running out."

Mina turned the TV off and filed behind the rest of the clique as they herded up the stairs talking over one another. Just before she slipped out the door, JZ's mother invoked the standard rules of using her truck, including seat belts, remembering to use the Bluetooth if he used the phone, and gassing it up if the tank went below a quarter full.

Mina shook her head, marveling at the things JZ's mother didn't ask, which Mina's certainly would have, like where all eight of them were going to in such a rush. An exhilarated thrill flooded her chest, thinking about the impromptu road trip and the prospect of seeing Brian. She barely remembered the forty minute drive, a blur of loud music, bad singing, and joke cracking. Squeezed in the third-row seat between Michael and Lizzie, she was more than ready to stretch her legs when they arrived on the campus of University of Maryland.

JZ's truck circled the vast parking lots, all full, five times before Michael cried out, "Son, park anywhere. It's mad cramped back here. Cinny, you're sitting back here on the way home."

"All right, all right," Jacinta said.

"Oh, I thought we had to sit boy, girl, boy, girl," Todd said from the second row. He turned around and grinned Mina's way.

She waved him off, laughing as Michael stretched his leg over the seat, dangling his foot next to Todd's head.

"This third row only good for like a ten-minute drive, not a forty-minute one," Michael said.

"Jay, dude, park quick," Todd said. "Mike's dogs are killing me."

"Everybody chill," JZ said, frustrated. "I didn't think about where we'd park."

"Groupie Love didn't tell you which lot to use?" Lizzie said, snickering.

"Oh, ha-ha." JZ rolled his eyes. He pulled the large Sequoia up to a curb. "Here, y'all girls go ahead and get out. I'll park and then we'll meet y'all back here."

The girls filed out of the truck. Michael hopped out of the back, like he'd been torched from a cannon, and took Jacinta's shotgun seat.

The girls huddled in the cold.

Several tall dorms stood to their right and a large lecture hall to their left. The campus was alive with activity as people passed in the dimming evening, their conversations hurried and excited as their pace in the cold.

"I love this campus," Kelly said. Her head swiveled from right to left taking in the expansive grounds. "It's pretty."

"Yeah, it's nice," Mina said, blowing into her gloved hands. "Where's the arena?"

"I think it's up that way," Lizzie said, pointing straight ahead. "I remember seeing it the tenth time Jay drove by."

Jacinta sunk her hands deep into her jacket pocket as she nudged Mina. "Excited?"

"Very," Mina said. "But all I keep thinking is we're gonna get to this spot and there's going to be like a million girls there waiting."

"Maybe not a million," Kelly said. She chuckled. "Fifteen thousand, maybe."

Mina elbowed her.

"You mean thirty-five thousand," Lizzie said. "His friend numbers are growing crazy."

"And I needed to be reminded of this because?" Mina said, her eyebrow raised.

"Sorry, Mi." Lizzie linked arms with her. "When we left, the game had just started. So we're here early enough. At least you'll be the first groupie there."

She and Mina shared a friendly squeeze.

"Wait, I know we not planning on standing out here till the game ends," Jacinta said.

She jumped when JZ came up and goosed her from behind. "Boy, don't do that," she fussed, turning to face him. "Are we standing out here for another hour?"

JZ sucked his teeth. "No."

"Oh, good," Jacinta said.

"Another seventy minutes . . . you forgot to calculate halftime," JZ said, jumping back as Jacinta took a swipe at him.

"So what are we supposed to do until the game ends?" Kelly said.

"Just jokes, baby girl. The game should be over in about thirty, so let's find the spot first," JZ said, walking in the direction Lizzie had pointed. "We'll decide after that."

The clique walked the path leading to the Comcast Center. Clouds of cold smoke rose above their heads as they analyzed the campus and speculated exactly how much longer the game had to go. Muted sounds of crowd noise and game music wafted in the air as they neared the large arena. A nondescript luxury bus sat in a large empty parking lot behind it.

"See, there's the Duke bus," JZ said proudly, as if someone had openly doubted him. His neck craned toward the arena and he squinted, taking in the back of the building. Suddenly he smiled. "Okay, right there. The players should come out right there."

Mina's neck snapped toward the building. She was relieved to see the area was empty. "Guess Brian doesn't have any groupies in Maryland," she said, cheering inside.

"Puhh, please." JZ's eyes rolled. "Watch. They'll be out here before the game ends. Wanna bet?"

Mina pursed her lips and smacked away his pinky. "No."

" 'Cause you know I'm right," JZ teased.

"Seriously, what now?" Jacinta asked. She scoped out the area, which was barren of seating or anywhere to stand without obviously loitering. "If we just stand here, won't security roll up on us?"

"Not like we'll be the only ones security gotta move," JZ said, head nodding toward the arena.

Mina's face fell. Even in the growing darkness, she saw a group of girls were gathering near the arena's back door. She counted five, but within minutes the numbers grew until she'd lost count. The campus's streetlights popped on and Mina was able to see that some of the girls had players' numbers painted on their faces, others had decorated tee shirts with the grinning Blue Devil mascot—bold since they were deep in Terrapin territory.

"Brian's the man," Todd said. He and Greg touched fingers in a light dap.

Mina frowned. "How do you know they're all for Brian?"

"Yeah, I guess you're right," Todd said. "It doesn't even matter. With all those girls lining up, even the benchwarmers bound to get a little action from the runover."

The guys howled and exchanged pounds and snickers of "I know that's right."

JZ embraced Mina for a fleeting second. "Come on, you know I wouldn't bring you all the way up here if I didn't have a way for you to talk to him."

Mina's eyes lit with anticipation.

Michael opened his cell phone. "The game should be over now. Where should we stand?"

JZ beckoned them away from the growing crowd until they were in a field of grass next to the parking lot, only a few feet away from the team bus. They stood in the shadows, just outside the nearest streetlight.

Mina waited, her heart simultaneously heavy and light. Her head tick-tocked between JZ and the crowd near the arena's back entrance.

Jacinta snorted. "Chicks is tripping. I'm not sitting around no door waiting on some dude just to catch a glance of him." She threw Mina an apologetic glance. "Sorry, Mi. I didn't mean you." She nodded toward the bulging crowd. "I meant I'm not doing that for some dude that don't even know me."

"I knew what you meant," Mina said quietly. She was too wired to argue or joke.

The crowd of girls finally drew security. They managed the crowd, pushing them away from the exit, forcing them to make a gauntlet on either side of the door. The girls were obedient, but their numbers kept growing. In minutes, it went from a single line on each side of the path leading from the door to several rows deep on both sides.

Mina looked around the empty field. People walking by paid them no mind, but she still felt as if she were a statue, on full display, in the large grassy area. "Jay, I feel stupid." Her eyes swept across the crowd of girls. "Cinny's right, I'm just as crazy as the other girls, waiting out here like I'm desperate."

"You are desperate." JZ knocked shoulders with Mina. "But he's your boyfriend. It ain't the same, so stop rummin."

Suddenly a high-pitched collective squeal burst from the gauntlet of groupies.

"Uh-uh, not screaming." Jacinta scowled. She covered her ears. "Umph, they act like it's Chris Brown or something."

"Oh, that would be you if it was Chris Brown?" JZ said, snickering.

Jacinta's eyes popped as she confirmed, "Hells to the yes."

The girls laughed.

"I know I would be too, Cinny," Mina said.

"The team's coming," Michael said.

Mina's heart raced. She was as nervous as she might be if it were Chris Brown. She stared at the exit. A sliver of light shone from the Comcast Center as the door opened wide. "What now, Jay?" she said.

He put his hand out to quiet her. "I got this. Chill. Mike, check your phone real quick, see who won the game."

The rumble of squeals grew. The clique's eyes were riveted on the guys streaming out the door, duffel bags over their shoulders, and the girls clamoring to touch them, holding out pieces of paper, tee shirts, and body parts for autographs.

"They won," Michael announced, closing his phone.

Mina blew out a breath of relief. She knew whatever JZ had planned wouldn't go down if the team had lost. She silently thanked God and waited for JZ's signal, whatever it was.

"Cool. All right, y'all stay right here, but when I hold my hand up, come over. Okay?" JZ waited for head nods. "And, Mina, y'all let Todd 'nem walk on the side closest to the side the guards are on, so they won't really pay attention to y'all."

He walked away without waiting on their consent, striding toward the players who were now just a few feet away from the bus. Unbothered by security, who were on alert for approaching females, he blended in with the players, walking beside them.

Mina grinned, her heart bursting, as she realized JZ was walking

beside Brian, talking. She'd recognize his head full of curls anywhere.

They exchanged a pound, then JZ pointed in the clique's direction.

"Was that the signal?" she asked, taking a step.

Jacinta pulled her back. "No. He said he was gonna hold his hand
up. Pressed much, Princess?"

Security held the screaming girls back, preventing any from following the players to the bus.

Mina squinted through the darkness. "Oh my God, is JZ talking
to Coach K?"

"You know Duke's recruiting him," Michael said. "He's met all
the coaches there."

"He *said* he was gon' get you the hookup," Todd said.

"What? Is he asking Coach K if we can come over?" Lizzie said,
eyebrows furrowed.

"Probably not. They're not allowed to even talk to him right
now," Michael said.

The players milled around the side of the bus taking their time
getting their bags loaded, and JZ began talking to a brown-haired
guy. JZ's head bobbed up and down as he talked, then without
breaking conversation, his right hand went up, as if he were waving
to a passerby.

"Now, *that's* the signal," Jacinta said. She pulled Mina toward the
parking lot.

"What if security says something?" Mina whispered.

"Remember, walk in the middle of us," Todd said, his long stride
shortened so the girls could comply.

Mina, Jacinta, Lizzie, and Kelly walked on the far side of the guys,
allowing them to "shield" their presence as they reached the parking lot.

"What do we do now?" Mina said, panicking.

"Say 'hey' or something," Brian said, suddenly in front of her.

Mina cheesed into his smiling face, her anxiety on pause. "I would say 'good game,' but I only saw like five minutes of it," she said.

Brian exchanged pounds with the guys, who remained rigidly in place, keeping Brian hidden from the coach, who was speaking to the driver at the back of the bus. The girls said a shy "hey" as they tried to remain out of sight of any coach or security guard.

Players milled by them, loading onto the bus. Others talked in small circles near the luggage areas and the back of the bus, on the down low flirting with the groupies from afar, reveling in the clowning allowed because of the win.

"I guess I can forgive you missing it this time," Brian said. He bent his head down and kissed Mina firm but quick on the lips. "I was thinking about you as we drove by the exit to Del Rio Bay earlier."

Mina's eyes shone. She wasn't sure what to say. The squealing of the groupies penetrated the air, giving the scene a surreal, dreamlike quality. She felt like screaming to see if it would wake her up, but before she could seriously entertain the thought, Brian pulled her close to him.

The clique did a supreme job of pretending to talk among one another as he spoke to her, his mouth near her ear, his voice low.

"I'm glad you came to see me."

"I guess I really am your number-one groupie," she said, unable to suppress a giggle.

It was as if she'd won some crazy contest—win five minutes with your favorite Duke player. She swallowed the urge to giggle like mad and yell, "I won. I won."

Brian's voice, husky in her ear, kept her grounded in reality. "I don't want no groupie." He lifted his head up, looking her in the eye for a fleeting second before leaning back down to her ear. "But you *can* be my number-one girl. Is that cool?"

She nodded, too giddy to respond.

Brian lifted his head and looked in JZ's direction.

"All right, Coach ready head this way," Brian said. "Holler at me later, all right?"

"Aren't you gonna be tired?" Mina said, finding her voice.

"Nah, I'm gon' sleep on the bus."

Before she could respond, his lips were over hers. She savored their warmth, falling into the familiar rhythm of his kiss. Forgetting her shyness in front of her friends and anyone who happened to walk by and notice, she kissed back, pressing her body into his. His arms wrapped around her, squeezing tight. She would have stayed that way until security forced her off, but Brian pulled away first.

"Damn, brother got a long trip ahead of him." He grinned as he palmed her butt. "Umph, let me go before I get myself in trouble . . . and I ain't talking about Coach K."

Mina reached up and pecked him on the lips. "See you."

He kissed back, letting the passion overtake him again but only momentarily.

"All right, Toughie. Love you." He reached over her and smacked hands with the guys before backing up toward the bus's door. He threw up the peace sign. "Check y'all. Deuces."

"Deuces, B," Todd said, returning the peace.

Mina's throat constricted. She waved as Brian disappeared, and managed a weak smile.

Seconds later, JZ was beside her. He waved at Coach K, then ushered the clique away.

When they were on the path heading back to the truck, Greg whistled, high and loud. "Okay, can somebody say violation of NCAA rules? Man, that was walking the line."

"Naw, it's all good. I only said hello, that's allowed," JZ said. "Plus, I did it for my girl." He chucked the back of Mina's neck. "I don't get a thank you for getting you some boo time?"

Jacinta pushed him in the small of his back and gave him a look.

"What?" JZ frowned.

Jacinta sped past him and walked by Mina, protectively close.

"On behalf of Mina, thanks, JZ," Lizzie sang.

"Why she can't thank me herself?" JZ tickled Mina's neck, oblivious to her silence.

"Thanks, Jay," Mina said, sniffing and swiping at tears.

"Aw man, you crying?" JZ said, louder than he intended. His voice rang in the cold, dark night, echoing between the campus buildings. He lowered it, grumbling. "Man, y'all chicks rummin. I thought seeing Brian was gon' cheer you up, Mouthy Mi."

"It did," she said, unsuccessfully working to stunt the tears.

"That's love for you," Michael said. He put his arm around Mina and squeezed.

JZ snorted. "And that's why I ain't messing with it."

"Yeah, yeah, yeah." Jacinta waved JZ off. "That only means you're gonna fall hardest of all, one day."

"Man, please," JZ said. He outpaced the group, steering them in the right direction, to the truck. He shouted over his shoulder, "It's gon' take a bad chick to make me all to pieces like that."

Eyes still leaking, Mina chuckled. "JZ meet Jacinta. Jacinta meet JZ."

The entire clique burst into a chorus of laughter.

"Aw man, forget y'all," JZ said. He jogged backward to the car. "Just for that, walk back to Del Rio Bay, punks."

His laughter pierced the night as the clique ran to the car, racing not to be left behind.

"I'm not that gay."

Up.

Down.

Up.

Down.

Mina's emotions were all over the place.

She had endured JZ's teasing of her constant mood swings all the way home on Sunday until finally giving in and cracking wise back. Dissing him had made her feel better—a little of the old, stable Mina at work—and also filled her with such a surge of love for him, for helping her see Brian, that she'd reached over the second-row seat and hugged him while he was driving. She nearly caused him to plow the truck into her parents' mailbox.

But that had been eight days ago.

The warm and fuzzies of last week's "boo time" with Brian evaporated as the days wore on. When it took five of the eight days to catch up with him again via text messages, the old insecure jitters filtered in, slowly at first, seeping into her mood like rainwater into a flower bed, then flooding her with a raging impatience even she didn't recognize.

Everything annoyed her. Her mother's request to "for the hundredth time, move your summer clothes downstairs before there's no point." Her coach's threat that if she didn't perfect her tuck, it was being taken out of the routine, and the wretched crystal heel sandals that refused to go on her feet, no matter how hard she dug her foot into them.

Exasperated with last year's prom shoes, which apparently no longer fit, she smacked the shoe down on her lap and pouted, using the time to take in the circus atmosphere of the Carter portfolio reviews.

If she'd ever had any hidden desires to be a model, they were gone now. The room full of Carter fashion hopefuls, abuzz with wannabe fashionistas and their models, was overwhelming. The room spun with activity. What was a large dance studio by day, was now a perfect replica of backstage runway drama—half-dressed models, harried designers, and last minute fashion fixes.

Annoyance with the shoe was replaced by awe, and some anxiety, about what she and Lizzie were about to do. Neither of them were models, by any stretch of the imagination, but they were about to get up and walk a pseudo runway for a panel of six judges who would then determine if Mike would get into the Carter.

Her stomach rolled with the burden of showing Mike's design well.

She grabbed the shoe and crammed her foot into it to no avail. The top of her foot, swollen like a sausage, refused to move past the blinged-out arc of the sandal.

Michael smacked her hand and repositioned the shoe. It locked into place on her foot.

"Ow, they hurt," she said, reaching to remove it until she saw his evil eye.

"Look, Deev, pain is beauty," Michael hissed. He sighed and sat down in the chair beside her. He leaned his elbow on the ballet bar, smiled and shrugged his eyebrows. "I'm sorry. I know I'm rummin. As soon as you finish, you can kick 'em off, throw 'em in the trash can, do whatever. Just rock 'em fierce for a few minutes, please."

Seeing the worry in his eyes, Mina put on a happy face, determined not to give in to her tumultuous emotions . . . at least until she'd rocked the runway.

"Sorry." She wriggled her toes. "Umm . . . can't feel my toes. But it's swazy."

Michael pinched her toe. "Must be nerves. They fit yesterday."

Mina nodded, resisting the urge to kick the shoe off and rub her foot.

Lizzie, decked out in the yellow pin-striped zoot suit, came up behind Michael and massaged his shoulders.

"Calm down, Mike." She looked up, scanned the room, and whispered, so only he and Mina could hear, "You totally have this."

Michael's eyes followed each corner, appraising the designs quickly.

"A lot of these are really good," he admitted matter-of-factly.

"Yeah, but your stuff is more intricate," Mina said, absently rubbing her foot against her leg to soothe the pinching. She nodded toward a little black dress. "I could have made that in Family Life class." She laughed. "Okay maybe *I* couldn't. But I'm saying, there's nothing that interesting about it."

Michael chuckled. "Good point."

"You'll fit into the Carter easy," Mina said.

"I don't know about fitting in," Michael said, rolling his eyes at one of the candidates passing by, a thin white guy with brown hair so neatly coiffed that it fell perfectly over his right eye. Too perfectly, in Michael's opinion. He wondered if it had been spritzed in place.

The guy was skater chic with skinny jeans, a black leather vest covered in zippers over a pink tee shirt that said "I was breast fed," and a pair of black and pink Chucks. The guy clapped his hand at his model, a prissy gesture, reprimanding her for sitting.

Mina and Lizzie giggled.

"I see a few designs in here I'll admit come close to mine. . . ." Michael shook his head, as he once again eagle-eyed every designer in the room, a handful of them girly acting guys. "But fitting in?" He snorted. "I'm not *that* gay."

Mina laughed abruptly, then put her hand over her mouth. "Sorry." She muffled a giggle, embarrassed when a few people stared their way, disapprovingly. She lowered her voice. "You're a trip. I didn't mean you'd fit in that way. I know you're not—"

The chuckle in her chest and the last word on her tongue died when she caught a look between Michael and Lizzie.

"Wait . . . are . . ." She frowned.

Lizzie shifted. She stood upright and brushed imaginary lint from her jacket.

Mina's gaze moved to Michael. His eyes, unflinching, bore into hers despite his neutral expression. His shoulders relaxed as he reached out and laid his hand on her thigh.

"Deev, don't be mad. I didn't want to make it a big deal when I told you." His chest heaved as he took a deep internal sigh. "But I needed to tell you . . . even though I figured you probably assumed." He smiled, weakly, at her wrinkled brow. "You're saying you didn't?"

Mina swallowed. She looked at Lizzie's plastered, pained expression and knew.

"You told Lizzie already, didn't you? Like way before today." Mina said, her eyes ping-ponged between her friends, reading the answer. Feeling it before either of them shook their heads yes. Her hands trembled as she smoothed out the blue satin prom dress that was suddenly making her sweat.

Michael was gay.

Lizzie knew. She hadn't.

It was hot.

Her head felt like it weighed a ton.

Her stomach pitched and she instinctively steadied it with her hand.

Michael shook a finger at her. "Don't you throw up on that dress, Diva."

Mina fought tears. "Why? I mean . . ." She pressed her hands to her cheeks, needing to feel the cool on her hot face. It calmed her racing thoughts.

This isn't about me, she chanted softly in her head.

She willed her thoughts to slow down. Forced her mind to focus.

Michael's hand patted her thigh. Lizzie's eyes sent apologetic waves.

The rest of the room probably thought she was having serious pre-runway jitters.

She closed her eyes for a second, steadying her mind, then looked Michael in the eye.

"It sucks that you didn't tell me." Her eyes welled and she held back the tears with the tightest blink ever. "I'm saying, if you couldn't trust me after twelve years of friendship, I'm seriously the world's worst friend. And—"

"Not about trust, Deev," Michael said softly. "It's about me needing to work through my own before getting everybody else in my mix. I told Lizzie 'cause me and her . . ." He considered it for a second before finally concluding, "We saw each other a lot because of Bay Dra-da. And when I got around you, it was nice just not dwelling on it." His smile was apologetic. "I guess telling Lizzie was enough . . . for a while."

Mina processed it, understanding but still stung by the secret. "Am I the last one to know?" she asked.

"Hardly." His eyebrow rose. "Does that make you feel better?"

Mina chuckled. "No. I was just wondering."

"Look, I have a lot going on right now," Michael said. He stood up, held out his hand, and helped Mina from the chair. He steadied her arm when her sausage feet made her wobble in the one-inch heels, and stepped closer to her. Lizzie closed in the circle. "There were a million and one ways I could have told you. A million times I could have picked besides today." He shrugged. "But I figured it like this. . . ." He leveled her with a classic Michael look, raised eyebrow, lips pressed in a fussy tight line. "No matter how much you trip over when and where I told you or in what order, in the end you're still my girl." He cocked his head and winked. "Is that what's up?"

Mina nodded. She gave Michael a gentle shove.

"Yeah, that's what's up. But don't think I'm not gon' bless you and Lizzie for keeping this from me." She gave Lizzie a look. "You know I hate being out of the loop."

Michael laughed. "Of course, 'cause it's all about you, Deev."

"And you know this," Mina said.

She wrapped her arms around Michael. He hugged her back, tight, and her emotions flared again. She cleared her throat as she stepped back, waving at her eyes to dry up any threatening tears.

"Real talk. I'm glad you told me, but you know it doesn't matter. . . . I mean, you didn't have to tell me." She winced. "Do you know what I mean?"

"Yup. I do." He nodded, opening his arms, and Lizzie and Mina walked into the group hug, their heads together. "Okay, now that our *The Hills* moment is over, can y'all please rock these outfits so I can get this over with?"

"You ain't said nothing but a word," Mina said. She pursed her lips and struck a pose.

Michael scowled. "Uh-uh, you better not do that when you walk."

Mina pouted. "Why? This is my first and last Tyra Banks moment." She popped her eyes. "Now, I'm smiling with my eyes." Her eyes lowered. "Now I'm not smiling with my eyes."

Lizzie and Michael laughed. They ignored the stares of the candidates, bothered by the interruption of their last minute fussing.

"Okay, Miss smiling-with-your-eyes." He nudged her shoulder, signaling Mina to turn. "Come on, let me fix the back of this thing." He shook out the dress, swiping it down with his hand as he scowled over at the door. "God, what's taking them so—"

"Michael James," a voice called. "You're on deck to present."

Michael's hands froze mid-nitpick. He blew out a deep breath. His head shook side to side in a tiny tremor. "Am I really doing this?"

"Yes," Mina and Lizzie sang.

Mina turned around, grabbed his left arm, and Lizzie grabbed the right.

"Let's do this, baby boy," Mina said.

"I feel like I'm forgetting something," Michael said, refusing to be led to the door.

"Everything's perfect," Lizzie said.

"Perfect," Mina echoed.

She felt Michael's arm shaking in her hand. She eased her hand into his and squeezed gently until he looked at her. "Mike, you got this," she said, nodding.

He repeated it, uncertain. "I got this?"

"You got this," Lizzie said, patting his arm.

He looked from Lizzie to Mina, his head going from a side-to-side tremor to a shaky, then firm, head nod.

"I got this."

Mina and Lizzie grinned.

"Yes," Mina said.

They took two steps toward the door when Michael stopped short.

Mina frowned. "What?"

"I got this," Michael said. "But if I don't . . . remind me later to talk smack about all these wannabe *Project Runway* rejects."

The girls promised as they made their way past the chaos and into the quiet hall of the Carter School.

"How come you don't call?"

"This love ain't gon' be perfect."
—Ne-Yo, "Mad"

Mina didn't care that Michael was gay.

Well, she didn't care *much*.

Bottom line truth, if forced to admit it, she'd confess that suspecting and knowing was like the difference between striding confidently into the shallow end of the pool and suddenly sinking in the deep end—daunting and a little scary.

One of her best friends was gay.

It was major, in a "I need to tell someone just to make it real" sort of way.

But she knew she couldn't and it was a struggle to know she couldn't openly ponder the ins, outs, and what does it mean with all her girlfriends.

Michael hadn't sworn her to secrecy or anything, but it didn't take a PhD to know that if he'd kept it from *her* this long, it wasn't something she was supposed to share.

Still, she wanted to tell Brian. There was nothing wrong with that. It wasn't gossiping, just sharing with her boyfriend, talking it aloud to keep herself honest about how she felt—which was she didn't care, but she was still just this side of freaked. After all, it wasn't exactly the same as Michael admitting to liking purple after years of claiming to like blue.

Later that night, after the portfolio review, she'd spilled to Lizzie, but only a little. It felt too gossipy, like maybe Lizzie would feel like, Dude, get over it, I've known forever. So she'd kept her conversation with Lizzie to a low-key minimum, mostly uttering, "This is really weird," and asking "So is Rob his boyfriend?"

Lizzie had nodded fervently to the former statement and shook her head no to the latter.

In time, they'd discuss it more, when she was solidly not freaked out by the sudden knowledge. For now, Mina needed to air the initial shock to someone.

She picked up her phone to text Brian, eying the clock on her PC as she did, mentally checking off where he wouldn't be. It was nearly midnight. He'd be long finished with classes, practice, and eating, hadn't had a game tonight, and likely wouldn't be goofing off with his teammates in the dorm, because this was the time he usually reserved for settling down before studying. This was one of the few open windows in his day for idle chitchat.

She crossed her legs in her desk chair and typed,

Hey B hit me back need 2 talk . . .

Then waited.

Minus a few very late-night text messages that had left her wilting in class the next morning, she hadn't spoken to Brian for days. Their Sunday rendezvous was weeks old, a hazy memory that only served to make Mina's heart ache when she thought about how little they got to talk since he'd returned to school.

She stared at the phone, willing it to chirp with a message. When it refused, she plucked at her PC's keyboard, signing on. Her screen was filled, within seconds, with hellos from a variety of friends. She laughed at the message from Vic.

Udontseeme: 'sup girl? Ur man must be busy. Ur away msg never goes off unless u already kno he's ghost or online 4 da nite

She laughed at her predictable-ness, refusing to own up to it.

BubbliMi: 4 ur 411 I just been 2 busy to log on
Udontseeme: yea right! miss u at work
BubbliMi: cut back on my hours during basketball season . . . 2 hard to cheer games, competitions, homework, and work.
Udontseeme: righ' righ' Jess miss u 2. lol

Mina rolled her eyes, chuckling as she eased into the conversation with Vic.

BubbliMi: I see her enuff at schl. So whut up?
Udontseeme: jus u ma-ma. March madness only 4 wks away, I kno u happy 'bout that.

Actually, she wasn't. Brian was barely able to call her as it was. She figured once the NCAA basketball tournament started she wouldn't hear a peep from him until it was over. The reality spiked her right in the chest.

A national championship better be worth it, she thought, smiling at the diva-like demand.

BubbliMi: happy? ::shrug::
Udontseeme: u b alright. U knew u was gon b a basketball widow when u hooked up w/dude. Take da good w/da bad, baby girl.
BubbliMi: gee thx Dr. Phil. lol

She stole a glance at her phone, as if it somehow rang without her noticing, before toggling over to Jacinta, who'd been beating down her browser trying to get Mina to answer.

CinnyBon: OMG look who's on!
CinnyBon: Hello! What's up Mi?
CinnyBon: ok u better b talking 2 Brian, icing me like dat
BubbliMi: OMG calm down. lol i was tlkg 2 vic
CinnyBon: w/his fine ass. Tell him I said 'sup?
BubbliMi: yeah cuz I have nothing better 2 do than pass msgs b/w u and vic
CinnyBon: u must not cuz u online tlkg 2 other people not named Brian James. What brings u online 2nite?
BubbliMi: dayum have I been ghost like that? Vic said da same thng
CinnyBon: thas y I luv u princess . . . so innocent. ;-) yes Mina u been ttly ghost. Only time u on is if u on tlkg 2 brian than u refuse 2 hold a real convo w/anybody else.
BubbliMi: ummm . . . sorry?
CinnyBon: LOL I ain't mean dog u out jus spitting truth

Mina sat back, absorbing the words on the screen.

Between school, cheerleading, work, family obligations, and kicking it with the clique, what little time she had left—mostly hours she'd usually spend sleeping—she used trying to catch up with Brian, emphasis on the word *trying*.

She hadn't intentionally igged her friends. A sense of regret nagged at her, but she kept her apology lighthearted.

BubbliMi: my b. life as a b-ball widow ain't all its cracked up 2 b
CinnyBon: b-ball widow?
BubbliMi: lol thas what vic called me. I like it.

CinnyBon: ::rolling my eyes:: w/e. u might b 1 but dam if raheem don't call my azz every day like clockwork.

Mina shook off the jealousy before it could dig its claws into her.

BubbliMi: somebody whipped ha ha
CinnyBon: he calls me b4 practice, after practice, b4 he study,
after he study LORD SAVE ME
BubbliMi: u crazy girl

Mina shook her head, laughing at Jacinta's antics, refusing to give
in to the little voice whispering, *I wish that were me.* She toggled back
over to Vic.

Udontseeme: ur welcome, my bill's in da mail. ay im dj'ing a
party this wkend in 1 of those burb hoods on ur side of town.
want come?
BubbliMi: o yeah? what nabe?
Udontseeme: folgers way
BubbliMi: thas where my girl kelly lives. how'd u get that hook
up?
Udontseeme: chick came into da store 1 day. thnk she's a
friend of Jess's . . . asian chick
BubbliMi: o i kno who u talking bout. Not really my clique.
Udontseeme: yeah but i cld use some company. it can get
lonely when its 1 of those rich kid parties. dont make a dude
beg

Mina pursed her lips, squinting at the screen, debating. Jill Ling
was one of the younger Glams, Jessica's snooty clique. A sophomore,
she was primed to be queen bee of the clique once Jessica and Mari-
Beth Linton graduated, this year. Not like Mina actually had plans
for the weekend, but there were a few dozen better ways to spend

her Saturday than be at a Glam party—jumping off a cliff was among them.

> Udontseeme: i'll owe u 1. ::on my knees:: see u got me begging
> BubbliMi: lol alright as long as I can hang at the dj table w/u . . . like rt by u. seriously I'll be ur assistant or w/e
> Udontseeme: done deal. i'll even let u pick some of the mixes
> BubbliMi: uh-oh BubbliMi on the wheels of steel lol
> Udontseeme: slow ur roll, ma-ma. i said pick da mixes not make 'em lol
> BubbliMi: o my b
> Udontseeme: cool i'll text u when i'm on my way saturday. c u
> BubbliMi: c u vic

She closed out the box and went back to Jacinta.

> CinnyBon: yes i am crazy insane in the brain frm him worryin me 2 death
> CinnyBon: if its not him then its JZ making me crzy got me wantin 2 jump his bones 4 real! lol i had 2 cut back goin down his house b/c it wuz getting intense
> CinnyBon: Mina? Whered u go?!
> BubbliMi: my bad. wrapping up w/vic.
> CinnyBon: o u see my last msg?
> BubbliMi: um-hmm somethin bout jumpin JZ's bones. lol. do it already then
> CinnyBon: shoot dont thnk I havent gotten close
> BubbliMi: sort of figured. Y havent u?
> CinnyBon: ummm cuz im not a trick! Dayum. thght u knew me better dan dat
> BubbliMi: didnt mean it dat way. Jus sayin its obvious u down 4 each other.

CinnyBon: yeah but i have a bf and as much as I play w/jz im not gon' cheat on raheem. U kno?

Mina nodded. She'd missed these brain dumps with her friends. She typed back, glad to purge her own fears.

BubbliMi: i kno. i hope brian feels that way
CinnyBon: do u thnk he's cheating?

The word *cheating* leered at her from the screen. She typed back quickly so it would scroll away.

BubbliMi: no I mean its not that jus sick of missing him n wondering if he misses me 2
CinnyBon: girl he misses u
BubbliMi: yea rght. even if he does he has 50,000 "friends" to keep him company ready 2 chat on groupie love
CinnyBon: lol not like he has time
BubbliMi: I guess. he sure doesn't have time 2 drop me a line. I texted him an hour go, Cinny, and nothing. NADA.
CinnyBon: da boy gotta study at some point. U want him to flunk out?
BubbliMi: do u think he would 4 me? LOL
CinnyBon: u tripping
BubbliMi: well at least I have something 2 do this wkend
CinnyBon: wht?
BubbliMi: vic asked me 2 come w/him to Jill Ling's jam
CinnyBon: eww y?
BubbliMi: eww to Vic????
CinnyBon: LOL no ewww to Jill. good luck w/all that
BubbliMi: tru dat. But better than sitting home
CinnyBon: true
BubbliMi: alright girl my eyes heavy like a mugger fugger

CinnyBon: if u want go talk 2 brian jus say so lol
BubbliMi: i wish. Naw rdy get some beauty sleep. c u
CinnyBon: grrr!!! There go my phone, raheem w/ his midnight
call. ::rolling my eyes::
BubbliMi: lol c u cinny
CinnyBon: c u girl

Mina closed out the message box and turned her screen off.

I'm too tired to be jealous, she thought, yawning.

But a simmering anger followed her into sleep. Hours later, an insistent buzzing intruded her slumber. Her eyes popped open, scanning the darkness for the giant bumble bee hovering over her bed until she realized the bee was her phone, lodged under her side.

She grabbed it, blindly punching the Send button. "Hello," she mumbled, her voice thick with sleep and impatience. She glanced at her bedside alarm clock, scowling at the red numbers. It was three A.M.

"What's up, Toughie? Were you asleep?" Brian asked, bright and alert as if it were midday.

"Yes. Until you went off to school, this was usually the time I did that."

His chuckling grated on her nerves.

"My bad. I thought you might be up."

Mina's fatigue fueled her sarcasm. "Usually I am, waiting on you to call. But you never do, so I figured tonight I'd actually do something wild and crazy like get some sleep."

"It's like that?" Brian said. "Let me let you get back to sleep then."

The phone went dead. Mina stared at it until the back light turned off, leaving her room in pitch blackness once more. She smashed the Send button and the phone dialed Brian's number.

"What?" he said, when he picked up.

Mina sat up straight in the bed, her back against the headboard, arms folded. "Did you seriously just hang up on me?"

"Oh, did I do it wrong?"

"Brian, it's no need to get smart."

"I know, that's why I hung up instead."

Mina closed her eyes and took a deep breath. She stayed quiet, hoping Brian would apologize in the silence, but he remained equally as mum. Her throat grew itchy and she fought the tears that typically followed the feeling. She had no idea how to steer the conversation in a better direction. She swallowed once, then twice, hoping either he'd say something or she'd find the words. None came and the silence on his end grew.

She sighed loudly, frustrated. "What did you want?"

He snorted and she knew her question had come out wrong. His answer came back flat and indifferent. "You texted me, so I was calling you back."

"I texted you at like eleven forty-three," Mina said, leaving the question of what had taken him so long lingering.

"I was in the library, Mina. My phone was off."

"Oh. Are you just getting back?"

Her heart leapt knowing he'd really been studying, but Brian's reply was even more sterile.

"No, Mina. I left the library at one-thirty. Went to Sonic. Had a burger with mayonnaise, onions, ketchup, mustard, and lettuce . . . oh, and cheese. Then . . ."

"Okay, I get it, Brian." Mina rolled her eyes.

"Like I said, I was hitting you back. What did *you* want?"

Mina sucked her teeth. She didn't think Brian heard her mumbled, "not this," but he said, "What does that mean?"

She hesitated, not sure whether to be dead honest—Brian's perpetual philosophy—or just let it go.

He persisted, angrier than before. "What? What didn't you want, Mina?"

"Nothing," Mina said quietly, refusing to be bullied into honesty.

" 'Cause if you didn't want me acting all bitchass on the phone, then you might have thought a little about how you came at me."

"I'm sorry," she said, managing to keep herself from bawling until Brian reprimanded her with a terse, "Why you dogging me out with all this attitude?"

She swiped at the fat tears wobbling down her face. Her silence served as fuel to Brian's rant.

"My schedule is mad crazy, Mina. When I have time to call you I do. When I don't, I *don't*." His words flowed fast, as if they'd been held back too long. "If I promised to call you every night at eleven and then couldn't, you'd be pissed. I'm trying cut the drama"—he scoffed—"or thought I was by calling you when I can. What do you want me to do, make promises I can't keep?"

Mina swallowed hard, refusing to let Brian hear the tears in her voice. "I didn't ask you to make me any promises, Brian." She hugged her knees to her chest and laid her head on them. It calmed her, drying the tears. "You act like you're the only one who's busy."

"Obviously you got time on your hands if you sitting around getting mad at me because I don't hit you right back. You need to get out more, Toughie."

Mina's head reared back, as if he'd smacked her. She scowled in the darkness. Forgetting the late hour, her voice rose. "I *am* busy." Her head shook side to side with every word. "And I try to only send you a message when I *think* you can hit me back. But you never do." She folded her arms, huffing. "When you finally have *time* it's hella late. I can't keep falling asleep in class 'cause I'm up late talking to *you*."

"Then don't," he said.

Mina forced back the lump working its way up her throat.

"What is that supposed to be, a breakup hint?"

"There you go, always reading into what I say." He chuckled snidely. "If I was breaking up with you, I'd say it straight out."

Mina's head slumped back onto her knees. She hated just how relieved she felt that he hadn't called her bluff. She closed her eyes and waited for her heart to beat normal before she said, "Then what are you saying?"

"Just what I said, don't stay up late talking to me."

She had no response to his wooden statement. Her pulse pounded in her temples. She ached from all she wanted and couldn't have—an apology from Brian for being pissy at her frustration, a promise that he'd do better to call or text even if it was just to say hello, a time machine to go back and answer the phone differently.

The silence between them grew, lulling Mina to sleep.

Brian's voice, irritated, roused her seconds later. "Mina? You still there?"

"Yeah," she said, forcing herself to attention.

"Look, you said you needed to talk to me. That's why I called," Brian said. "I wouldn't have called back so late, but I thought maybe something was wrong."

Just like that, the storm passed.

The concern in his voice touched Mina. But her mind was too muddled to dredge up the multitude of emotions she'd been feeling about Michael's bombshell. The urgency she'd felt to share with Brian was long gone. It seemed almost like it had been ages ago instead of only four hours.

"Nothing's wrong," she said simply.

"You just wanted to give me grief for not calling enough," he said, but Mina heard the joke in his voice.

She chuckled. "Something like that."

She stretched out her legs and slid back down beneath the covers. The phone stayed put on her ear as she lay there, the chill of the pillow cooling her other cheek. Her eyes grew heavy again and a yawn escaped before she could bite it back.

"I'm not gon' keep you up. . . ." Brian said.

His reluctance to simply hang up made her smile. "I didn't mean to come at you like that," she said.

"It's a'ight. I know how nasty you get when you're sleepy."

"Me?" She snort-laughed. "I know you're not talking."

"Hmmph, yes I am too. At least I don't get all spoiled and snippy like a toy poodle." He yapped like a small dog and Mina had to laugh into her pillow to muffle her voice.

"That's not right."

"Go 'head to bed, Toughie. I ain't messing with you no more."

"Do you love me?" Mina asked softly. She caressed her pillow, wishing Brian were beside her.

"What you think?" He snickered. "That I just enjoy getting bitched out at three-thirty in the morning?"

"No. But can you answer anyway?"

"Yeah, I love you, Mina. You be dogging me out sometimes, but I love you."

"I love you too," she said dreamily. Her lids drooped.

"Go 'head before you end up falling asleep on me . . . again."

"You hung up on me," Mina said in a drowsy pout.

His chuckle was sweet. "I'm sorry."

Mina smiled. "We swazy?"

"All day . . . till the next time."

"Very funny," Mina said, alert for a second.

"Bye, Toughie. I love you."

"Love you too. See you," Mina said before hitting End.

Seconds later she was in a deep sleep, the phone curled under her chin. Later that morning, it would be the only proof that her late-night exchange with Brian hadn't been a dream.

Ante Up

"'Cause you dig the hole you're in."
—Eye Level, "The Hole You're In"

JZ's hand jumped across the paper as his father's voice rang throughout their large house like it was a cottage.

"Jason, get down here."

JZ cursed at the blotchy scratch the pen left on his homework, something to add to the thousand other things Mr. Collins would have over his head in Advanced Placement Calculus. He couldn't avoid getting the prissy theatre instructor for math to save his life.

He balled the paper up and threw it in the trash can. He'd have to redo it. *I don't feel like hearing his mouth,* JZ thought sourly.

"Jason," his father roared.

"Speaking of hearing somebody's mouth," JZ muttered.

His grumbling belied the fear pounding in his chest. His father was angry. JZ didn't know why, and if he could have put off finding out he would have, but he couldn't. He trudged down the stairs, putting pep in his step as he got closer to the kitchen, where his parents stood.

His father's eyebrows were a unibrowed scowl in his cinnamon-complexioned face; his mother's a worried knit. She sent waves of sympathy JZ's way in her tiny smile.

His father held a thin sheaf of papers in his clenched hand.

"Yes?" JZ asked.

"Boy, what in hell is wrong with you?" his father said, the uni-brow wrinkling further.

JZ leaned on the counter in the middle of the kitchen, keeping his distance. "What did I do?"

His mind raced over the possibilities and kept going back to Mr. Collins. Mr. Collins hated him. But JZ couldn't think of anything he'd done to incur his wrath recently. He was maintaining a solid B in AP Calc.

What more do they want? he thought, annoyed.

"Did you ride up to College Park a few weeks ago?" his father said.

JZ's adam apple jumped as he swallowed. His hand went to his head and slid down, rubbing his low cut, over and over, a sure sign he was anxious. "Yeah . . . I drove Mina up there to see Brian," JZ said.

The elder Jason Zimms looked at his son with an expression of scorn usually reserved for idiots and bad drivers. "And you talked to Coach K while you were there?"

"All I said was hello, for real," JZ said. His hand brushed at his hair. Up, slide down, up, slide down—speeding up when his father slammed down the papers he held in his hand.

"You're not stupid, right?" His father's lips pursed as if he felt JZ was just that.

JZ remained silent.

"Jason," his mother said, seeing her chance to play peacemaker. "You know it's evaluation period. The coach isn't allowed to have any contact with you unless it's planned."

"Ma, I know that," JZ said, rolling his eyes. "No contact beyond hello. I said hello and then I started talking to a few players I met last year when we visited the campus."

His eyes jumped nervously to his father, whose nostrils flared as he shook his head, clearly disappointed. "I . . . I didn't violate the rules . . . you know I know the deal," JZ said.

"No, what you think you know is how to do what you please," his father said. He leveled a look at JZ that made his head ache. "I've got eyes and ears everywhere. One of the assistant coaches called me, said you hadn't violated the rules, but that he thought he better give me a head's up, remind you to steer clear to keep rumors at bay." He picked the papers back up, tapping them against his palm. His voice took on the condescending tone of a parent intent on pointing out just how stupid his kid's actions were. "When he called, I was like nooo, Paul, you must be mistaken. I know *my* son didn't do anything that stupid, like go to the campus of one of Duke's biggest rivals and parade up to Coach K for all the world or any Terrapin staff member to see. . . ." His right eyebrow stretched so high JZ thought it might get stuck. "Noo, not *my* son. Because if a Terrapin staff member saw that and recognized him, since they're *also* recruiting him, it wouldn't be anything for them to claim Duke was violating policy. Oh sure, it would mean the recruit is dead to them too . . . but what the hell? If Maryland can't have him, may as well not let their biggest rival have him either. No loss; moving on to the next hot recruit."

JZ's mouth went dry. His hand dropped from his head to the counter with a meaty thud. "I . . ."

"You what? Didn't think about that?" His father stared him down until JZ looked away.

"I know you didn't think about it. It doesn't matter that you didn't violate the rule, Jason. If someone reported it, by the time the whole matter was resolved, you'd be out of the loop, sitting out the season at some Division Two school or worse, a small-time college in the boondocks because you wanted to play big shot." He brushed his shoulder and popped his collar, imitating a young buck with lots of swag. "Yeah, look at me, man. I know the coaches. Watch me go up and say hey. I'm cool as hell."

"I . . . it wasn't like that," JZ said, lamely. "I . . . Mina wanted to see Brian and I was helping her out."

His father nodded. "Well, Duke plays North Carolina next week in the finals. You want to give her a ride down there, so she can see him? Give UNC the chance to turn you in too?"

Anger and shame welled in JZ's chest. He chewed on his cheek, gnawing at it until it hurt. "My bad," he mumbled.

"Pssh, your bad." The anger in his father's face was palpable. "No, your bad is going to be you sitting in some tiny, no-name college dorm room reading over the recruitment letters from all the big Division One schools that *used* to want you. Wallowing in what could have been if you hadn't been playing Mr. Big Dick."

JZ's mother blanched.

JZ grit his teeth, looking his father in the eye as he finished.

"Do something that stupid again and you won't have to worry about somebody turning you in. I'll send you to a little school in the boonies just because, Jason." He gritted on JZ one more time for good measure. "Don't think I won't."

He walked out of the kitchen, his long confident stride a duplicate of his son's assertive swag.

When his footsteps reached the stairs, JZ's mother walked to the counter. Her cool hand rubbed his. "You know he doesn't mean it, Jay." Her eyes smiled reassuringly. "He's just angry about how bad this could have gone."

"He doesn't know what he wants." JZ scowled. "One minute he's talking about keeping my grades up and having a plan besides professional ball. Then he's sitting there tripping about this." Horrified to feel tears burning his eyes, he blinked furiously, fighting them off. "If education so important, than why is he tripping so hard? I can get an education and play ball at *any* school."

"Because he does want you to play ball at a school where you might have the chance to get picked up by a professional team. He just doesn't want that to be your only goal." His mother's hand patted his gently. "Don't let the way he tells you things cloud the message, Jason. He's angry because you could have ruined your chances. But don't go getting mad because you were told the truth . . . what you did wasn't very smart."

JZ hung his head. He stared down at the granite countertop, letting his mother stroke his hand a few seconds longer before standing up straight, sliding his hand away.

"Maybe it wasn't, but I didn't violate the rules." His jaw jutted stubbornly, but his eyes pleaded with his mom. "Isn't that more important than what didn't happen?"

"Only because no one saw you, Jason. And we don't know that, for sure."

The thought sent panic racing across JZ's chest. "Well . . . it was dark. Nobody could have seen me," he said, mind churning, thinking back to the night. It was too fuzzy, too many days gone, but he still felt somewhat confident there'd been no spies lurking to report on a single passerby saying hello to Coach K.

"No sense worrying about it now," his mother said, reading his fear. "Just don't do anything like this again. You'll be declaring your school soon; don't endanger your options."

She walked around the side of the counter to where he stood. He towered over her, a full foot and a half. She reached up and held his chin in her hand. "You have homework to do?"

He shook his head, lying. "Can I run out?"

She tugged gently on his chin and he obliged her with a peck on the cheek.

"I'm cooking dinner in a bit, so don't be long."

"Okay, I won't."

"Have fun," she said, as he walked out of the kitchen and through the front door.

His legs pumped, conquering the long driveway in record time. Normally, he'd shoot some ball, go jogging, or lift weights to work off the wiry ball of fury lodged in his chest. But the thought of touching a basketball made his mouth upturn in a bitter grimace.

He didn't want to hear the word *basketball,* much less play with one, right now.

His father was always sending him mixed signals. One minute practically disavowing the importance of basketball in JZ's life, then, the next, going out of his way to ensure JZ remained on track to strengthen his hardwood skills. Keeping up with which mood his father was in left him emotionally spent, and working as hard on his schoolwork as his athletic prowess added to the burden.

He needed to do something that didn't require thinking.

His stride long, he quick-stepped up Dogwood Street, unbothered by the shadows thrown by the spidery limbs of the naked trees looming overhead in the dimming sunlight. The street was deadly silent until he came to the neighborhood's park. A few parents were out with their kids on the playground, taking advantage of daylight's last remnants. Otherwise the park was quiet. Even on cold winter days, like today, there was usually some action on the courts or fields. But both the basketball courts and baseball diamond were devoid of anything athletic.

Grim satisfaction quelled some of his anger.

If I'm not playing today, nobody is, he thought smugly.

He walked until Dogwood brought him to the center of the community, an intersection leading out of the Woods, back to his house or down the main road, which broke off into three cul-de-sacs. Michael lived in the second, Mina in the third. JZ walked the main road, intending to turn to Michael's. Maybe game a little to get his mind right. . . . But his pace quickened past Michael's street, then Mina's.

There was only one thing beyond the third cul-de-sac, more road and twenty more houses, one of them Jacinta's. When he was twenty yards away from her house, he slowed down long enough to put his cool back on. It's not like he was going to cry like a sucker on Jacinta's shoulder. He just needed to get away from his own crib for a hot minute.

He walked casually up the empty gravel driveway toward the small, white house and knocked on the door. He leaned closer to the door, listening. Hearing nothing, he went to knock again and jumped when Jacinta opened the door.

"Dang, girl, you ain't have to open it that fast."

"I wasn't aware there was a special speed to open the door." Jacinta smirked.

JZ's heart bumped in his chest. He looked down on Jacinta, from half-closed eyelids—his cool face—taking in all of her curves. She had on a pair of navy blue cotton shorts, the kind the cheerleading squad always wore to practice, knee socks with blue and gold stripes, and a Blue Devils Track tee shirt. His eyes lingered on her naked thighs, savoring the peek of skin.

Jacinta's right eyebrow popped up. "Ahem. So you're coming in or I'm supposed to freeze to death while you wait for an invitation?"

JZ sauntered in. "An invitation would have been nice."

Jacinta walked into a small family room and plopped down on a love seat. She spread her arms out wide. "Consider yourself invited."

JZ sat beside her, taking up what was left of the small space on the half couch. "What's up, girl?"

"Shoot, I was gonna ask you," she said. "You coming to see me? Wow, what did I do to deserve this?"

JZ slid out of his coat and draped it over the arm of the love seat. "Real talk, my parents were straight buggin' and I had to evacuate." He breathed noisily through his nose, glad to get it off his chest, telling Jacinta the short version of his father kirkin' out. She listened without asking questions or pressing for additional information, which was why he enjoyed her company. There was a moment of silence, at the end of his tale, and he became aware how quiet the house was—no television or radio played. "So you chillin' solo? Where's Mina and the girls?"

"Mina had extra practices for Nationals. Lizzie's at rehearsal and Kelly with Greg."

"I'm glad I didn't go see Mike then. He probably wasn't even home."

Jacinta shoved him. "Oh, so I wasn't your first stop? That's wack. How you gonna second choice me?"

JZ grinned. "I said I didn't stop by."

"But you were thinking about stopping by his place first," she said, pouting.

JZ flicked her bottom lip. "Look at you, all cute when you pout."

Jacinta's eyes rolled. "Knucka, please, I'm cute when I do anything."

"All right, officer, I'm not arguing," JZ said, throwing his hands up in surrender.

Their chuckling died down, filling the room with the surreal silence left only by lack of white noise.

JZ smoothed his palms out over his jeans. "It's all quiet in here. What were you doing?"

"Upstairs on the computer."

"Did I interrupt homework?"

Jacinta shook her head.

JZ smirked. "Oh, was you IM'ing your boy?" He laughed when she rolled her eyes, and kept teasing. "What then? You not gon' tell me?"

"Why are you all up in my business?" Jacinta's hands flew to her hips.

He knocked shoulders with her. "Why are you being all super spy?"

She waved him off. "If you must know, I was checking out college Web sites."

JZ's eyebrow popped in surprise. He didn't move fast enough to dodge Jacinta's smack to his shoulder.

"Don't be acting all surprised." She folded her arms tight against her chest, making her breast jut in the tight tee shirt. "Yes, the ghetto chick plans to go to college too."

His eyes lingered on her chest as he laughed. "I wasn't even thinking that."

"Uh-huh. Yeah right."

"No, I'm serious." He shrugged. "You been living over here for almost four years. Why you think we still see you as the 'ghetto chick.' I never did, really."

Jacinta's shoulders hitched.

"You're just Cinny . . . big mouth, always got something to say, phat ass Cinny."

He jumped up, skittering away before Jacinta could strike. She chased him into the kitchen until he scooped her up, carrying her back to the family room, tickling her sides.

"Stop, Jay." She kicked and flailed. "Stop, for real. Oh my god, I need to pee."

He dropped her on the sofa.

"I knew that would make you drop me," she said, laughing.

" 'Cause I know you're crazy enough to do something like pee on my head to make me put you down," he said, taking a seat on the floor in front of the love seat. He rested one elbow on his tented knee, the other on Jacinta's leg. "So what schools were you checking?"

"Spelman, Florida A and M, and Clark."

"Word, all HBCUs, huh?"

She nodded. "Yeah, DRB High been all right, but I'm ready to be in Chocolate City again."

JZ snickered. "I hear you."

Jacinta ran her hand over his head, going with the grain of his waves. She did it a few times before saying, "You should let your hair grow."

JZ's eyes closed at the soft stroking. He kept his answer short, unwilling to break the spell. "Why?"

"Just curious what you'd look like with braids."

His shoulders shook as he chuckled. "Naw, that ain't me."

"I think you would look cute."

"Oh, no doubt." JZ smiled. He couldn't open his eyes. Her hands felt too good.

"I would braid it for you if you let it grow," she said.

He cocked one eye open in her direction. "And what else would you do if I let you?"

She sucked her teeth. "Umm . . . let me think . . . *nothing*."

JZ turned toward Jacinta and tugged her calf. She resisted, weakly, so he tugged until her butt hung between the love seat's cushion and his shoulder.

"Nothing at all?" he asked, staring her in the eye.

"Nope," she said, holding his gaze.

There was defiance in her eyes, typical Jacinta, but JZ saw curiosity as well.

He gave her calf one more playful tug and her butt landed in his lap.

"So if . . ."

The house phone, loud and shrill, pierced the quiet. Jacinta jumped up out of his lap, more startled than anything, and snatched the phone off its cradle. Her chest heaved as she answered, "Hello." She rolled her eyes to the ceiling. "Raheem, my phone is all the way upstairs. I didn't even hear it ring . . . because I'm downstairs." She sucked her teeth. "Are you seriously gonna sit up here and fuss me out about not answering the phone, when you finally did reach me on another line? That's stupid. . . . No, I said *that's* stupid, not you're stupid."

She shook her head at JZ, as if to recruit his sympathy. He pretended not to see. Instead, he pushed himself up from the floor and grabbed his jacket. Jacinta held her hand up, gesturing for him to wait, but he threw up the peace sign and headed to the door.

"Deuces, Cinny," he said, louder than necessary.

Jacinta's eyes bucked. She mouthed "oh my god, Jay," before explaining into the phone, "That was the TV, Raheem. Why are you tripping?"

JZ didn't stick around to hear how she was going to get out of the bind.

Machismo

"You think you hard, you think I'm soft."
—T-Pain, "Church"

Michael held the ivory-colored envelope in his hands. It was on good, heavy parchment paper, the kind of paper stock that said, this ain't no Office Depot brand. He smoothed it over for the hundredth time, reading the address of the Carter School under his breath.

This was it.

After a month of angsting over it, another month preparing for it, and a few weeks of pure agony as he awaited word on his acceptance or rejection, this was really it. He balanced the envelope on his fingertips, testing its weight. The lore was when dealing with correspondence from colleges, heavier envelopes meant acceptance while a slim envelope was a sure rejection.

His heart sank at the light feel of the envelope.

He placed it on the white bar table, refusing to look at it again until the clique arrived. Frowning, he checked his cell phone. They should have been here by now. He'd called everybody forty-five minutes ago. Just like them to be late.

All the times I wait around for their butts and they can't even show up on time just once, he thought, furious.

He stole a glance at the envelope, its ivory a contrast to the pure white of the table. He stared at it, wishing for X-ray vision.

A thunder of footsteps poured down the stairwell, jerking him out of his fantasy.

" 'Bout time," he yelled.

"Money, money, money, Mikey . . . money," JZ sang. He shook hands with Mike and gave him a back pound. "What up, son? So you in or what?"

Michael scowled. "I told y'all I'm waiting for y'all to open it." He looked beyond JZ to the stairs. "I thought you were picking up Mina and Cinny?"

JZ pursed his lips, scowling. "No. They were at the top of the cul-de-sac when I rolled in."

Michael chuckled. "Man, you ain't give 'em a ride?"

JZ shrugged. "They a'ight."

Mina scurried down the stairs, fussing before she hit the landing. "JZ, why didn't you pick us up?"

"Oh, was that y'all walking?" JZ said, feigning ignorance.

"That was foul," Mina said. She smacked his arm and gave Michael a hug. "Hey, Mike."

"Hey, *Mike*," Jacinta said. She sat in the bar stool opposite him and threw darts with her eyes at JZ. "Oh, hey, JZ."

" 'Sup?" JZ said. He went and sat on the sofa.

Michael raised his eyebrow at Jacinta and she shrugged. He looked to Mina and she threw her hands up like, "I'm not in it." He shook his head, not interested in whatever crack had arose in the JZ/Jacinta facade.

"All right, where are Lizzie and Kelly?" he said.

"Right here, right here," Lizzie said, hustling into the room as if she were being chased.

"Late much?" Michael said.

"Sorry," Kelly said. She waved to everyone as she walked over to the bar table.

"Oh my God, you guys forget that Kelly and I don't live in the Woods. Hello," Lizzie said, flustered. She shed her scarf and jacket, throwing them playfully on JZ's head. He swiped them off and draped them over the back of the sofa.

"Okay, can we please do this?" Mina said. "I mean, I know you got in, but let's get the formality over with."

Michael blew out his breath. "I don't know. The envelope is really light."

Jacinta scowled. "It's not a college acceptance, Mike. How many pages do the people need to say 'yeah, you're in' or 'naw, see ya'?"

Everyone, except JZ, teetered nervously. He shouted over his shoulder, "Yeah well, Cinny the expert on acceptance and rejection. She should know."

"Man, forget you," Jacinta said, rolling her eyes.

"Err . . . huh?" Lizzie said, frowning at Mina.

"Girl, no one knows," Mina whispered. She joked, loudly, "Lovers' quarrel, I guess."

"Shoot, we're hardly lovers," Jacinta spat.

"Got that right," JZ said. "Come on, Mike. Do the damn thing, man."

Michael picked up the envelope and held it up to the light in the ceiling. "Maybe I can just read it through here."

"Mike, come on," Mina pleaded. "Band-Aid style. Just rip it open and read it."

"I hate that I'm even pressed," Michael said.

"Well, it is sort of funny considering you weren't really worried about going at first," Kelly said. She chuckled at Michael's dead-eye stare. "Okay, I'm totally not saying anything else today." She mimed zipping her lips and laughed when Michael winked at her.

"All right . . ." He tapped the envelope once on the table, then ran his finger under the lip of the envelope, breaking the seal. He slid his finger all the way across, ripping it open, then plucked out the letter. He held it out. "Okay, Jay, you read it for me, son."

JZ got up from the sofa, walked over, and took the letter out of Michael's hand. Everyone's eyes were on the paper as he unfolded it.

"Good luck, kid," JZ said.

Michael's breathing was so shallow that his slight head nod looked like a trick of the eye.

JZ's eyes skimmed the words as he read them aloud.

" 'Dear Mr. James. As you're aware, there were many candidates vying for the limited spots in our new fashion design program.' " JZ cleared his throat. He frowned at the text, causing the clique to step in closer, as if to see better for him. " 'Over one hundred seventy-five candidates showcased their work. Our desire to select only the most promising students . . .' "

"Oh my God, who goes on this long without saying yay or nay," Mina said, startling the others.

"Deev," Michael said, frowning. "Go ahead, Jay."

" 'Our desire to select only the most promising students made our decision very difficult. There was much potential among all of the candidates. However, only those with the unique combination of potential, talent, and a special quality that one cannot quite define were chosen. We're"—JZ grinned—" 'pleased to inform you that you're among them.' "

"Finally," Lizzie shouted.

"Mike, oh my god, I'm so happy for you," Mina said. She threw her arms around his neck.

Michael closed his eyes. His temples throbbed from the girls' screaming and JZ pounding him on the back, congratulating him. Adrenaline raced to his head so fast, he felt like he was going to swoon right out of the chair once Mina let go. Luckily she held on for dear life, preventing him from falling and anyone else from getting in an embrace.

"Go, Mike!" Jacinta cheered, rubbing his arm.

"Congratulations," Kelly said, beaming.

"Mi, you plan on letting go anytime soon?" JZ said.

She let go and dabbed at her eyes. "Sorry." She chuckled as the tears streamed. "Well, this means you won't be with us next year. That sucks."

Michael smacked the top of her head with the empty envelope. "Uh-uh, don't do that. Happy thoughts. Happy." He laughed, choking back tears he felt rising in his throat. He knocked fists with JZ.

"You gon' blow up, son," JZ said, moving over as Lizzie barged her way in for a hug.

"I know that's right," Mina said.

"So, I'm wondering how big a discount we gonna get," Jacinta said.

"Wait, we gotta pay for our stuff now?" Mina said, laughing through her tears when Michael nodded vigorously.

"Is this a pizza night?" Kelly said. "We haven't been to Rio's Ria in a while."

"I could go for something," Lizzie said.

They all looked to Michael for confirmation.

He smiled sheepishly. "How 'bout a rain check? I promised Rob I'd swing by rehearsals tonight and give him the news."

JZ frowned. "Man, just text him."

"Naw, it's cool. A promise is a promise," Mina said, sniffing, her tears seeming to dry at JZ's suggestion. "Mike, we'll do pizza tomorrow or Sunday."

"Wait . . ." JZ looked at Michael. He lifted his palms up and shrugged, his smile fragile. "Money Mike, I know you not gon' dip out on your peeps who been with you since the ice age. I mean, if dude really pressed, tell him meet us over there."

Michael stood up from the bar stool. He kept his voice neutral as his stomach dropped twenty feet. "Man, it's not even like that." He smiled, hoping to defuse the challenge in JZ's tone. "He has rehearsal, then a masters class, so he can't roll out . . . plus he don't have no ride over here."

JZ's head reared back. "Why you know his schedule and shit?"

Lizzie and Mina's eyes sent frantic messages back and forth. Finally Mina jumped in again.

"Jay, oh my goodness, stop rummin. Michael knows your schedule too. . . . Don't we all know where everybody gotta run off to and—"

"No. All I know is sometimes we all together and sometimes we're not." JZ gave her a look, daring her to challenge that notion. "I don't know y'all exact movement from one place to another."

Michael's ears burned. He felt JZ's storm brewing, but he had a storm of his own kicking up good too. He fought it by walking to the back of the room and grabbing a scarf and hat off the rack. He took his time putting it on as JZ continued.

"Look, Mike, I'm just saying, we want to help you celebrate." He scowled in realization. "You're going to the Carter now, you'll see Rob all the time." He laughed his boyish aw-shucks chuckle. "What? We can't get down one last time for old time's sake?"

Michael walked back and stood in the original spot next to JZ and the table. He adjusted the skull cap so it covered his ears.

"I'm not leaving for the Carter tomorrow, you know?" Michael teased, looking at all of his friends, one by one, as if to ensure they understood that, before looking at JZ again. "I mean, if I had promised to meet up with y'all somewhere and Rob was like—Naw man, forget them—you'd be cool if I just bounced on y'all?"

"No." JZ rolled his eyes, annoyed that he had to explain. "But why would you bounce on the friends you've had since kindergarten for somebody you've only known for a few years? It ain't like dude your boyfriend, is it?"

"Jay, it's not that big a deal," Lizzie said, green eyes flashing. "I'm not even that hungry."

"A friend is a friend, Jay. Three years or thirteen," Michael said, ignoring the last crack. His jaw clenched and he released it, sawing it gently back and forth before going on. "See, if y'all had come as soon as I called you, I would have had time to hit the Ria with you.

But as usual, y'all took your time, cause you figured Michael don't have shit else to do but wait on his friends, right?"

"It wasn't even like that." JZ frowned. "I was finishing up some homework. I came as soon—"

Michael sucked his teeth. "Man, you've split on homework for less than this. So . . ."

"Punk, I got grades to keep up," JZ said, raising his voice. "I got real classes to take, not no fancy-ass arts and crafts bull."

"No, don't do this," Mina said. She immediately placed herself between Michael and JZ.

Lizzie stood by JZ, tugging his arm, begging him to stand down.

Kelly and Jacinta remained frozen in place, outsiders trapped on the inside, eyes skating from the guys to the girls.

"See, that's why I decided to apply," Michael said. His nostrils flared. " 'Cause I couldn't take another year of it being about your punk ass. Wake up, son. It ain't about you all the time. I know you think it is, but it ain't. And that's real."

"So what, it's about you?" JZ smirked. "You and your colored sketches and fabric swatches? And your gay dancer friend?"

Mina placed her hand on Michael's chest and he looked down at her, as if just realizing she was there. Her eyes brimmed with tears. She shook her head at him, then at JZ.

"Mike, JZ, don't do this." Her head ping-ponged between them. "Please," she pleaded.

Michael shook his head at her. "No, Mina . . . that's the thing. I keep not doing anything. JZ not gonna be the only one who gets to do something, this time."

"Man, what you spitting?" JZ said, his eyes gleaming with disdain. "You were one of the best ballers in middle school. All-county point guard. You're the one who left that behind. We could have been running DRB High together, dominating. I ain't make it about me, you did when you punked out and stopped playing."

Michael snorted. "Jay, basketball was cool, but it wasn't life or death." He shook his head. "You don't get it. I don't miss it. I ain't like you. I don't have that fire to play it day and night and worry about what some recruiter say about my skills."

"Hell naw, you not like me. 'Cause you soft and you can't take it," JZ said. He folded his arms like, "yeah, I said it."

Lizzie groaned beside him.

Michael smirked through the pain piercing his chest. His heart thumped against Mina's hand, reminding him once more that she was there, a tiny branch between two trees. He wrapped his fingers around hers, squeezed lightly, then let her hand go.

"All right, whatever, Jay. Whatever, kid." He walked away.

JZ reached out and grabbed Michael's shoulder. "Naw, don't turn your back on me, son."

Michael whirled around and punched JZ in the mouth.

"Now who soft, punk?" he yelled in JZ's stunned face.

The girl's screamed, scattering as they hustled out of the way.

JZ wiped at his bleeding lip, then shoved Michael hard into the bar table. The table fell over, taking Michael down with it. JZ was on him, pummeling him with his fists.

"Oh my God," Mina said. She screamed. "Y'all stop. Stop fighting."

"Kelly, run and get Miss Mae Bell," Lizzie said. She wrapped her arms around a shaking Mina, unsure what else to do.

Michael shoved JZ off balance and rolled on top of him. He punched him once, in the face, then got up. He stood over JZ, fists at his side.

"That's how it is, son?" Michael wasn't aware he was crying until a tear ran into a split on his cheek. He winced, but otherwise ignored the wound. "That's how we gon' end this?"

"You made that choice," JZ huffed, out of breath, waiting on Michael to make a move. When he didn't, he pushed himself up.

They stood inches from one another, glaring.

"See, 'cause to me, any dude that ice his lifelong friends for another dude he only known for a minute . . ." JZ snorted and turned his lip up. "Well, like I said, you made a *choice*. It ain't us, so be gone. Go with your boy . . . *friend*."

"Don't talk shit you don't know," Michael said, shoving JZ again.

JZ shoved back and drew his hand back to punch, but Jacinta caught it.

"Stop, Jay. Just stop," she said.

JZ looked back in surprise. He snatched his arm away, but Jacinta's action had the right effect. He didn't attempt to hit Michael again. Instead, he and Michael stood there, a sorry state of bruises and cuts, looking at each other until Michael turned heel.

He bent over, picked up his hat and scarf from the floor. He snuggled the cap on his head and took his time winding the scarf with trembling hands. When he finished he turned back to JZ, his eyes dark with sadness.

He looked around the disheveled room, as if wondering how it had gotten that way, then shook his head. He walked to the stairwell, stopped and turned again.

"Jay . . . you was my boy, man."

Still posturing, JZ jut his chin. "Yeah, *was*."

Mina cried out and Lizzie squeezed her, rocking her like a baby.

Michael closed his eyes. His breath came out in a low hiss from his nose. He felt his heartbeat in his temples and behind his eyeballs, as if it were trying to ooze its way out altogether. Gray and black dots danced behind his lids. He stood there, at the steps, letting the shaded dots go from a frenetic vibration to a standstill; then he opened his eyes, staring at JZ, sending a silent message.

JZ's eyes flinched, just barely, before steeling themselves again.

"Okay, was," Michael said. He threw up the peace sign. "Deuces."

He walked up the stairs, just as Kelly and his grandmother were coming down.

"I gotta go, Ma," he said in answer to his grandmother's worried inquiries about his face. "I gotta go."

No Means No

"You don't think so, but this is where you belong."
—Dave Hollister, "What's a Man to Do?"

JZ extracted himself from Michael's house as politely as he could, under the circumstances. Miss Mae Bell lectured him, but not much. When she saw the state the girls were in, especially Mina and Lizzie, she let him off with a firm, "You two boys know better. Been friends since you were practically babies. Make sure you come back here tomorrow and you two work it out."

He nodded, promising that he would, knowing that he wouldn't. And leaving Michael's grandmother to get the truth out of the girls. He swung the door open to his mother's Volvo and folded his tall body into the compact, sporty four-seater. He turned the ignition and gunned the engine, startled when the passenger-side door opened.

"Man, what you want?" he asked Jacinta.

She slid into the front seat and closed the door. "JZ, stop being an asshole," she said matter-of-factly. She fixed him with a look that he understood to mean she wasn't getting out.

He rested his head on the steering wheel. The bumpy texture of the wheel ground against his forehead, as he shook his head back and forth. "This is messed up," he said.

"Yeah, it is," Jacinta said.

He waited for the lecture, but Jacinta said nothing else, relieving him and irritating him at once. He didn't want nagging, but would have welcomed Jacinta pointing out how wrong Michael was to dip out on them like that.

He jerked his head up. "What do you want, Cinny?"

Her eyes searched his face, never wavering. "I don't want anything. I thought you might want some company."

He stared at her, working to read between the lines but finding no hidden messages. He rubbed at his eyes, digging harder than necessary. The pain kicked him into gear.

"Well, let me take you home 'cause I don't want company." He looked at her. "All right?"

Jacinta shrugged.

He put the car in reverse and gunned it, nearly crushing Miss Mae Bell's azalea bush. He kept up the mad pace, barely yielding at the stop sign at the top of the cul-de-sac, and was at Jacinta's within two minutes. The gravel popped and clicked under the car's wheels until he came to a stop in the middle of the drive. He waited a few seconds, but Jacinta made no move to get out.

He slammed the car into park and leaned his head back on the headrest.

"Jay, I know you—"

"Don't say nothing, all right?" He blew out a deep breath. "You don't know anything . . . not about me or what just happened. So don't say it." He softened his tone. "I just don't feel like hearing no lecture right now. I'm sick of lectures."

"All right," Jacinta said.

The submissive agreement made JZ look up at her. The cold serenity of the car and Jacinta's calm presence cleared his head. "I'm sorry," he said.

"Tell Michael that."

"No, I mean I'm sorry I dogged you out the other day and been acting shady."

Jacinta sighed. "I'm used to it."

"I didn't need to act like that." JZ leaned his head back again. "Did I get you in trouble?"

"Weren't you trying to?" Jacinta said.

The smile in her voice made JZ chuckle. "Yeah, I guess so," he admitted.

"I can handle Raheem." She laughed. "Especially when I don't have to actually see him. He was mad for a few hours, but he called back later, apologizing."

"That's good," JZ said.

Jacinta's abrupt laugh was ear-piercing in the small car. "You don't even mean that, JZ."

He shrugged, talking up at the car's ceiling. "I meant I'm glad you're not hurt or whatever."

He looked back up when she'd been silent too long. Even in the darkness he could feel her eyes on him. "What?" he said.

"See, I think you mean that."

He hesitated for a second before leaning toward her. Jacinta closed the rest of the gap and he kissed her, first soft, probing, then energetically sucking. His hands went to the back of her head. Jacinta softened in his arms and he gently pressed their faces together.

Heat surged through his body, despite the frigid air in the car. His right hand slipped from her head to her back, then eased to the top of her jeans. He rubbed the skin on the small of her back where her jacket and pants gapped. His lips moved to her neck, while his left hand explored under the front of her jacket.

She moaned and his hand lifted her shirt.

"Jay . . . Jay, stop," she said, pulling back.

Caught up, JZ leaned in more. The gear shift bit into his thigh as he tried to penetrate Jacinta's side of the car. Jacinta pressed her hands against his chest. Her head reared back, smacking into the window.

"Jay, stop, please."

The words got through that time, slowly. He withdrew, first his lips from her neck; then one limb at a time—his right hand from her butt, his left hand from her breast—until all of him was back on his side of the car again. He sat immobile, his breathing going from a heavy pant to a labored sigh. He steadied his elbow on the sill of the window and the fog from their making out squelched under his leather jacket. When he'd gotten himself together, he squinted over at her.

"What's up? Seriously, why you playing me?"

She ran her fingers through her pixie cut bob. "I'm not. . . . I mean I don't mean to."

He snickered. "You doing it well for somebody who ain't trying." He adjusted himself in the seat to relieve the aching in his lap. "All right. I gotta dip."

"Jay, wait," she said, turning in her seat to face him. "Can we talk about it for a minute?"

He looked her in the eye, his gaze wooden. "Baby girl, it's three things we can talk about right now, and they all start with B." His fingers ticked them off as he listed. "Blow job, bare that ass, or buh-bye."

"You always gotta get rude." She sucked her teeth.

"Okay, that sounds like you chose buh-bye." He waved. "See ya."

"Jay, stop," Jacinta shouted. She folded her arms, refusing to leave. "So what, you making sure you ruin every single friendship you have tonight?"

"Naw, I'm just realizing that some of my friendships wasn't as solid as I thought." He rolled his eyes.

"Why you gotta talk to me like I'm a trick?" Her head shook side to side in disapproval. "We *are* friends. But not if you keep dogging me out."

"Then stop being a dick tease." He grabbed the steering wheel, shoulders hitching. "How 'bout that, Jacinta?"

She rubbed her eyes. "It takes two to flirt. I thought we were just . . . playing around."

"We were." His chuckle was nasty as he pretended to pull her hand toward his lap. "But you never wanna play with the right toy."

She snatched her hand away. "JZ, I have a boyfriend."

"So break up with him." His fist pounded the steering wheel, making Jacinta jump. "Okay, yeah, we were just playing around. But I feel like I'm tripping. Are you saying you don't want it to be more than that?" He grilled her, raising his voice. "Huh?"

Her fingers ran rampant through her hair. Cold smoke puffed out of her mouth as she breathed hard.

"I would . . ." She blew out a deep breath, as if the answer were a burden she had to dump. "It could be more if it wasn't for Raheem."

"All right, so then we're right back where we always are." JZ shook his head. His hands swept back and forth on the steering wheel, rocking it side to side. "I know you're always talking about wanting to stay friends with Raheem. But sometimes . . ." His voice trailed off, then came back with a gritty determination. "Sometimes friendships die."

Jacinta looked up at him in alarm.

His hands stopped their frenetic dance on the steering wheel, as he faced her. "Sometimes friendship die." He held Jacinta's surprised gaze. "If you can break up with Raheem and be friends, that's cool. But if you can't, it is what is, Cinny."

She turned her head and looked at her frosted window, steaming it more as she spoke. "You're asking me to choose between you and Raheem?" Her head shook in a tiny tremor. "JZ, don't make me do this."

"Why?"

"Because."

"Because what?" He touched her shoulder.

She turned around and JZ frowned at the pain in her eyes.

"Because even if I break up with Raheem, it doesn't mean I'm down with us doing the exclusive thing."

His hand dropped away like he'd been burned.

Anger welled up from the pit of his stomach and burned to his cheeks. He wanted to lay them against the cool, fogged up window.

"I told you not to make me choose," she said softly.

"Yup. That's my b," JZ said, smiling. He saw in Jacinta's face that she saw the lie in his eyes. But by the time she saw his hand coming toward her, he already had her by the hair, pulling her toward him. "Cool. I'll settle for being friends with benefits then." He went to kiss her hard on the lips, but their teeth clanked together in a painful collision.

She smacked him in the face. Her eyes, glossy but dry, were wide with shock. "What is wrong with you tonight?"

Bile rose hot in JZ's throat. He stretched his neck, forcing it back down. He heard the tremor in his voice, but lowered his eyelids, putting his cool face on. "You were the one who said I'd fall the hardest." He chuckled. "It's nice being right, ain't it?" Jacinta jumped when he pressed the button to unlock the doors. "Bye, Cinny. I gotta dip."

Jacinta made one last attempt. "Don't . . ."

"Bye, Cinny, damn," he barked, and that got her moving.

She opened the door, angrily, but took her time getting out, maybe hoping JZ would cop to some elaborate, very early April Fool's joke. He only waited patiently for her to step out. Before she had a chance to levy any last words or shut the door, he backed down the driveway, gravel popping. He shoved the car into gear so hard, the door shut on its own.

All Hail the Clique . . . The Clique IS Dead

"The end of the world it seems. You bend down and you fall on your knees."
—Kate Voegele, "It's Only Life"

Mina was sick.

She raced into the house, past her parents in the sunroom and up the stairs into her room.

The entire evening was a patchwork quilt of ugly words and images seared in her mind so deeply, her stomach lurched whenever they flashed. She laid across her bed and dialed Michael's number again. She smashed the End button when his voice mail came on for the fifteenth time.

He wouldn't text her back.

He wouldn't answer her calls.

She had to talk to him.

Michael was the reasonable one. Once she talked to him, they'd figure out how to get at JZ, bring it all back together. She dialed Michael's number again, waited patiently for the voice mail message to end, and left a message, "Mike, please call me . . . please."

She jumped when her mother's face appeared in her doorway. "Hey, baby girl," her mother said, instinctively treading lightly. "Wanna talk?"

Mina shook her head no, then threw herself into her pillow and bawled. She lifted her head long enough to wail, "Ma, it's a mess. JZ and Michael are fighting and . . . Cinny just sent me a text saying she's mad at JZ." She dumped her face back into the pillow. "What's happening?"

Mariah Mooney stroked her daughter's back, letting her cry until the tears turned to dry hitches. "Tell me what happened." She pressed gently on Mina's shoulder until Mina sat upright.

Mina relayed as much of the story as she could bear, leaving out the more hurtful words and only scratching the surface of the story Jacinta had told her about JZ taking her home. Her voice hitched, "It's . . . it's like we're falling apart." She placed the pillow on her lap and hugged it. "I knew that if Mike got into the Carter, we'd miss him and all but—I didn't think it would mean we wouldn't be friends."

"You'll always be friends," her mother said. "Maybe just not like you are now."

Mina wailed. "That's not enough."

Mariah smiled. "It might have to be."

Mina sunk her face into the pillow, smashing her eyes and her mind closed against what her mother was proposing. The clique not friends anymore? The words were as foreign to her as another language.

Her mother's hand raked gently through her hair. "Tonight sounded pretty bad." Mina nodded and Mariah went on. "It might be bad for a while. But you guys will bounce back, I bet."

Fresh tears streamed down Mina's face as she thought about Michael and JZ using the term *was* in reference to their friendship. She shook her head, lifting it up only enough to be heard. "Not from this, Mommy. I just have a bad feeling."

Mina's mother leaned down and kissed the back of her head. She stroked Mina's back until her breathing took on the steady rhythm of sleep, then she repositioned her in the bed and stepped out.

The chirping of Mina's phone awoke her several hours later. She reached blindly for it, finding it on her nightstand.

"Hello," she whispered, squinting at the clock. Her vision was too blurred to make out the time.

"Mi, it's Jay."

"JZ?" Mina's eyes, sore and puffy, fluttered until her vision steadied. She rolled onto her back. "Jay, what's going on?"

"Can you meet me outside?"

She peered at the clock. "Jay, it's one o' clock."

"Thanks, Time Lady. Are you coming out or what?"

"Just come to the door of the sunroom. I'll let you in."

"All right, peace."

Mina sat up, staring around her room, dazed. She was still dressed. She didn't remember falling asleep. She got up, went to the door, and listened to the sounds of the house. Her father's light snoring confirmed what she needed to know. She eased down the stairs and went out to the large sunroom. Her parents must have turned in only a bit earlier; the room was still warm from the gas stove.

She walked to the main sliding glass door and waited for JZ to appear. Even staring straight out the window, he startled her when his face popped up. She slid the door open as quietly as possible.

"Where's the car?" She peered behind him in the frigid night.

"I walked," JZ said. He rubbed his hands together and blew into them.

"You're crazy. It's pitch black out there."

JZ snickered. "We've lived here our entire lives, Mina. When was the last time somebody got jacked walking in the Woods?"

Mina shrugged. Far as she knew never. Still, she wasn't about to walk down the street alone at night. She went over to the sofa and sat down.

JZ sat beside her. He held his hand up. "Don't say anything, okay?"

She obeyed.

They sat in the dark silence, listening to the last cracklings of the gas stove and the creaks of the house settling, until JZ said, "You know I hate . . . talking about feelings and shit." His eyes were wide and white in the darkness. Mina focused on them, nodding. "But I gotta get some things straight. Be real with me, all right?"

She nodded again. A sliver of cold curiosity lodged itself in her spine and she shivered.

"Is Michael gay?" JZ said.

Mina's gasp was a tiny sip of air, but JZ heard it. His eyes locked on her lips before closing heavily. He shook his head. "Tell me, Mina."

"I . . . you should be asking Michael this, Jay."

He hung his head. "You know that's as much of an answer as you gasping." He was scowling when his head came back up. "But I said be real with me. I need you to answer."

Mina's throat tightened. She shook her head no as she answered, "Yes."

JZ's hands went to the crown of his head, then slid down to his forehead again and again, first slow, then quickly, in a back and forth motion until his hair stood up in tiny, fiberlike spikes. He blew out a deep breath as if it were taking a lot of effort to go on.

"When did he tell you?" he asked.

"A few weeks ago."

"Guess you weren't going to tell me, huh?"

Mina's face cracked. "It . . . he . . . no."

"How y'all gonna . . ."

Mina pressed her finger against JZ's lips. "Look how you acted tonight. Are you seriously going to catch a 'tude that Mike never told you?"

JZ rubbed his hands on his thighs, squeezed his knees, then shrugged. "All right, yeah. But I was his boy. It's like . . ."

"Was?" Mina said, choking on the word. "Can't y'all still be friends?"

"Were we ever?" JZ's eyebrow rose.

"Why would you say that?" Mina said in a high-pitched whisper. She could barely contain her frustration. "We've been friends since we were five years old and . . ."

"And Michael never bothered to tell you until recently and he never told me. So did we really know him?"

"I can't pretend it didn't hurt to know he'd already told Lizzie," Mina said.

JZ's eyes popped wide. "So Lizzie knew? For how long?"

"Since freshman year, apparently," she mumbled.

JZ shook his head up at the ceiling. "See, that's what I mean. Man, secrets is bull." He cocked his head and squinted at Mina. "Now the two of them kept this from us and we're supposed to be like this." He held two fingers together. "Come on, Mina, that's not right and you know it."

Mina touched his thigh. "I don't disagree, but it's not anything we should end our friendship over."

JZ chuckled. "Only you would say that, TV Land."

Mina hadn't heard that nickname in a while. In middle school, Michael and JZ used to torture her with the name, teasing her for her belief that everything could be wrapped up nice and neat, ideally in thirty minutes like the old-school reruns on TV Land. She hated being teased about being a bright-eyed optimist, but had grown to feel it had to be somebody's job to be the optimist, so she embraced it and admitted as much to JZ.

"Well, you and Michael are beefing right now but you'll work it out." She shrugged at his skeptical glance. "If I don't believe it, no one else will. And if no one believes it, it won't happen." The pain in JZ's eyes made her heart ache.

He flicked her under the chin with his knuckle. "Go 'head and believe it, Mi. But only me and Michael can make it happen."

Her eyes welled. "Are you saying you're not going to try?"

"Just saying . . ." JZ looked past her for so long, Mina was tempted to turn and see what was behind her. Finally he cleared his throat and said, "Mike was right. He need to get his. Do his thing. Go some place where he's not the sidekick." He chuckled, wistfully. "That's why Batman works alone."

"What does that have to do with y'all making up?" Mina frowned.

"Sometimes friendships die, Mi." He swiped angrily at his eye. "Mike gotta dip and I gotta respect that."

"But y'all can do all that and still be friends."

Mina's heart raced as JZ shook his head, disagreeing.

"I don't know Mike no more, Mina."

Mina pulled JZ's arm, as if physically trying to bring him to her place of thought. "Jay, don't say that." She tugged on his arm, then smashed it down, angry. "Don't say that."

JZ leaned forward, resting his elbows on his thigh. He spoke toward the floor. "So is Rob his . . . boyfriend?" His body flinched on the last word.

"No," Mina said, dully. "They're just friends, like you and him were . . . *are* friends."

JZ turned his head toward her. Mina looked him in the eye.

"Real talk. They're just friends."

She turned away, wiping at a stray tear, when she saw JZ's eyes glisten.

"I know Michael's mad right now, but he . . ." she stopped when JZ stood up abruptly.

"All right, Mouthy Mi, time for me to jet."

"So that's it?" Her eyes gleamed fiery accusation. "You just gonna break up the clique like that?"

JZ stretched. He put his hoodie up on his head. His voice was tired. He was over the conversation, Mina could feel it.

"The clique not broken up, Mina. We're all off doing our own thing most of the time anyway. . . . I bet after a few days you won't even know the difference."

Mina started to refute him, but stopped. Lately, their get-togethers with all of them present were far and few between. It was hard enough coordinating against six schedules to get together, but even random, spontaneous gatherings among two of them at once were near extinct as demands from their lives mandated attention.

JZ dangled his arm around her in a choke hold, then moved it around her shoulder.

"You still my girl, though, Mouthy Mi."

Mina wrapped her arms around him, clinging until he returned the embrace.

She looked up at him. "What about Cinny?"

His mouth was a half-moon smile. "She ratted me out already, huh?"

Mina nodded.

"I'll set things right with her if she ever talks to me again."

"Why can't you do the same thing with Michael?" Mina pleaded.

JZ squeezed her once, then let go. He took several long-legged steps and was out the door before Mina could say anything else.

Umma Do Me

"'Cause life is way too short and I can't wait no more."
—Lesley Roy, "I'm Gone, I'm Going"

Michael awoke early the next morning. It was Saturday, but he had work to do.

His hand instinctively rubbed his jaw. *JZ got a good right hook,* he thought, wincing.

He grimaced as the pain shot through his entire face. He didn't even want to know what he looked like. No need to see the representation of the stinging, aching, and itchiness that buzzed across every inch. Besides, if Rob's reaction, the night before, was any indication, his face was probably a good mix between Will Smith in *Hitch* when his face swelled up from eating seafood, and any Ultimate Fighter, winner or loser.

Unable to resist, his hands roamed the terrain. His left eye was soft and puffy. His right cheek jagged. His jaw swollen.

Good thing it was the weekend. By Monday . . . he stopped himself from thinking about Monday, Tuesday, or any day he and JZ would have to roam the halls together. His stomach rumbled and he forced himself out of bed.

He padded over to the mini-fridge in his room and grabbed an orange juice. The sting from the acid tore into his lip, squelching his appetite immediately.

Okay, so I'm not going out or eating today, he thought.

It was just as well. He had to finish one final design. He thought he'd have the entire summer to finish it, but the fight with JZ changed the priority of the outfit.

He turned on his iPod, placed the volume as loud as he dared without waking his grandmother—he definitely didn't feel like going there with her questions—and headed to the costume dummy in the far right corner.

He'd always wanted to be able to spend all day just designing and sketching, designing and sketching. But class work, Bay Dra-da fittings and meetings, and kicking it with the clique often kept him from tackling some of his more ambitious ideas.

Today was the day to make good on the dream.

He walked to the work table and laid out some charcoal fabric. The scissor made a whispery *schk, schk* sound as it ate across the material, emphasizing how quiet the room was.

He looked up and scoped out the spacious basement bedroom. The room felt huge without the clique. Images of them hanging out while he worked on his latest project flashed in his mind. Their hyper overtalking both distracted and fueled him.

The room's silence tormented him.

He turned up the music a few notches, willing his mind to focus.

In three more months he'd be staying in the Carter dorms in DC anyway—might as well get used to something new.

He shut out his thoughts and let his hands take over.

Getting Out More

"**S**tupid phone," Mina said, sending invisible hatred waves to her cellie. She hoped they reached Brian's phone in Durham. She'd been calling him since she awoke an hour before, but his phone was dead or off. She hung up, sent him a text message—Life here sux!—then plopped down cross-legged on the floor in the middle of her room and stared insolently into the closet.

A sea of clothes stared back and yet she still had no idea what to wear to Jill Ling's party. The idea of having to put too much thought into choosing an outfit for a party she didn't really want to go to only made her want to flake on Vic and cry cramps or flu or something. But as soon as she considered sending Vic a message begging out, she thought about Brian telling her to get out more.

She'd get out all right, with sexy Vic, and see how much Mr. Brian James liked that.

She would prove to him she had plenty to do, even though the last place she wanted to be was at a party with the Glams.

It would have been just bearable, if all was right in her clique, but watching Jessica, Mari-Beth, Jill Ling, and the other Stepford friends enjoy themselves as a tight group tonight would be hell.

Her eyes took in the variety in her closet—miniskirts galore hanging on one bar, blouses and dressy shirts next to them, dozens and dozens of folded tee shirts, more jeans than she knew what to do with. But her mind couldn't put an outfit together.

She brightened when her cell chirped. It was Lizzie.

R u up?

She typed back eagerly, glad for a distraction.

Yup. Whut r u doin up so early?

She nodded in agreement to Lizzie's response:

Cldnt sleep. 2 much drama last nt

And commiserated: me either been up since 7. blegh! JZ came by last nt.

A message came in immediately, surprising her.

Dag, Liz, your fingers burning up the keyboard today, she thought, laughing, until she realized the message was from Brian

'sup, Toughie? Y ur life suck?

Her fingers flew over the keyboard: hey 2 much 2 say but mike n jz got into it lst nite.

She immediately responded to Lizzie's:

he did? dish!!

With: asked me if mike was gay and I had 2 tell him the truth. its just a mess

She scooted over until her bed brushed her back, then leaned onto the mattress, into the text conversations for the long haul. The rhythm of the two exchanges relaxed her.

She read Brian's message: wtf? Got into it like jus tlkg shit or throwing bows?!

She mulled over how to explain last night to Brian as she responded to Lizzie's: I kno. Mike isn't ansrg his phone. dreading monday!, with: who r u telling?! jz is our ride 2 school. no idea if hes goin 2 jus leave mike behind or what.

She rested her head on the edge of the mattress and stared at the ceiling a few seconds, before responding to Brian with a simple: throwing bows.

Lizzie hit her back: do u thnk they'll make up?

Mina inflated her cheeks with air. She held her breath a few seconds then blew it out noisily as she answered: truthfully?: No. jz acted like done is done, son. Not sure abt mike but u kno how jz can get . . . all stubborn!

Her heart ached with understanding at Lizzie's response: yeah I feel same way. they said stuff they cant take back. sux majorly!!!!!

Mina had no response. It did suck majorly, no need to restate the obvious. She chuckled at Lizzie's next message: what? no infamous Mina plan 2 fix things?!

Mina wished she had a plan and she admitted it: nope, wish there was.

Seconds later she followed it with: but its still early u never know ;-)

She didn't feel as confident as her message, but no need to close the door on the possibility that she could work some magic and get the two best friends back on track. She checked back on the last message from Brian: dam 4 real?!

She didn't feel like rehashing the whole thing, via text or a phone call. She wanted to forget yesterday or at the very least not have to relive it. She typed back: yeah. its bad. dont feel like goin into it rt now. Kno what I mean?—and hoped Brian didn't take offense. She smiled, grateful, when he responded: yeah those ur road dogs, I kno u tore up. Feel better baby girl, they'll wrk it out. U kno how guys do.

I sure do, Mina thought. That's exactly why she didn't think it would be as simple as them working it out like nothing ever happened.

She happily switched subjects: called u earlier was ur phone off?—and then fretted that she came off needy. Brian's "you need to get out more" echoed in her ears.

But his response was a simple: dead. Sitting here now cant move cuz its on the charger.

She laughed as she typed back: ah-ha got ur azz on lock down lol

He played along: I kno rt! lol

So whut u doin 2day? she asked, hoping that wasn't yet another needy question.

But any annoyance Brian had with her earlier in the week was gone.

Already had prac. Prbly catch a nap, hang out w/pop and jingle.

She chuckled, laughing at the nicknames Brian had given his roommates. Pop was another freshman starter on the team, whose real name was Damian, from upstate New York, where they still called beverages soda pop—something Brian found hilarious. And Jingle was a freshman benchwarmer who had apparently been made to carry the entire team's keys one day on a huge ring. Brian said he jingled everywhere he went and people heard him coming a mile away.

any plans 4 da nite? she typed.

She debated sharing her own plans, especially when his response came back: nope. nuttin.

Oh, so I have something to do and you don't, she thought, giddy, deciding she'd only share if he asked what her plans were. She typed: whut no hot frat parties 2 go 2?

He replied: Plenty 2 go 2 jus 2 dam tired. Rdy 2 hit the road 4 the tourney soon, got mad work 2 catch up on.

Her heart went out to him. She couldn't imagine how hard it must be for him to travel as much as the team did, practice as often as they did, and still have class work to tackle.

Poor baby, she typed, cracking up when he wrote back: u shld come down here and give me a quickie.

Her fingers danced over the keyboard as she laughed: u want me 2 travel 6 hours away 4 a quickie?!?!

LOL quickie, longie jus come down here, he wrote back.

Her heart soared. He wanted to see her. She'd be so glad when March came and went—they could talk more—and then before she knew it, he'd be home early May. Before she could respond, he typed back: gtg Toughie. pop heading out 2 get some grub n im gon roll w/him.

Ttyl she typed.

She closed her eyes, savoring the joy of a normal conversation with Brian and during the hours she was usually awake to boot.

She checked for Lizzie's last message, saw none, and resumed the stare-off with her closet. Needing an excuse to call him, she dialed Michael under the guise of wanting fashion advice. The call was two rings in and she was about to give up—he certainly hadn't returned her last twenty calls—when he picked up.

"What's up, Deev?"

He sounded as tired as Mina felt. Still, she infused her voice with cheerfulness. "Hey, Mike. I need a fashion consult."

"Dial it down a notch, Diva, you're blowing up my eardrum."

Mina giggled. "Sorry." Without the false cheer, her voice broke. "I just really need your help. I'm going to this Glam party with Vic and I don't know what to wear."

"A Glam's party? Found a new set already?"

He chuckled and Mina burst into tears, caught back in the reality of the other day.

"Diva, I was joking."

"Mike, I can't do this. It hasn't even been twenty-four hours and I feel like I've landed on Mars or something."

"We're still cool, Mina."

"But we're *all* not cool and it's wack." She wiped her face, determined to be stronger. "Can you at least come over and help me?"

"Seriously, are you really gonna make me leave the house when you know my face looks like a plate of hamburger?"

Mina sniffled as she laughed, surprised that Michael sounded so normal. She attempted to evoke the same stance. "You're gonna let vanity stand in the way of finding me a tight outfit?"

"And you know this," Michael said, laughing. "No. It's not that. I'm in the middle of something and it's sort of important. Can't I just talk you through?"

Mina sucked her teeth and pouted.

Michael read her mind. "Stop pouting, girl. I know your wardrobe like it's my own."

"Yeah, whatever," she said, refusing to be cheered up.

"Look at you doubting my skills. You're lucky I'm busy or I'd come over there and boot you in the butt."

Mina giggled. "Boot. Ha."

"That's more like it," he said in a fatherly reprimand. "All right, let me think for a second. . . ."

"I could wear jeans. That's nice and easy."

"Shhh. How you gonna call me and ask for a consult, then tell me what you should wear?"

"Sorry," Mina said. She waited silently, browsing the closet from the floor.

"Wear that black cotton mini with the big buttons down the middle, black tights, black boots, three quarter length or knee . . .

the yellow V-necked long-sleeved shirt. You know, the one that looks like a sweater but isn't?"

Mina stood up, walked to the closet, and immediately plucked out the shirt. "Yeah."

"And then wear that black and white houndstooth vest."

Mina wrinkled her nose. "Black and yellow . . . I'm gonna look like a bumble bee."

Michael sniffed. "A *fly* bumble bee."

Mina grabbed all the pieces, holding them up to herself in the mirror, while holding the phone with her chin. She smiled at her image. "All right, all right. Yeah, it's fly."

"Hmph, doubting me twice gon' cost you two boots in the phatty."

"Thanks, Mike."

"Welcome, Deev."

"Next time, though, come over. I don't like this phone consultation."

"Get used to it," he said.

Mina stuck her tongue out at the phone. "What'd you say?" he said, as if he'd seen her.

She laughed. "Nothing. I said our connection breaking up."

"I hook you up and you pull the old lost call thing on me. You're not right."

Mina let his nagging ring in her ear. She confessed, "I never thought I'd enjoy hearing you lecture."

He chuckled. "And now you know."

"Yeah." Mina dropped the clothes on her bed. "Mike . . ."

"Deev, I gotta go for real. I gotta finish this."

"Wow, could you be a little bit more concerned about crushing my feelings? Dipping out on me all fast."

Michael dismissed her with a snort. "No time for drama, Mouthy Mi. Just call me later and tell me all the juicy bits from the party. I know those Glam hags gon' act a fool tonight."

"Don't remind me," Mina said.

"Love you, Deev. I gotta go."

"Love you," Mina said into the dead phone. She dropped the phone and went to take her shower. The hot water lifted her spirits enough to keep her motivated. She went to the sunroom and sat on the sofa between her parents, so deep into Saturday mode they still had on pajamas, unusual for them.

Her father raised one eyebrow. "Nowhere to go?"

Mina snuggled against him, loving the comfort emitted from his body heat. He put his arm around her.

"Nope . . . not until tonight anyway," she said.

"That's right, you're going to a party with Vic from work," her mother said. "I think it's good that you're widening your circle."

Mina scowled. "I'm not widening anything, Ma. Vic just didn't feel like being with all those boogee snotty kids and I'm keeping him company."

Her mother's eye roll didn't hide the fact that she was genuinely glad Mina was getting out.

"Now, who is this Vic guy?" her father asked. "Brian's no longer?"

Mina sucked her teeth. "Daddy, Vic is just a guy I work with. Me and Brian are fine."

He chuckled. "Awfully defensive for someone who's 'fine.' "

"Jack, stop teasing her," her mother said, grinning. "You know Brian's the great love of her life."

"That's right. When's the wedding again?"

He squeezed Mina with one arm as he laughed. She let their jokes, an ongoing thing with them about her and Brian's long distance romance, bounce off her. When the conversation eventually turned to Michael and JZ's fight, she tried to hear their advice, about time healing wounds, without getting depressed. They spent the entire morning and most of the afternoon together, a rare slice of spontaneous family time only broken when Mina realized she'd left her phone upstairs. When she went to retrieve it, breaking the vibe of the slow-moving day, her parents chose that moment to get dressed and up for the day. Mina politely declined their invitation to hang out while they ran errands and grabbed a bite to eat and was dressed and waiting for Vic by the time they returned seven o'clock that evening.

His knock on the door prompted a set of jitters that Mina hadn't felt in a long time. She'd be attending a party with a group of people she mostly disliked without the armor of her clique. It was unnerving.

Her mother beat her to the door.

"Hi, Mrs. Mooney," Vic said politely, extending his hand for a shake.

He looked handsome in a pair of dark-washed jeans, a striped button-down shirt, and a pair of fresh white-on-white Nikes. His hair was freshly braided in twenty neat simple rows.

"Hi, Vic," Mina's mother said, gripping his hand in a ladylike handshake.

Mina's father stepped up behind Mariah and extended his hand, shaking harder and firmer. "Hi Vic, I'm Mr. Mooney, Mina's father. I don't think we've ever met."

Mina chuckled inside, laughing at her father's alpha male vibe.

"Mina and I work together, sir," Vic said politely, not intimidated. "Mina's doing me a favor, hanging out with me while I DJ a party."

"Well, she has a curfew," her father said.

Mina rolled her eyes, stepping in. "Daddy, okay, Vic knows what time I need to be home. See you guys later."

She hustled Vic out the door after giving both her parents a kiss on the cheek.

When they got in the car, Vic wiped his brow. "Whew, your dad is like . . ." He deepened his voice, imitating Mina's father, "She has a curfew, you know."

Mina laughed. "He's all bark and no bite. It's my mother you gotta really watch."

"I'm not even surprised," Vic said, smiling. "The way you stand up to Jessica at work, I can tell you got some fire up in you."

Mina's eyes rolled. "That's just from years of dealing with her."

Vic backed the car out of the driveway, then steered it out of Mina's cul-de-sac.

"You know I don't feel like going to this thing," Mina said.

"Me either, that's why I needed a sucker, I mean volunteer, to go with me."

Mina smacked at his arm. "Misery likes company, huh?" she said.

He winked at her. "For real, for real."

There was a comfortable silence. Mina watched the bare trees whip by, then the stores of Main Street and the high school. Kelly's neighborhood was only a seven-minute drive from the Woods and they were at the guard's booth of the gated neighborhood in no time.

Vic put his window down. "Victor Adams visiting the Ling residence."

The guard eyeballed a list on his clipboard, saluted Vic, and hit a button that opened the gates.

"Victor Adams visiting the Ling residence," Mina teased, mocking him.

Vic's smile was sheepish. "Come on now, that's my professional voice. I can't be acting a fool rolling in a neighborhood that has its own rent-a-cop."

"True," Mina said. "Just not used to hearing you all polite."

"So here's the deal for tonight," Vic said. He rolled the car slowly through the neighborhood of mini-mansions as his eyes ping-ponged between an address on a piece of paper on the console of his car and the mailboxes on the street. "You can hang out by me, but if you want dance or kick with it anybody, that's cool too. I just wanted somebody there to break up the monotony every now and then."

"No worries. I don't plan on kicking it with anybody," Mina said.

But an hour into the party, she was having more fun than she expected. She stationed herself at the extra table Vic used for his additional equipment. She had the perfect view of the entire party. It was wall-to-wall people, many of them friends or associates. She'd already talked to Sara, Cassidy, and Meggan from the cheer squad; Jake, Tommy, and Conner from the football team; and Julius and Kelvin, two hottie skaters. There were a lot of people there that Mina would have invited to any party she had.

She'd forgotten that despite most people despising the Glam's reign of terror, a party was a party. People were enjoying the night out and Vic kept them moving with his deafening music—mixes flashing from house music to hip-hop in a fluid streak that made her tired, and she wasn't even dancing.

Mina sat, legs crossed, laughing at the antics of her classmates, mentally taking note of some of the total illegal hookups—a few people who were normally coupled up were there without their partner—and leaning over to holler-whisper at Vic as they tripped off some of the more rhythmically challenged dancers.

Once people realized she was there with the DJ, she was practically the center of attention. People kept coming up to her to talk and give Vic a pound, complimenting him on the music.

Sara, Jessica's twin, came back to Mina for the third time. Her brown curly hair was stuck in wisps to her face. "Oh my God, Connor is totally trying to kill me," Sara said, taking a seat next to Mina on the table.

Mina laughed. "And you're totally loving it. Connor is hot to death."

"I know, right." Sara's laugh was lost in a sonic boom from Vic's mix, which immediately revved into a dance mix of Rihanna's "Shut Up and Drive." The dance floor was a mass of gyrating pandemonium.

Sara leaned over, yell-whispering, "But he's a junior. I'm not trying to start anything new."

"Date him, Sara, don't marry him."

She and Sara exchanged a girly pound.

"I can't believe you and Jess graduate this year," Mina said. "I'm gonna miss you so much next year."

Sara threw her arm around Mina. "Same here. But truth up, aren't you going to miss Jess too?"

Mina leaned away and gave Sara a look. "Hell to the no . . . no harm."

Sara laughed. She was well aware of the love/hate frenemyship between Mina and her sister. As if conjured up by their conversation, Jessica sashayed over to the table. She stood in front of Mina and Sara, legs spread wide, hands on her hips.

"Mina, I swear to God." She tossed her weave of jet black curls. "I heard you were here and nearly tore Jill a new asshole until she said she hadn't invited you." Her eyes skated to Vic, who blew her a kiss, making Mina laugh, before settling back on Mina. "Work's been so awesome with you only working two days a week."

Used to Jessica's venom, Mina only stared at her passively, trying not to laugh as Sara kept nudging her slyly.

"So what, are you and Vic dating?" Jessica asked, her lip up-turned. "Did Brian finally break free?"

"Vic and I are just friends," Mina said as if speaking to a two-year-old. "I only came with him because he thought you and the rest of your clique might tie him up and perform voodoo if he came without a witness."

Sara's loud laugh pierced a momentary lull in Vic's mix.

Jessica rolled her eyes. "Same old Mina, always dogging my foot-steps, wanting to be where I am," she said with a snide smile.

"Kiss, kiss," Mina said, and made a kissy face at Jessica.

Devin, an attractive senior with a stutter, came up behind Jessica and he put his arm around her shoulder. "C-c-come on, Jess," he said, and steered her toward the packed dance floor.

Jess tossed her hair. "Gotta go. Some of us didn't come here to

work as the DJ's pack mule." Her Glam Stepford laugh floated in the
air as she walked away.

"Oh my God, are she and Devin dating?" Mina asked.

"I think so," Sara said. "She denies it. But he's been by the house
a lot the last few months. And they're always texting."

Mina frowned. "Why deny it? Devin's hot."

"Because he st-st-stutters," Sara said, laughing at her lame joke.

"Whatever." Mina rolled her eyes. "He's still hot. Jess is lucky
somebody would even tolerate her snotty butt."

"She's actually pretty sweet around Devin. You wouldn't know
her if you saw it."

"I would pay to see that. Call me next time he comes over," Mina
said, cracking up at the thought. She watched Devin, who was a
pretty smooth dancer, and Jess dance, noticing that Jess gave him a
slight nudge, pushing him away, when he got too close. Mina shook
her head. Jess was so superficial it wasn't even funny. She might be
turned off by Devin's stutter, but Mina was certain that Devin's cute-
ness and the fact that his father owned ten Chick-fil-A's throughout
the state kept Jess from totally dissing him. Devin lived just next
door to Jill Ling, in one of Folger's Way's largest houses.

Now what Devin saw in Jess, Mina didn't even want to know.

She started to say so politely to Sara when Vic's voice boomed
over the mic, "I got my girl Mina in the house, my little DJ girl in
training."

He smiled Mina's way, laughing at her wide-eyed horror. "Y'all
want hear my girl Mina mix?"

There was a raucous cheer of "yeah" from the crowd.

"Mina, girl, come bless 'em with a mix."

Sara giggled. "Hidden talent?"

"It better choose now to come out," Mina said, easing her way
off the table and over to Vic.

"What are you doing?" she said to him. "I have no idea what
to do."

Vic motioned her over. She stood in front of him and he placed his hands over hers on a record, helping her to mix it.

"Go, Mina. Go, Mina," Vic shouted into the mic until the entire house went along.

Mina laughed, letting her fingers do whatever Vic's directed her to. The mix was hot, she had to admit. He nodded toward the mic and Mina frowned, shaking her head no. But he insisted.

She put her mouth closer to the mic, shy at first, "What's up, y'all?"

Mina laughed at the mangled, unintelligent answer emitted from the crowd.

"Is Folger's in the house?" she said, tickled when those who lived in Folger's answered with a lusty, "hellllll yeah."

"Is Falcon's Nest in the house?" she said. Getting into it, she shouted out all of the burb Del Rio Bay communities, then led a rowdy, "Rep your nabe. Rep your nabe. Rep your nabe," until everyone was jumping to her beat, yelling out their neighborhoods.

Vic was cracking up behind her.

"Look at you, girl. Don't be trying steal my job." He bumped her from behind and nudged her gently out of the way. "Now that my girl got it crunk up in here. . . ."

He let a mix explode, changing the tempo to a crazy fast beat. The crowd roared with approval. Mina stood by Vic, nodding along to the insane beat. She gave Sara the thumbs-up when she waved to her from the dance floor with Connor.

Vic bumped her lightly with his hip and she swayed along with him. He leaned in close to her ear. "Go dance if you want."

She shook her head, talking up to his ear, "I'm cool."

"You scared somebody gon' go tell your boy you were out having a good time?" He smiled at her rolled eyes.

"Whatever, DJ, just play the music," she teased.

Vic did just that, bending back over the turntables, choosing his next selection while Mina returned to her perch on the table. At the mention of Brian's name, she thought about him, wondering what he'd ended up doing with his night. She felt bad for him and a little ashamed that she'd been so insecure lately. Whenever she gave him grief he reminded her how tough it was to juggle classes and basketball. Something he shouldn't have to do. She totally understood. Some days she was so tired from her day, it was all she could do to keep her eyes open at work or during class.

She vowed to end her clingy neediness, right here, right now.

She was glad she'd come out with Vic. She'd proven she could enjoy herself, having fun with another guy, platonically. Surely Brian was doing the same thing, if he even had this kind of free time.

She'd do better, if it killed her.

1@1

"Once you move forward, there's no turning back."
—Daylight West, "Better Friends Than Lovers"

Forget a man in uniform, ladies loved DJs, if the number of girls approaching Vic after the party was any proof. Once the party was over, Mina was more than ready to go. She'd had a good time but was ready to roll. She helped Vic pack his equipment, then waited impatiently as he talked to a gaggle of girls claiming they needed his digits because they were all having parties.

Mina knew for a fact that Janell Clark had just had a party, the weekend before. Standing with her back against the wall, Mina gave Vic her best "let's go" face. He finally broke from the girls after Mina popped her eyebrows in a clear sign of exasperation.

"Sorry," he said, laughing as they got in the car. "But you know word of mouth is my best advertisement."

Mina yawned. "And if any of those girls actually has a party within the next three months, I'll be a monkey's aunt."

"Party or date . . . I'm open to either."

"Obviously," Mina said. She jumped as her phone vibrated in her pocket.

"You all right?" Vic said.

Mina laughed. "Still had my phone on vibe." She raised her butt and pulled the phone out, reading the text from JZ: u up?

She texted back: yeah. Heading home.

"That went better than I expected," Vic said.

Mina yawned again. "Dag, sorry. I can't wait to jump in that bed. Yeah, it was nice."

"Why you dog all those dudes that asked you to dance?" Vic gave her a mock scowl.

Mina chuckled. "Just wasn't in the mood. Most of 'em were buddies of mine, they understood." She squinted down at JZ's next message: o when u get home log on 2 groupie love.

"Pssh, why?" she said aloud.

Vic frowned at her. "Huh?"

"Oh, I was just talking to JZ," she said, typing back: y?!?!

"Thanks for kicking it with me. I owe you," Vic said.

"No problem." She stared down at the phone as she finished. "If I hadn't had a good time you would owe me two."

Vic put his fist out for a pound, saying, "I hear that," and Mina tapped it.

He pulled the car into Mina's driveway and asked, "When do you work again?"

Mina frowned at JZ's message: Brian is da 1@1.

She looked away from the phone, realizing Vic was waiting on her to answer.

"Huh? Oh . . . um, I think I'm on the schedule for Monday. How 'bout you?"

"Yeah, Monday, Thursday, and Friday. So I'll see you Monday, then."

"Yup," Mina said. She opened her door. "See you."

"Thanks again," Vic said. "You're all right no matter what Jessica says."

He laughed and Mina managed a chuckle as she shut the door.

Her legs scurried to the front door of her house. She wrestled with the key until she realized it was the wrong one. She put the house key into the door, turned it and pushed the door open, closing it louder than she meant, locking it behind her. She moved quietly across the hardwood floors and tiptoed up the stairs. Closing her bedroom door quietly, she threw herself into her desk chair and logged on. As soon as it connected, she IM'ed JZ.

BubbliMi: wht in da world is 1@1?!
Jayizdaman: dam did u make vic speed?!
BubbliMi: what's 1@1?
Jayizdaman: groupie love has a chat every month at one a.m. on the 11th w/whoever is the #1 hottie of the month. Ur boy is it.

Mina rolled her eyes.

BubbliMi: y would I log on? I don't even have an account.
Jayizdaman: I figured u'd want 2 make 1 and let all them chix kno he got a girl LOL
BubbliMi: w/e
Jayizdaman: u not even curious? aw man my girl growing up

Mina read his message several times.
Curious.
Growing up.
Her heart thudded loud in her ears.
Curious.
Growing up.
The promise she'd made herself at Jill's party rang fresh in her mind.

So what if Brian was on this site chatting? In some (very) weird way, it was an honor that he'd become the number-one hot guy on their Web site, considering the site included guys from colleges all over the nation. And it was *just* a chat.

Too bad she didn't mean a word of it.

JZ's message broke her thoughts.

Jayizdaman: im proud of u Mi.

BubbliMi: give me the sign-in 4 ur cutieboomd account

Her heart raced as she waited for his response.

Jayizdaman: no. if u gon do it jus create a new 1.

BubbliMi: jay jus let me have it! please

Jayizdaman: i only tol u cuz I thght u wuz gon log on as u. don't trap him by pretending. thas foul.

BubbliMi: 4 real? 4 real u gon' come at me abt stuff thas foul?

Her chest heaved as she felt herself slipping out of control. The chat had started, she didn't have time to fill out a bunch of bogus info for a new account. She needed the cutieboomd account. Why was JZ tripping about it?

Jayizdaman: w/e im not gon help u set him up

It was already five after one. If she was going to log on, she needed to get to it. Tired of playing with JZ, she pulled out her heavy artillery.

BubbliMi: im not setting him up. jus gonna check it out. so ur choosing 2 b loyal 2 brian over me?

Jayizdaman: not even like that!

BubbliMi: then what's the big deal?

Mina shook her head as she read his message. Sometimes JZ was too hypocritical for his own good.

Jayizdaman: fine. if some shit pop off i don't want no parts of it.

BubbliMi: yeah I wish I could say the same abt the shit that popped off ystrday but im knee deep in it w/u

Jayizdaman: its cutieboomd and the password is jtg363
BubbliMi: thx
Jayizdaman: not wlcome!
BubbliMi: w/e

Mina put up her Away message and logged into Groupie Love. The entire page was lit up with pictures of Brian and comments from his seventy-five thousand plus friends. Mina stared in awe at the page.

I'm just curious, she thought, telling herself she wouldn't be if Brian had told her about the chat when she'd asked about his plans for the day.

She clicked on the private chat link, a privilege given only to those who'd been members at least thirty days. The Groupie Love server put her in the chat queue, sending her a message saying the chat room was full to capacity and she'd have to wait until someone logged out.

The message released the tension she'd felt since JZ explained what 1@1 was about.

It was full—a sign she wasn't meant to log on.

What were the odds any of these stalkerazzi fan-girls were going to willingly bow out of the chat with their #1 Hottie?

She took her Away message off and sent JZ a message.

BubbliMi: happy? I couldn't get on. Plffttt
Jayizdaman: good. use ur investigative skills 4 good, obi wan
BubbliMi: LOL w/e im hittin da bed. tired as a mug
Jayizdaman: c u

She signed out and was about to click the close button on the Groupie Love page when her screen changed from the queue message to a bright white screen filled with dozens of messages in a variety of colors. Symbols and chat speak scrolled a mile a minute as person after person added their chatter to the mix. Her eyes froze on the chat moderator's message:

> Heather Head-lee: Welcome Cutieboomd. Say hi to Brian aka Sexy#8. That name's no lie, right ladies?! ;-)

Mina's throat dried. She felt like ducking when she saw the next message.

> Sexy#8: Hi Cutieboo. Wht part of MD u frm?

Her hands froze over the keyboard. She had no idea what JZ, Todd, and Greg had put in Cutieboomd's profile. She typed Del Rio Bay, then quickly deleted it. No way they would have been honest, since they made the account to lurk on the down low. She took a deep breath and dove in.

> Cutieboomd: suitland
> Sexy#8: word? I used 2 live in Potomac.
> Heather Head-lee: So Brian, naturally all the ladies are dying 2 kno r u single or taken?

The chatters went into a frenzy.

> Luvmesome#8: omg pls say SINGLE
> Hotgurl890: wouldn't matter. Gf's r meant 2 b cheated on ;-)
> Ballergirl: heard u have a gf back home in DRB
> Sexigroupie765: well if u got 1 the ques is r u lookin 4 a chick on the side. i live in Durham! Bet ur gf doesn't.

Answer after answer poured in. Mina had to scroll up several times to see Brian's actual answer. Her heart dropped to her stomach.

Sexy#8: totally single

Another round of frenzied responses poured in. Mina could barely keep up, until she realized Brian's answers were a bolded dark blue and the moderator's a bolded black in a sea of lighter colors and shades.

Heather Head-lee: So how do u feel about groupies?
Sexy#8: LOL ummm . . . for 'em

Mina rolled her eyes. She was surprised when Brian addressed Cutieboomd directly again.

Sexy#8: Cutieboo how big a fan r u?

Mina squinted at the screen. What the heck did that question mean? She debated how to answer as the chatters grumbled about the light shining on her.

Sexigroupie765: come on B I kno MD is ur hometown but dont play favorites! Durham ur new home, show me some luv.
Luvdudeswhoball: LOL dont 4get the west coast. Cali got luv for #8 too.

Still uncertain what to say or even if she wanted to deal with another forty minutes of this, Mina finally responded, playing along.

Cutieboomd: a huge one. Still have a program frm game u played in @ Flowered Arms Academy. On my wall now . . . kiss it every nt.

She grinned, caught up in her own cleverness. These girls might be fans of Brian now, but how many of them knew much about

Brian before Duke? The thought of Brian asking which game put her in a panic. She had no idea who Flo-A played.

> Heather Head-lee: Woah got a ringer, somebody who knows u from back in the day.
> Sexy#8: Damn thas hot!

I know it is, Mina thought. *Take that, Sexigroupie765.*

She watched as the other chatters tried to one-up her, justifying their fan-hood. She seriously hated Sexigroupie765 and Hot-gurl890. If this were an in-person chat, they would be naked by now. She almost forgot to be mad at Brian. The chat was so over the top, it was obvious he was playing a role—worshipped god among his groupies. She wasn't going to hate on him for that, though the words "totally single" were singed in her brain.

She laughed as Lovemesome#8 and Sexigroupie765 got into an argument and Heather Head-lee had to remind the ladies of Groupie Love's "rules."

Do the rules include "must be a total slut?" Mina wondered.

She sat back, enjoying the drama when a message popped into the right-hand corner of her screen.

> Sexy#8 requests a private chat. Do you accept?

"No he didn't," Mina said, jaw dropping. She bit her top lip and stared at the message.

JZ had said not to set Brian up, but she hadn't lured him. She'd been the quietest one in the entire chat. She . . . Mina snorted. He approached her and she was the one feeling guilty.

She clicked yes and waited.

> Sexy#8: so u frm suitland huh? Do I kno u?
> Cutieboomd: no we've never met

Sexy#8: but u saw me play? Suitland beat Flo-A pretty bad my soph yr . . . must not have been my best game. LOL

Mina blew out a huge breath of relief, her worries about details gone. She swung with the chat, letting the words come naturally.

Cutieboomd: u still looked hot tho
Sexy#8: thx. whut abt u? whut u look like? U don't have pics on ur profile

Mina's stomach clenched. She hated how deep he was getting himself, but she couldn't stop playing her part.

Cutieboomd: u been checking me out?
Sexy#8: lol a lil bit.
Cutieboomd: tell u what, if ur serious I'll post a pic l8r
Sexy#8: what's serious?
Cutieboomd: jus wondering how bad u want 2 see me
Sexy#8: jus makin sure u aint a dude

If I were, that would be good enough for you, Mina thought, typing back angrily.

Cutieboomd: def'ntly not a dude. U'll see if u play rt
Sexy#8: dam u got game girl. its over 100 girls in the chat rm who would send me their 1st born if I asked and u teasing. thas cool. i don't mind the chase.
Cutieboomd: all dogs like 2 chase tail
Sexy#8: ouch! its true . . . but it still hurt
Cutieboomd: lol j/k
Sexy#8: naw its aight. so how old r u?
Cutieboomd: 17. I'm a sr. at Suitland High School. so y did u msg me? U got chix in there rdy 2 fight

Sexy#8: lol its crazy in there. im still in there chilln but most of da chix in there not bein real

Cutieboomd: r u being real?

Sexy#8: always

Mina's eyes rolled. She wanted to kill him.

Cutieboomd: so r u really single? heard u had a gf

Sexy#8: how u hear that?

Cutieboomd: cant tell u all that. but wht kind of groupie wld I b if I didn't kno all the details of my fave player?

Sexy#8: righ' righ' well I had a gf but its 2 hard 2 do that ldr thing. kno what I mean?

Mina snorted. She sure did.

Cutieboomd: yeah

Sexy#8: u have a bf?

Cutieboomd: does it matter? if i did—i wouldn't da nite u dipped by

Sexy#8: umph thas what im talkin bout. so u gon post that pic or what?

Mina scrolled to the top and read the chat from the beginning, dissecting every word, turning them over, inspecting them for interpretation, wishing there was a way for Brian to be innocent. When she confirmed the verdict for herself she responded.

Cutieboomd: yup. putting 'em up now.

She posted several pictures of herself and one of her and Brian together that only she had, so he'd know without a doubt it was her and not someone playing a prank, then logged off.

"You played yourself."

"Lately, I get the feeling we're not the same."
—16 Frames, "Everything Around Me"

Mina cut her computer off and took her time undressing.

She dropped the clothes on the bottom of her closet, turned her light off, and got into bed. The darkness nestled her in its bosom and she let the tears flow, soft and hot onto her pillow. Brian's betrayal hurt, but the reality of what she felt hurt more.

She was empty.

She'd wanted so badly to believe that she was the nutcase worrying needlessly about Brian cheating that discovering the truth only left her exhausted.

Her phone buzzed angrily beside her, as she expected it would. She let it buzz three more times, then hit Send calmly.

"What the fuck? So you set me up?" Brian's angry voice said.

"Yeah, that's it, Brian," she said quietly. "I set you up. I made you message me privately. And I forced you to ask me for a picture. Then I put a gun to your head so you'd say you broke up with me because it's too hard to do that ldr thing, know what I mean?"

Her bluntness threw him off. His breathing came hard and heavy over the line. Mina remained lying down, the phone sitting on her top ear. She pressed it closer so she could hear better when he talked.

"Why'd you do that, Toughie?"

Mina's tears flowed harder at the regret in his voice.

"Why'd *you* do it?" she asked with equal remorse.

His silence stretched forever. She waited, wondering if Brian would practice what he preached when it came to honesty and being real and wasn't surprised when he did.

"I don't know. I know I messed up."

Her voice hitched. "You were gonna . . . h-h-hook up with this girl? Some random girl you met online?"

"I was just . . . messing around. Seriously."

"Brian, stop. If I had given you my phone number or arranged a time for you to drop by once you got home, you would have totally acted on it." Her voice rose angrily. "Don't lie anymore."

"I can't believe you did this shit," he said, astounded. "All I asked was for you to let things run its course, Mina." His voice squeaked in his anger "Why'd you do this?"

"Why are you blaming me?" she said, crying harder, unsure whether to be angry or apologetic.

"Because we had a good thing going," he spat. "I'm three hundred miles away. You can't keep me in check from there and I can't check you. When I got home for the summer it was gon' be cool, we were gonna be together. But you couldn't let shit be. Damn."

He continued to curse and mutter under his breath. Mina nearly apologized until she remembered him glibly agreeing he was like a dog chasing tail.

"It's not my fault." She sat up, lighting into him as loud as she dared. "And you know what? It was only a good thing for you. I've been a basket case since you left for school. Half the time I can't eat or sleep wondering what you're doing. I wanted to believe we could do this, Brian, but I couldn't . . . I can't."

"Then why didn't you break up with me?"

"Why didn't you break up with me?" she spat. "You're the one chasing slutty groupies."

"Because I thought we could each do our own thing and still be cool when I was home."

"What is our own *thing*, Brian?" Her voice bounced off the dark, quiet walls and she lowered it to a fierce whisper. "We never agreed to see other people."

"Not officially, but you knew I wasn't going to be down here twiddling my thumbs in my dorm room every night."

The words stung Mina. "So then you've been cheating the entire time?"

He sucked his teeth. "No."

"Yeah, excuse me if I don't believe that," she snorted.

"Believe what you want," he snapped.

"So you haven't gone out with anyone in Durham?" she asked, hating herself for caring.

"Gone out? Grabbed a bite to eat or went to a party with somebody . . . yeah. But I haven't sexed nobody."

Mina's arms folded across her chest. "And how come you never told me about any of this?"

"Because it wasn't a big deal." His voice was incredulous. "So you've been sitting home every weekend doing *nothing*?"

"I've been busy, Brian, and when I go out it's with the clique."

"Well, I don't really have a clique anymore. I'm just chilling, meeting new people and enjoying school."

"Well, when you come home you can enjoy Cutieboomd," she huffed, adding snidely, "Oh that's right. She's not *real*. You're burnt."

"Man, you're so . . ."

"So what?" Mina said, challenging.

"Obsessed. You never let shit go, Mina. All you had to do was trust me and—"

"Trust you?" She snorted. "I did trust you and look what happened."

"No, you didn't trust me and that's why this happened."

Mina took the phone from her ear and looked at, as if she'd heard wrong. Brian was still talking when she put it back up to her ear.

"You played yourself," he said.

Her body shook with fury, then trembled with cold doubt. She rubbed at the goose bumps on her arms. She had brought this on herself, but it must have been meant to happen, whether she liked the end result or not.

She took three deep breaths, then closed her eyes.

No, this wasn't happening. When she opened her eyes she'd be back at Jill Ling's party or at JZ's New Year's Eve Party, the last time she and Brian had been happy . . . anywhere but here. She pinched her eyes closed, willing this to be a dream, scared to open them to reality. But his voice reached into her haven.

"I'm sorry, Toughie. I honestly thought we had an understanding that what happened while we were apart stayed in the past."

Tears leaked from Mina's closed eyes. She let Brian talk, unable to speak.

"Mina, I know I messed up. But I wouldn't hurt you on purpose." He paused, waiting for her to respond, but she refused.

His voice, gentle and pleading, coaxed her. "I don't want to lose you."

Mina sniffed and it seemed to give him hope.

"Can we work it out?"

Her eyes fluttered open. She spoke low and tentative. "Remember you said I was obsessed?"

He rushed to explain, "I didn't mean—"

"No. You're right," Mina said. "But that's just me, Brian. I get . . . so into something and it's like, I just want to throw myself into it all the way. I don't know how not to do that." She took a deep breath, letting the words find their way out. "I wanted so bad not to care what you did at school. And when I saw you at Christmas time, I almost didn't. But then I would care and when I did, I needed to hear that you still loved me. I waited for any tiny sign or signal that you still loved me—"

"I do," Brian said.

"But it's not enough." Mina sighed. "I keep needing more and more proof and it's driving me crazy." Her voice hitched and she waited until the feeling to bawl passed. "I'm letting shit go this time."

"So you're breaking up with me?" Brian said, strangely calm. His voice grew angry when she didn't answer. "Mina, are you breaking up with me?"

"Yes," she said softly.

In her head she screamed, *No, I didn't mean it,* as Brian coolly played the whole thing off.

"All right, cool," he said. "See you around then."

He seemed unable to stand her silence.

"What? You speechless now?" He snorted. "You had plenty to say online. Where's all that mouth from earlier, Cutieboomd?" He waited for her to respond and the silence hung between them until he sighed loud and exaggerated. "Bye, Mina."

The line went dead.

Mina fell back on the bed, smashed the pillow on her face, and cried herself to sleep.

Epilogue:
Beginnings and Endings

"Where do we go? I don't even know."
—Keane, "Bad Dream"

All due respect to her parents' advice, time wasn't healing Mina or the wounds of the clique fast enough. Every day, Mina awoke praying that some or all of Bloody February, as she'd come to think of it, had been a dream, and every day she had to face the grim truth that it was real.

The day after she broke up with Brian, he called her every half hour begging her not to end it. Too weak to resist his calls, she spent the entire day in her bedroom arguing with him, torn, wanting to forgive him but knowing her insecurity would be worse than before if she did. His pain ripped through her. She'd never seen him lose control and wasn't used to being the "strong" one in the relationship. Hearing him cry and plead weakened her defenses, but the words of the chat were seared in her brain. She could literally quote from it. In the end, those words and what they represented were stronger than Brian's pleas, eventually pulling her through the emotional torrent of his calls until they stopped.

The fight left her too weak to doctor the wounds of JZ and Michael's friendship. But true to JZ's words, their busy lives made it hard—though not impossible—to tell the clique was fractured.

Three weeks after "the implosion," she sat in Jacinta's family room, on the floor, browsing a magazine.

"Ooh, turn that up," she said, nodding her head to T.I.'s latest jam.

Jacinta made a big deal of moving two inches to turn up the music. "How long am I supposed to be at your beck and call while you're in mourning, Princess?"

"At least another three weeks," Mina said, smiling through the pain in her chest. She wasn't quite ready to joke about it but appreciated Jacinta's ability to be normal under any circumstance.

They both looked up, startled, at a knock at the door.

"Who is it?" Jacinta said, as she got up from the love seat.

"FedEx, ma'am."

Jacinta frowned, then snorted when she opened the door to JZ's grinning face.

"Hey," JZ said. "Is it cool for me to pop in? I been looking for y'all."

"Yeah," Jacinta said, leaving the door open as she walked away.

JZ walked in. He put his foot on Mina's back and rubbed gently. "What's up, Mouthy Mi?"

"Nothing," she said, pretending to be into the magazine.

Although JZ continued to give her and Jacinta a ride to school every morning—Mina riding shotgun—this was the first time JZ and Jacinta had said more than "hey" and "good morning" to one another since "the implosion."

"Can I holler at you for a minute, Cinny?" JZ said.

Jacinta shrugged.

Mina kicked JZ's leg with her heel and he removed it so she could sit up.

"I'll give y'all some privacy," Mina said. She grabbed her magazine and went into the kitchen, just off the family room, where "privacy" consisted of her simply not being in the middle of the conversation. She could still see and hear everything.

JZ sat on the edge of a fat overstuffed chair next to the love seat. He cleared his throat and rested his elbows on his thighs. He stared down at the floor, seeming to get himself together, then looked up at Jacinta suddenly.

"You're one of the coolest chicks I ever met, Cinny."

Jacinta's eyebrows hitched.

"It was mad swazy hanging out with you at my crib." His hand shot up to his head, then slid down. He looked down at the floor again. Mina saw his broad shoulders heave once before he looked up at Jacinta again. "Nobody was more surprised than me when I started digging you . . . more than a friend. I should have just come correct with my feelings from the start but . . ." He looked off at the wall behind Jacinta, shaking his head. "That's not really me, you know?"

Jacinta nodded. The cool indifference in her eyes softened to warm understanding.

"But that didn't give me no right to go all date rapist on you." He chuckled nervously, wiped his hands on his jeans, and sat back in the chair. "I'm saying, I'm man enough to apologize . . . even if I'm hella late with it. But I'm sorry I came at you like that. I hope we can be cool again."

A tiny smile played at the corner of Jacinta's mouth. "Dang, so I had to ice you for three weeks just to get an 'I'm sorry'?" she said.

JZ's hand went back to his head for a new round of hand brushing as he admitted sheepishly, "I'm just not good at this apologizing shit."

"You can start by not calling it shit," Mina hollered from the kitchen, unable to resist.

JZ and Jacinta laughed.

"Gee, thanks for the privacy, Mina," he said over his shoulder.

Jacinta beckoned Mina back into the family room and she came over eagerly, relieved for them . . . for the clique, what was left of it.

Pleased to have one brick of her friends' foundation back in place, she threw herself into cheer Nationals, state basketball championships, work at Seventh Heaven's, and homework with a fervor she'd forgotten she had. She watched Duke play in the NCAA tournament, alone (at the protests of Lizzie, Kelly, and Cinny), crying through every game until they were knocked out in the final four.

The end of college basketball season brought closure, and shades of the old Mina made an appearance, two weeks after Kansas was crowned the NCAA national champion.

She sat at her desk, laughing her head off at Vic's IM.

BubbliMi: ROFLMAO
Udontseeme: im like dam tht shiggity burned into my brain! ugh!
BubbliMi: u wrong 4 dat
Udontseeme: naw she wrong 4 tryna rock a bikini. wrong like a mug. lol

Mina looked down as a text message from Jacinta popped on her phone: can u come down jzs pls? now!

Mina's heart fluttered. She texted back: OK

What now?

She almost didn't want to know. JZ and Jacinta had been cool since he'd apologized late February, and Mina was finally starting to deal with life's new "normal."

What now?

BubbliMi: gtg see u at work 2morrow
Udontseeme: aight c u V

She smiled at Vic's version of the peace sign and sent it back.

BubbliMi: V

She logged off, not sure whether to race down to JZ's or take her time. She slipped on a pair of blue and gold spirit flip-flops, hollered her destination to her parents, grabbed the keys, and headed out. Seeing Lizzie's car in JZ's driveway sent her heart and feet racing. She shifted from right to left as she waited for someone to answer the buzzing of the doorbell.

Mrs. Zimms's smile was warm. "Hey, Mina. Wow, everyone's here . . . haven't seen all of you guys in a while." She hugged Mina. "They're downstairs. Must be a super-secret meeting of the clan."

Mina's smile was plastic as she walked away as fast as she could without being impolite.

Everyone was there? Even Michael?

She scampered down the stairs, not sure what she'd see when she turned the corner, expecting the worse but praying for the best.

They all looked up when Mina burst through the doorway, chest heaving, head whipping left to right as she scanned the room, sweeping it, wanting to see Michael standing there, his dark chocolate face scowling, fussing her out for being the last one to arrive. Disappointment kicked her in the chest.

JZ sat on the edge of the pool table, his shoulders hunched, his gaze on the floor. Jacinta and Kelly stood to his left, Lizzie to his right, faces somber, but no Michael. She battled tears as she joined them at the pool table.

"What's wrong?" Her eyes skated from one friend to another, then took another sweep of the room, still expecting Michael to pop out of the bathroom or out of the storeroom with the juice bar supplies.

Jacinta plucked a large white index card out of JZ's hand and gave it to Mina.

Mina frowned at it. "What is . . ." She skimmed the card, frown deepening. Unwilling to break the eerie quiet, she read it aloud in a low voice, breaking when she realized it was from Michael.

Jay,

I know you care what people think and that's why you're tripping right now. Maybe one day you won't. Maybe one day you'll realize that our friendship was one of the most important things in the world to me and it ain't have nothing to do with me secretly digging you. 'Cause that's what you think . . . I know it is. Maybe one day you won't.

You ain't even my type, punk. LOL

A tear dropped on the letter and Mina swiped at her face to avoid ruining the card. She swallowed the tears in her voice and kept on.

But I can't wait. That's the thing. I can't wait on you to get right about this. This is me, son. I was going to wait until senior year, then get ghost. Figured we'd just slowly lose touch and then do that 20-year reunion thing, where we catch up on things in our life. By then some things wouldn't matter no more. But I couldn't wait. I couldn't do 365 more where I was scared it might come up. But you still my dude, son. So I made this for you.

Mina looked up scowling. "Made what?" she asked.

Jacinta's head nodded to a suit hanging on the door of the supply room.

Mina walked over to the charcoal gray, pinstripe suit. She touched it lightly, caressing the fabric of the bold striping on the black vest. It was so JZ it made her heart ache. Unable to take her eyes off it, she stared at the suit until she realized she hadn't finished the letter.

How fly you gonna be on stage, shaking the NBA commissioner's hand in this? You know the answer, punk—fly as hell!

Do your thing, player. Umma do me.

Deuces,

Mike

Mina gazed at the suit again. She stepped toward it and caught the scent of Michael's bedroom, vanilla apple candle mixed with the Sean Jean cologne he always wore. Her resolve broke and she cried like a baby. She jumped, startled, when JZ came up behind her. His arms wrapped around her, filling the ache in her heart, a little but not enough.

"I'm sorry," JZ said in her ear. "I'm sorry I messed things up."

Mina cried harder, because in JZ's apology she knew what he hadn't said. That he knew Michael was right. JZ wasn't ready to accept Michael and Michael had moved on, no longer waiting for it. The bromance was over and there wasn't anything she could do about it.

FLIPPING THE SCRIPT

A Del Rio Bay Novel

PAULA CHASE

ABOUT THIS GUIDE

The following questions are intended
to enhance your group's reading of
FLIPPING THE SCRIPT
by Paula Chase

DISCUSSION QUESTIONS

1. Whether you have the type of relationship Jacinta had with Raheem or Mina with Brian, long distance romances (LDRs) are challenging. Are you for or against them? Debate your point presenting why or why not.

2. List five good reasons to remain in a LDR. Then list five reasons it's best to break up rather than continue a relationship with someone who lives far away.

3. Mina caught Brian cyber-cheating, but what was worse—her pretending to be someone else online or him putting himself in the position to take the bait?

4. Michael has always remained on the edge of the clique, often lost in the shuffle as the clique deals with their various dating issues. Were you surprised when he finally admitted that he was gay? Why or why not?

5. Have you ever withheld something from a good friend because you feared their reaction to it or you? Describe how it felt to keep that secret. Describe how you handled what happened, if you ever revealed the truth.

6. JZ's hang-up isn't with Michael's sexuality but how Michael's sexuality reflects on him. Why do you think some people, even those who seem outwardly confident, are so afraid of "guilt by association"? How would you feel if a close friend revealed he was gay? Would it impact how you felt about him as a friend?

7. Why do you think it was easier for JZ to apologize to Jacinta than to Michael?

8. Do you agree or disagree with JZ's philosophy "sometimes friendships die"? Explain your position.

9. Friendships definitely change as we get older. How have you handled a friendship that changed drastically?

Resources

www.gaystudentcenter.student.com—A site for high school and college-aged gay, lesbian, and questioning students.

www.saclibrary.org/teens/yaglbtlist.html—A list by the Sacramento Public Library of books featuring characters who are gay, lesbian, bisexual, or transgender.

www.sexetc.org—A site for teens by teens about sex education. Includes resources on relationships, teen sex, teen pregnancy, and sexually transmitted diseases.

www.stayteen.org—Facts on dating, relationships, waiting, breaking up, and more.

Catch up with Mina Mooney from the beginning!

Turn the page for a preview of
Paula Chase's Del Rio Bay series,
now on sale at your local bookstore.

Prologue

"They wanna know. Who's that girl?"
—Eve, "Who's That Girl?"

Popularity is a drug. You get a taste of it and suddenly the looks you get from people, the way you get treated, the things you get away with . . . you need it. You honest to God need it. People make pretend that being popular is no big deal. Either those people aren't popular and know they'll never have a chance at tasting its sweet addicting juices, or they're lying.

I got my first taste of popularity when I was four. No, seriously. My boy, Michael, and I attended Sunny Faces, a day care run out of his grandmom's house. The day care was downstairs in her basement, a kiddie wonderland of toys in every corner and hugantic paintings and colorful decals on the walls. There was also a big playground out back.

Now the basement is Michael's, remade over into a bedroom/gameroom/den of boyness.

But back then, when it was our playpen, even with all the dazzling odds and ends and kidgets, the one place we all wanted to go was upstairs. We never got to see the rest of the house. It was off-limits. So naturally, that's where we wanted to go. The stairs went up forever, gobbled up in the darkness near the top, with only a sliver of light coming from beneath the door.

With me leading the pack, we'd make up adventures about conquering the fantasy land beyond that door. Like, maybe it opened up into a lake of ice cream and trees of chocolate—since that's where Ms. Mae Bell came from with snacks. That became our favorite fantasy and eventually, the truth, as far as a bunch of four-year-olds were concerned.

If only we could get beyond the dreaded baby gate, we could take a dip in a big creamy vat of vanilla and take a bite out of one of the choco trees.

You know, to his credit, Michael never said a word to dispel any of our myths about the rest of his house being a candy land. Then again, why would he? How cool would that be to live in a land of candy?

Since his grandmother ran the joint, Michael was always allowed to go upstairs. Sometimes he'd toddle after her and she'd let him help bring down the snacks. If anyone else tried, Ms. Mae Bell would scoop them up, plop them down at the bottom of the stairs, and secure the gate with a firm, "You're gonna break your neck on these steps. Stay here. I'll be right back."

Man, but that gate made it irresistible. Some days we'd park right next to it and play because it was as close as we could get.

So, yeah, anyway, popularity and how it found me.

I became popular thanks to workaholic parents climbing the corporate ladder. Thank you, Fifty-hour work weeks! My mom had just started her own PR firm and my dad was a techie at a big company based out of Northern Virginia. They were mad busy scrambling to the top.

One day my mom called. She was running late and she couldn't reach my dad. Could Ms. Mae Bell please keep me a little later than normal? Of course, she'd pay whatever penalty was required for having Ms. Mae Bell work beyond her usual grueling twelve-hour day of screaming toddlers and crying babies.

So as everyone else was leaving, Ms. Mae Bell announces, to no one in particular, I'm guessing—we were a bunch of four-year-olds—that I'd be having dinner with her and Michael. She lifted the latch on the baby gate and ushered us upstairs to watch television, while she waited for the parents of the three other kids still left.

My stomach sang and danced as my chubby, four-year-old legs carried me out of the dark coolness of the stairway into heaven. I was so excited walking up those stairs, so caught up in what I'd do when I got to candy land, that it took me a few seconds to realize that the plush brown carpet wasn't, in fact, a river of chocolate.

Michael's house was just like mine.

Where were the gummy rocks? The Reese's Cup benches? The clouds of cotton candy (don't ask why he'd have clouds in his house)?

I'm not sure, but I think I cried. I really only remember Michael showing me his room and watching *Teletubbies*. I was too shocked to ask him where the candy stuff was hiding.

The next day, I was all set to report that candy land did not exist. But when everyone crowded around me, anxious to know what it was like, giving up their snack if I sat by them to share my adventures, wanting to team up with me for play circle . . . well, I discovered something better than candy land.

I had something everyone wanted—a glimpse into the other side—and it made me the It girl of Sunny Faces day care. It put me on the pop side or at least as popular as you can be with a crowd with very short attention spans. I think Shelly Mason was popular two days later for bringing a puppy in for Show-'n'-Tell.

No matter, my taste for popularity was born and my quest to remain ever the It girl sprouted roots.

I remember making up some story about not being able to talk about what was upstairs because it was top secret. Which was cool with them; they just wanted to be near someone who had crossed over.

I've never looked back.

Why would I? Being popular rocks!

When my rule of middle school came to a close, naturally, I had to hatch a plan to remain on top at Del Rio High School. Del Rio High is full of cliques. What high school isn't? But it's more full than most and the fate of your existence depends on where you get stuck, labeled, categorized, and otherwise boxed in by the governing clique—the Uppers.

So you see my dilemma?

Me and my crew have always been popular—but that transition from middle to high school is inevitable—and we're about to go from Middle School Royalty to High School Ambiguity. So, you know, I'm thinking I've gotta handle that.

It's not the same as starting over. Popularity carries over. So it's not that I'll be totally unknown. The Class of 2009 will know what's up and some of the sophs knew me before they left middle school. It's the junior class I'm worried about. I'll have to scrabble my way to the middle of the pack—which is to be the most popular in your class and more popular than some sophs and juniors. But, of course, never more pop than the reigning senior class. Lesson #10 from Pop 101.

All of this and classes too!

I'm an old pro at the tricks of becoming and staying popular and I could pretend that there's a true formula, or I can be real and let you know, it's a lot of work. Work that started the minute my pink Nellie Timberlands left Del Rio Middle School and strutted a few blocks down to the one and only high school, in the 'burbs of the DRB. Samuel-Wellesly, Del Rio Bay's only other high school, is another story. And we'll get to that later. But the best laid plans of popularity can and are disrupted by real life. So let me back it on up and let you peep how plans go right, left, back and forth before they land you at your destination . . . or at least somewhere really close.

The Frenzy

"Shorty, I want you to be my entourage."
—Omarion, "Entourage"

U down?

Mina Mooney stood, hunched over the back of the chair at her desk, staring at the three words on her monitor. Her stomach rumbled. From hunger or anxiety, Mina wasn't sure.

Two seconds ago, it was definitely hunger.

Sick of leftover turkey, mashed potatoes and all the other food they'd eaten on Thanksgiving and all yesterday, she'd been ravenous at the thought of sinking her teeth into something that wasn't stuffed or covered in gravy. When her mom burst into the room and plopped down on the bed, rousing Mina from a sound sleep with a tickle to the neck and a proposal that they cook a very un-Thanksgiving family breakfast, Mina had eagerly shaken off the early—if you could call ten-thirty A.M. early—morning haze fogging her head.

That was five minutes ago. Now . . .

She wanted to be sure that she understood Craig Simpson's words correctly. He *was* asking her out. Wasn't he?

Mina swiveled the chair with her knee and let her butt hover over the seat in a half-sitting, half-standing stance. She scrolled the screen and read the short exchange again.

Bluedevils33: Ay what up?
BubbliMi: Nuthin' ready to go eat
Bluedevils33: O. U know 'bout the Frenzy?

Mina knew. It was all JZ had talked about the last two weeks since football season had ended. It was the big bash Coach Banner held for the varsity football team at his McMansion in Folger's Way, Del Rio Bay's ritziest neighborhood, to celebrate the season.

BubbliMi: yeah. heard they had strippers last year
Bluedevils33: LOL. whatever. people b x-ageratin! It's not that bad
BubbliMi: I figured . . . but u never know! Y'all ballers can get out of control—ha ha
Bluedevils33: tru dat. But naw it ain't nothin' like that.
BubbliMi: I'll have 2 take ur word 4 it
Bluedevils33: No u can see 4 urself. u want 2 go w/me to the party?

And that was when Mina had shut down, unable to move, type, blink or breathe. It was while she was trying to come back to her senses that the last message came in . . .

Bluedevils33: R U down?

Mina stared at the screen, letting the words sink in. She wanted to type "seriously?" but figured that sounded stupid.

She rested a knee on the chair, a big grin on her brown sugar face. Craig was finally asking her out. Exactly four weeks ago they had spent the night bumping, grinding and getting their dance on at a party Mina had given for her best friend, Lizzie. Since then she and Craig talked more at school than they had before and IM'ed when they were on-line at the same time, but nothing drastic had changed between them.

Now, he was asking her out. And not just any date—no movies or grabbing a slice at Rio's 'Ria, the hot hangout spot in Del Rio Bay. Craig was asking her to go with him to the annual Blue Devils' Football Frenzy. She ignored the images the word "frenzy" brought to mind and instead tried to picture the forty-member football team playing rowdy rounds of spades, Madden football or checkers.

Yeah, right.

JZ had already given her and the clique an earful about the Frenzy. Board games and Playstation were never mentioned.

JZ and a few other select junior varsity football players, those who were definitely making varsity next year, were invited to the Frenzy. JZ was the main reason the JV football team had gone on to win the county championship. The invite to the Frenzy was a not so subtle acknowledgment that next year's tryouts were only a formality. JZ's future place on the varsity food chain was set.

The only reason JZ wasn't on varsity football this season, as a freshman, was because of his father. He wanted sports second on JZ's priority list. But JZ was a die-hard athlete—football in the fall, basketball in the winter and track in spring to stay in shape. He trained like a pro, running several miles a day and lifting weights several times a week. Even if sports were second on JZ's schedule because Mr. Zimms said so, football and basketball were first in his every thought.

And being on JV had actually brightened JZ's star, not dulled it. The minute he'd stepped on the field in September, it was obvious to the coaches he was varsity material. They'd been drooling over the thought of having him move up ever since.

Now the varsity basketball coaches were going to get the chance the football team hadn't had, because when football season ended, JZ's dad had relented and agreed to let him try out for varsity. JZ made the team easily. The only "catch," if JZ's grades suffered even a little, his father was going hardcore and making JZ cut out the sports until next season. So all JZ talked about, lately, were basketball and the Frenzy.

According to JZ, the Frenzy was wild. Coach Banner basically let his "boys" have the run of the house for the night, no chaperons. JZ also mentioned nude foolishness in the hot tub and drinking, *Real World* high school edition.

Other than pointing out to JZ that she thought the details of the party were probably rumors or overexaggerated, Mina hadn't given the Frenzy much thought. Until now. Now she had an invitation from a varsity football hottie.

Was she down?

Mina wanted to type YES, all caps just so Craig would know how down she was.

She couldn't believe that only three letters stood between her and her first date with the guy she'd crushed on for months. Her first date, period.

It wasn't even eleven A.M. and this day was quickly moving toward best-day-ever status.

And to think, in her haste to throw down on some pancakes and bacon, she'd almost walked right by her computer without as much as a glance.

Thank goodness she'd logged on to see if Kelly had sent a message confirming whether she could come over later and hang over at JZ's with the rest of the clique. Mina was anxious for the six of them to get together. They'd squeezed in only a few IMs and phone calls over the weeklong break. Mina didn't mind family time, but five straight days of it was enough. She was ready to kick it with her friends, especially now that she had something more interesting to share than an account of her family's insanely competitive game of Trivial Pursuit on Thanksgiving night.

Mina's head turned toward the loud clanging of pots and pans coming from downstairs, her attention slipping, just for a second, from the three words on the screen. She tipped over to her bedroom door, leaned her head out of the room and waited on her mother's call asking for (requiring) help cooking breakfast. When it didn't come, Mina scurried back over to the desk and sat down, her heart pounding and her hunger completely forgotten.

The loud tinkle of another IM from Craig rang out.

Bluedevils33: Yo, Mina u there?
BubbliMi: Sorry! Listening out 4 my mom . . . I'm supposed to be downstairs cooking
Bluedevils33: Word. I let u go if u answer me. U down w/the Frenzy?

This time Mina didn't think. She typed, quickly.

BubbliMi: Mos' def!!
Bluedevils33: Cool. U be @ the Ria tonite?
BubbliMi: Trying to be. Not sure tho'
Bluedevils33: I can give u a ride if u want

The thought of being in the car with Craig made Mina's heart race. Everything was moving so fast.

BubbliMi: Naw I'm cool. If I go it'll be w/my girls. I see u there if we go.
Bluedevils33: Aight. Later
BubbliMi: C U

Mina stared at the conversation on the screen, reading over it quickly again and again. It felt like a dream. If her heart wasn't practically beating out of her chest, she would swear she was still sleeping.

"Mi-naaa!" her mother called from downstairs. "What's taking you so long?"

"Coming, Ma!"

Smiling like an idiot, Mina closed out the IM box and signed off. She stood up and jogged down the hall to the bathroom. If Craig could see her now, bed head and stank morning breath, he'd run screaming in the other direction. She laughed out loud at her fuzzy-headed image in the bathroom mirror.

Stank breath and all, she had a date!

She had a DATE . . . and one problem. Her parents didn't allow her to date yet.

Waking the Sleeping Giant

"They hate to see you doing better than them."
—Field Mob ft. Ciara, "So What"

Jessica Johnson glowered.

She stood mannequin-still in the school's long hallway at the floor-to-ceiling glass panes surrounding the fishbowl—the café, Del Rio Bay High's outdoor Beautiful People Only section of the cafeteria. Her eyes, focused like hazel laser beams, glared catlike in her coffee-bean complexioned face.

She couldn't take them off the scene outside.

About forty people milled around the square, no larger than two average-sized bedrooms. Some huddled around the five tall bistro tables—sometimes six people deep. Others stood atop the sandy-colored concrete benches that anchored the corners, while still others were content leaning against one of the two brick walls that enclosed the area. So used to being gawked at from the hall or cafeteria windows, no one paid her much mind. Everyone was enjoying the budding warmth of the early spring—many going jacketless in the fifty-degree Maryland day.

Winter had been short but fierce. Two ice storms had walloped the area, closing school for a total of seven days in February and nearly sending everyone stir crazy from cabin fever. Fifty degrees was almost hot in comparison, the open air addicting.

The thick glass made it impossible for Jess to distinguish any conversations, but she could almost feel the buzz of the various rowdy discussions. Now and then a loud laugh or exclamation would erupt from one of the hubs. Jess assumed it was loud—it had to be if she could hear it from inside. She imagined that the talk was of the Extreme Beach Nationals, the big cheerleading competition taking place in a week, who was heading down to Ocean City with who, which hotel people were staying at and what madness they could get into with their parents lingering nearby.

Typical day in the café, the school's powers discussing who and what was important in DRB High land, in their own version of politicking and strategizing.

The café, twenty feet wide, twenty feet across, and accessible by a single door at the far end of the cafeteria, was nothing more than an island of concrete surrounded by a patch of grass just wide enough to be a pain for the maintenance crew to cut. But it was the students' slice of heaven. No teachers patrolled it. And nobodies stayed away from its door, choosing instead to a) act like the café didn't exist or matter, or b) gaze inside from the windows, like Jess was doing now.

Only she wasn't a nobody. Jess was a café regular, an Upper whose right it was to lounge in the café at her leisure during lunch.

And until that very second, the café had been Jessica's safe haven from wannabes and nobodies, specifically the one wannabe nobody who annoyed her more than anyone in the world . . . Mina Mooney.

Jessica's eyes squeezed into slits, piercing Mina from the shadows of the hall as Mina's head bobbed up and down excitedly, deep in conversation with Kim, the varsity cheer captain, and Sara, Jessica's twin.

Seeing Mina there, all smiles and grins enjoying life in the fishbowl, shouldn't have jolted Jessica. But the flash of heat she felt boiling in her chest was anger—pure and powerful. It grew as she remembered how lightly Sara had mentioned Mina's new "status."

"I was telling Mina that we're gonna kill it at the Extreme," Sara had said, bubbling with a mix of anxiety and excitement at the thought of Nationals.

"Look, I know you two cheer together now, but I'm over hearing you talk about *her*," Jessica snapped. She tossed her hair, a well-kept straight weave that hung just below her shoulders, a ludicrous auburn that almost shimmered next to Jess's dark face, and fixed her twin with a defiant stare.

Sara's light cocoa-complexioned cheeks darkened slightly as the crimson spread through her face. But her voice was neutral as she answered, "I know you guys don't get along." She hesitated for a second, then swallowed a sigh before finishing. "Nothing I say will matter, will it? You love to hate Mina."

Jessica laughed, her dark face brightening at Sara's truthful declaration. "Yup. I do."

"Well . . . you know Kim and I invited her to sit in the café, right?" Sara cleared her throat as if admitting it out loud had dried her mouth.

Jessica's smile quickly turned into a sour-lemon scowl and this time Sara's mouth did dry out. Her tongue stuck to the roof of her mouth as she quickly added, "We have a lot of cheer strategy to go over. So you know . . . I mean, you knew Mina was going to get the call to the café eventually, Jess. She's the JV cheer captain . . . she . . ."

"Is a total wannabe, Sara," Jessica huffed. Her finger wagged in Sara's face like she was lecturing a young child, something she did often to her twin when it came to social etiquette. "I know you like hanging out with any and everybody. But Mina is . . . the way she rolls with her . . ." Jessica rolled her eyes and sneered, "clique." She shook her head as if warding off some sort of bad word cooties. "Like they're running things at DRB High." Her next words were thick with venom. "I hate how she thinks her little Miss Nice-Nice act is going to make everyone like her."

Sara giggled. "So let me get this right. You hate her because she's nice?" hadn't bothered Jess. She knew that sitting in the café didn't mean much to Sara. Neither did DRB High's whole social hierarchy thing. So it was easy for Sara to dismiss it all as silly or ridiculous. But it wasn't silly to Jess. She rolled with the Glams, the snotty, mostly rich kids, and took her status as a member of the ruling class serious, deadly serious. It hit Jessica where it hurt that Mina—neither rich nor snotty—had always managed to sniggle her way in with the right circles.

Jess had tried, God knows she had, to keep her out. She'd even tried to get her schedule switched around so she'd have the same lunch as Mina this semester, solely to keep Mina on the outside of the fishbowl. None of it made any sense to Sara, who considered Mina a friend. She'd once told Jess, all she wanted was for Jess and Mina to peacefully coexist in the same circles at DRB High.

Peacefully coexist, huh? Jess thought, already nurturing the seed into an idea.

She stared through the thick glass, registering back to the present just as Brian James walked over to the table where Mina sat. He was cute with a capital C, his toffee complexion smooth, eyebrows thick, soft brown eyes accented by thick lashes and a head full of hair so black and curly it made Jess's fingers squirm at the thought of touching it. He stood behind Mina's chair, his six-foot-three frame towering easily over the three-foot high wrought-iron bar chairs, and wrapped his arms around her waist.

Jess averted her eyes from Mina's insanely idiotic grin and focused on Brian. He was telling a joke, she guessed, because all the cheerleaders at the table giggled and Sara gave him a high five. Just as quickly as he came, he whispered something in Mina's ear (more insane teeth-grinding grinning) and sauntered over to a table where a few gaming geeks (award-winning gamers, of course) happily welcomed him into their conversation.

Jess closed her eyes and tried to block out the image of that wide, "I'm such a lucky girl" grin on Mina's face. She tried to force the one word that kept coming up, to describe Mina, back into the far reaches of her mind.

It couldn't be.

Mina was not, could not be . . . an Upper.

No!

True, she was sitting in the café and was dating one of the school's hottest guys. Jess didn't even want to think about Mina's sudden fame as the high-school's "Pop" reporter, as people were calling her since she'd snagged the position as writer of her own column, "Pop Life," which showcased the school's up-and-coming stars. Some people were even courting Mina, hoping to get a little ink in "Pop Life."

Blegh!

It was definitely a ridiculous level of freshman beginner's luck. But it didn't make her an Upper, necessarily. Far as Jess was concerned, Mina was popular by association and Jess was being generous by admitting that much.

No, Mina wasn't officially an Upper yet. And if Jessica had anything to do with it, Mina never would be . . . not while they roamed the halls of DRB High together, anyway.

If Mina wanted popularity she'd have to go through Jess first.

Popularity cost, and Jess was going to make sure Mina paid dearly.

The Fifteen-Minute Make-Out

"I hate how much I love you boy."
—Rihanna ft. Ne-Yo, "Hate That I Love You"

It feels too good.

It feels too good.

It feels too good.

Lizzie chanted to herself to break the spell of the warm frenzy building between her and Todd as he nibbled at her ear and stroked her side. Her breath hitched. Every time she attempted to move an inch or say something to slow the rush, he'd do something magical with his fingers or lips.

She tried again, managing to move her head an inch.

Victory.

She parted her lips to say something (anything), and Todd's lips moved to hers. She instinctively kissed him back, rolling the icy cool taste of Orbit spearmint around her tongue, savoring it. It was hard to chew gum now without thinking of Todd and flushing.

As a matter-of-fact, it was hard to do a lot of things without thinking of Todd.

The realization struck her dumb.

No matter how hard she tried, it was hard to connect that a practical, straight A, theatre geek like her not only had a serious boyfriend, but a popular, honest-to-goodness hot guy as well.

Six-foot one; blue eyes; unruly, light walnuty hair highlighted blond; and ready with a joke the second he opened his mouth, Todd had a hot surfer dude look going. Truth be told, even when he let the blond grow out, he was easy on the eyes. He was also a full member of Club Six-Pack. And his biceps and chest weren't bad, either. If Lizzie hadn't seen his body change with her own eyes, she would have never believed someone could go from skinny to sculpted in two years.

Yet it still took her by surprise when girls went out of their way to flirt with him or give her nasty looks when she and Todd walked down the hall together. To her, he was still the goofy, too skinny T who used to shadow JZ like a puppy when they were ten years old. Because of that, and their middle school friendship, she and Todd were a comfortable couple. She never felt self-conscious around him because whenever her nerves would attempt a takeover, like worrying that she had food stuck in her teeth and she had to get it off before he saw it, Todd would poke fun at it, reminding her that he didn't care about her being the perfect girl.

Everyone seemed to know Todd was hot, except Todd.

That made it easy to get caught up in his charm.

Except . . . Lizzie wasn't ready to be completely gaga.

She was changing, and some of the changes felt good. Really good, in fact.

But mostly, they were unsettling. Like now. Why couldn't she open her mouth to say, "Hey, let's take a break?"

How come her brain was directing her body to move, get up, put some space between her and Todd, and her body wouldn't obey?

Todd was becoming a priority in ways Lizzie had always secretly vowed no guy ever would.

Flubbing lines in theatre when he popped into her mind. Getting a B on her Chem test after their first real argument—she didn't recognize herself sometimes.

But things were about to take a turn if all went according to plan.

Todd's kisses rained down on her in quick pecks, like a yappy dog nipping at her heel. She met his lips with her own slow, but firm kisses encouraging him to gel with her, easing him back a little until their kissing was in sync. Her resolve melted. It always did around the twelve-minute make-out mark. Instead of panicking that things were going too far, Lizzie gave in, savoring Todd's warm breath on her neck, ears, then his lips on hers.

Step one of her plan would kick in in exactly five . . .

Todd's tongue darted in her mouth for a quick visit, then was gone.

Four . . .

His hands pushed her shirt up just enough so Lizzie could feel their coolness on her warm belly.

Three . . .

He stroked her waist, careful not to go near her armpit (he'd learned the hard way that she'd burst into a fit of giggles, busting up the mood) but working closer to her bra.

Two . . .

Lizzie inhaled sharply as his hands made soft, smooth circles on her belly.

One . . .

Todd's fingers were on the front clasp of her bra just as Lizzie's cell phone blared "One" from *A Chorus Line,* filling the room, "One, singular sensation, ev'ry little step she takes."

Todd hesitated for a fleeting second.

Lizzie pushed herself upright. Her chest heaved as she ran her fingers through her tousled hair.

Todd's eyes, wide with surprise, skated from Lizzie to the phone in confusion.

Lizzie kneeled against the sofa, picked the phone up, and turned off the alarm she'd set right before she and Todd began making out. She was getting so good at doing it, fingers flying to set it before the kissing began, he never noticed. Smiling, she dipped her head and bunched her cascade of blond hair into a quick and dirty ponytail before standing up. She put her hand out to help Todd up from the floor.

His long body unfolded into a standing position where he tow-ered a full foot over Lizzie.

"Dude, I hate your phone." Todd shook his head, eyeing the phone with disdain. "It rings every time we . . ." He dropped down onto the sofa dramatically, pouting.

Lizzie pretended to check the missed call, even though there was none. "It's Mina. JZ should be here any minute to get us," she prac-tically sang, giddy that once more, her fifteen-minute make-out alarm had done its job.

Todd ran his fingers through his unruly locks, gathering himself. He looked shell-shocked and Lizzie almost felt sorry for him.

Almost.

She felt (a little) bad for having to trick him, but she couldn't trust herself anymore to untangle herself from the increasingly hot and heavy make-outs. At some point, they were going to stop work-ing. Either Todd was going to throw her phone out the window—he was eyeing it now like he wanted to—or simply not let her jump up like someone had lit her pants on fire to check it.

She knew the day was coming. That's why it was time for the virginity pact.

Satisfied with herself, she plopped down beside a silent and pouty Todd.

"I'm starved. You?"

"Yeah, but not for pizza," Todd said, making googly eyes at her.

Lizzie planted a prim peck on his lips, allowing it to turn into a bit more before pulling away. Todd reached out to pull her back, but Lizzie was up in a flash, laughing as his hand swiped her tee shirt, catching only air.

He scowled, chiding her playfully. "Tease."

"Sucker." She sprinted clumsily as he chased her up the stairs.

The door bell rang as they reached the landing.

She hadn't planned it, but the cavalry had arrived right on time anyway.